P.I. FOR HIRE

Skena looked at me significantly. "Could you stand to have a secret client for a few months, one who pays you a lot—in cash?"

"With a big risk of getting killed," Ariadne pointed out.

"And a good shot at Blade of the Most Merciful? Maybe even a chance of tracking them back to where they came from?" I grinned at them. "Oh, yeah, I'm in. Just try and keep me out!"

From the way they both laughed, I knew I had finally found my own kind of people.

Patton's Spaceship

JOHN BARNES

HarperPrism
An Imprint of HarperPaperbacks

🏰 HarperPaperbacks
A Division of HarperCollins*Publishers*
10 East 53rd Street, New York, N.Y. 10022-5299

This is a work of fiction. The characters, incidents, and dialogues are products of the author's imagination and are not to be construed as real. Any resemblance to persons, living or dead, is entirely coincidental.

ISBN 0-06-105659-3

HarperCollins®, 🏰®, HarperPaperbacks™, and HarperPrism® are trademarks of HarperCollins*Publishers*, Inc.

Cover illustration by Vincent Difate

First printing: January 1997

Printed in the United States of America

Visit HarperPaperbacks on the World Wide Web at
http://www.harpercollins.com/paperbacks

❖ 10 9 8 7 6 5 4 3 2 1

This one's for David Wintersteen

Patton's
Spaceship

1

<hr />

"*I get bored really easy,*" I explained to the kid. "Easily, I mean."

"And this isn't boring?" She was a nice kid, as kids go, sitting at the kitchen table in the little temp suite I'd gotten us as a safe house. I liked the fact that she didn't make any noise or run around much—it's a pain to have to guard something that runs and zigzags unexpectedly.

"No, this is dull, but it's not boring." Anything but; I'd been up all night while ten-year-old Porter Brunreich, who wanted to know if it was boring, and her mother were sleeping their first safe sleep in several days. I'd been sitting here, at this cheap wood-grain table in an anonymous apartment building, a .45 in my shoulder holster, a little auto button on my cellular phone that would dial 911 and tell the cops where to come, waiting for her crazed father to turn up and try to break in.

In books they always say a kid looks "solemn," when

all they really mean is "serious" or "not giggling." Porter just looked like she was thinking about something very important. "So it's dull because there's not much to do, but it's not boring because there's danger."

"Something like that," I said. Actually, not boring because there was a good chance of getting into a brawl, and just possibly of having to beat up her father. But that didn't seem like a nice thing to tell her.

Porter looked pretty much like any other skinny blonde ten-year-old. In a few years she might be sort of handsome or elegant in a horsey kind of way, like her mother. Or rather like her mother usually looked— right now Mrs. Brunreich had two black eyes, some nasty abrasions on her face and neck, and her nose under a piece of steel that was being held on with a complicated bandage. Things Mr. Brunreich had done to her two days before; reasons why she had hired a bodyguard.

"You're carrying a gun," Porter said. "Are you going to have to shoot Dad?"

Mrs. Brunreich stirred at that, and I let her have the chance to answer, but she just took an extra-deep drag on her cigarette and continued to stare at the wall. So I had to answer. "I don't shoot people, usually," I said. "I carry the gun so I can protect you and your mother, because since I have it, they can't get rid of me by waving a gun in *my* face. That's why I carry such a big, ugly-looking one—to help keep them thinking straight about that."

It's a Colt Model 1911A1, the "Army .45" you've seen in a million war movies and private-eye movies, and people recognize it instantly; it says "Blows big holes in people." Saying it is nicer than doing it, I guess, and if you say it loud enough, you don't have to do it as much.

She didn't look successfully diverted by the comment, so I added, "I hope I won't have to use it, ever. And I don't want to use it on your dad. I guess if he came after you or your mother with a gun, I might have to. But only if it was your lives at stake, Porter."

"But you do shoot people."

"I've never had to. I've never fired this thing at a person."

Mrs. Brunreich stubbed out her cigarette and said, "Porter, don't ask so many questions."

The kid nodded and gulped the last of her milk. It seemed unfair—she was just worried about her dad—but considering all the marks he'd given Mrs. Brunreich to remember him by, I could see where the lady might prefer the subject was dropped.

On the other hand, Porter wasn't the kind of kid who'd ever been subjected to much discipline that she'd had to pay any attention to. "If you've never shot anybody, how good a bodyguard are you?"

"*Porter!*"

"It's all right, ma'am, it's a fair question." I was keeping an eye out the window for the van we were using for this job. Robbie and Paula were complete pros, and they wouldn't be one minute off either way from the set time of 8:37 A.M., still nine minutes away, but we were running the pizza routine, and that has to be done quickly. "I haven't shot anyone because there hasn't been any reason to. Shooting people is not my job; keeping people safe is. And the people I guard are *safe.*"

The kid nodded.

"If anyone even *thinks* they need the bathroom," I added, "go right now. It might be a while before there is another chance."

Porter got up and went down the hall to the pot; she

did it just as I'd told her always to do it, with her little bag (two changes of clothes, two books, one very old teddy bear) with her.

As soon as the bathroom door closed, Mrs. Brunreich said, "You can shoot the son of a bitch for all I care."

It came out "sunuffafish" because of the way her mouth was swollen from where he'd beaten on her face with his fists.

I nodded to indicate I'd heard her. I didn't say anything because I didn't want to encourage her. No matter what one of them's like, I hate it when one parent bad-mouths another in front of the kids.

She lit another cigarette, and said something I had to ask her to repeat. "You're a quiet man, Mr. Strang." She blew out smoke in a way they all learn to do from movies—I guess it's supposed to look sophisticated, and maybe she needed that considering what she looked like just then. "Is that because it's more professional?"

"I'm just quiet." I kept my eye out the window, on the street. Robbie and Paula had just a couple of minutes to go.

I just had to hope that *Mr.* Brunreich, if he was watching or even still in the state, didn't figure there was something weird about a pizza delivery at this hour of the morning.

It wasn't the cover we'd have used if we'd had a choice. But Robbie and Paula had had to do surveillance the night before from the parking lot, and the only company that I had a standing cover arrangement with was Berto's Pizza.

This was the second apartment Mrs. Brunreich had been in within the past three days; the other one had been one of the secure houses for Steel Curtain, a big bodyguard company here in the city. The trouble with a big agency is that there are a lot of people around who know them, and lawyers especially tend to know them—that was how Brunreich had found out where it was, or so everyone guessed.

Brunreich, besides being a lawyer, was a big, dangerous, crazy bastard with quite a bit of martial arts training—the kind of training you can buy if you're lucky enough to inherit the money, which also gives you time to train a lot when you're young. I knew—I had the same kind of training, and, in fact, I'd sparred with him a few times.

I wasn't looking forward to doing it for real. Hal Payton, who ran Steel Curtain, had been escorting Mrs. Brunreich on a quick trip around the block—supposedly his men had swept it first—when Brunreich had just popped up from behind a yew bush, slammed poor old Payton in the face with one hard fast one that put him out for the count, and started whaling away on Mrs. Brunreich. Payton's backup had jumped right in, but that still gave Brunreich time to land four or five savage blows on his soon-to-be-ex, and from the look of things she would have to be lucky to avoid seeing a plastic surgeon before it was over.

Hal Payton's assistant was a burly guy, my height but with a lot more muscle, and he'd given Brunreich a good hard one upside the head with a police flashlight. He said it seemed to startle him more than hurt him— "at least Brunreich didn't run off like a man who was hurt."

I couldn't exactly remember which of us had won when we'd sparred. I think I had a slight edge in speed, and I know he had a big one in strength.

I like to pretend it's all just a job, and I don't worry more about one guy than another, but the fact was the job before this one had been chasing off a 130-pound computer nerd who was pestering an underage girl for a date, and I had liked that job a *lot* better.

Mrs. Brunreich's lawyer hadn't liked me much, either, but when she insisted on taking Payton off the case (bad move—Steel Curtain was a good outfit and anyone could have rotten luck, and her lawyer knew this but couldn't win an argument with his client just then), he'd asked Payton whom to hire instead, and Payton had said me. One more thing I owed the old fart, along with my training, my experience, my life, and the lives of my sister and father. I buy him a beer now and then.

Her lawyer had not asked the "ever shot anyone?" question. I wondered if he would have hired me if he had. Especially if he'd found out that although I'd been in business five years, this was really just a temporary job, while I was taking a little time out from doing a doctorate in art history, just a little time to get my head a little more together . . .

The toilet flushed. Porter came back, still carrying her bag, balanced and ready. I glanced at her and gave her a little smile, hoping it looked encouraging—I mean, I don't know anything about kids, except it's hard to keep the parent that doesn't have custody from grabbing them—but there was something about the way she was behaving . . . more adult than most adults I had guarded, certainly more adult than her mother—

She nodded at me but didn't smile herself. Maybe she had nothing to smile about, or was just very serious. You never really know unless you've known them for a while.

Lately I hadn't known anyone for more than a few weeks.

I was getting extremely morbid in my thinking. Bad before going into action, I reminded myself, and Hal

Payton could tell me that this was likely to be bad action. I scanned the street again; nothing but six-block flats and row houses, high stoops and barred windows, like any other Pittsburgh street. It was a cloudy spring day, so the street seemed to be almost in black-and-white. They film a lot of horror movies in this town—the mood is right.

The big van marked "Berto's Pizza" came around the corner and parked at the curb; I'd have known it in any paint job, and it had had plenty, because Robbie and Paula supplied what I thought was the best secure-vehicle service in the city, and I always used them when I could. You couldn't have put a shot into that van at point-blank range, or into its engine, and various other things were set up in it to make it a bit tougher to stop than a light tank.

Paula got out with the red box; red meant she'd seen nobody but wasn't perfectly sure the area was secure.

She's a big young woman, halfway between "Rubens" and "East German Swim Champ," and though she can look pretty good when she wants to (she only wants to on a job), right now she looked thoroughly up-all-night bored and tired, which was just what you would have expected.

Through the tinted windows you couldn't see Robbie sliding into the driver's seat, but I knew she was, the way I knew the .45 in my shoulder holster already had a round chambered. Paula had left the engine running; if we could get to it, we had the ride for the getaway.

I motioned Mrs. Brunreich and Porter to follow me downstairs, with their bags, and they obeyed instructions, not turning out any lights. Paula rang the door-bell behind us, an obnoxious buzz designed to be heard on the street and make things look convincing.

When Mrs. Brunreich and Porter were directly behind me, I opened the door. Paula dropped the empty pizza box and stepped to the hinge side of the door, facing outward; I moved to the lock side, my back toward Paula. As we'd rehearsed, Mrs. Brunreich and Porter came through the door, and Paula and I closed up ranks with them between us.

I really had to give credit to Porter—she stuck right by Paula's right side, where she was supposed to be. (I was grateful for the millionth time that Paula is a lefty.) I was on the other side because the main threat was supposed to be to Mrs. Brunreich.

We were almost down the long flight of concrete steps to the cab when he came charging out from between the buildings behind us. He must have stood there with his gut sucked in all night—the space between the row houses was barely a foot—and maybe that was why he stumbled a little, and it made some noise.

I got a glimpse of him and whirled to get up on the step behind Mrs. Brunreich; Paula got another glimpse and reached out to hurry the mother and daughter down the steps to the van. Robbie kicked the automatic open on the van, the door slid open, and behind me I could feel Paula practically lift both of them up by the scruffs of their necks and *heave* them across the sidewalk and into the van.

Brunreich was ignoring me and heading straight for the open door of the van, right down the grassy slope.

My job is always to be between the client and trouble. I grabbed the old pipe railing, vaulted onto the dew-wet grass, braced myself hard, and aimed a shoulder into Brunreich's chest.

I had just an instant to think that tripping him would be more effective, and another to realize that if I had missed the trip, he'd have gotten right through me, before he hit my shoulder hard enough to knock the air out of me.

He was a big guy, as I've said, and he was running full tilt downhill, so the impact was quite a shock. But in my favor, I had the better position—to control himself coming down, he'd had to let his feet get a little in front of him to steady him, and I was leaning forward, with my feet well back of me. We compromised; I was driven down the slope but remained on my feet, and he flopped backwards and slid, legs sprawled and ass first, right into me.

He was reaching for me as he came, and I grabbed for a counterstrangle; as a result I fell on top of him, with each of us clutching the other by the collar, neither with quite the grip to squeeze a windpipe or close a carotid.

Brunreich's momentum was more than enough for both of us. With me on top, he went careering down that grassy, wet slope on his back.

The push-and-pull grip I had—basically pulling his lapel down with my left and trying to force his collar over his windpipe with my right—wasn't tight enough to put him out, but it at least let me keep both hands on him. I can recommend it highly if you ever go mud-tobogganing on top of a lawyer. And give some credit to L.L. Bean as well—his shirt never tore in the process.

But I really can't recommend the experience.

As we hit bottom I was thinking I'd just disengage and run for it, get enough space to use my tube of Mace or even the can of NoBear I keep in my car, when I realized that there was a lot more yelling than just me and Brunreich, and the van hadn't left yet.

I didn't have time to assess what the matter was, but it meant I had to keep fighting.

I got my feet planted before he did and kicked myself upright, but I didn't quite break his grip—he caught one lapel of my jacket with both hands and started the quick climb hand over hand that ends with an elbow whip and a brutal headlock, if not a broken neck. It forced my head back down toward him, and his feet moved in around mine to get better balance.

In self-defense class the students always ask why you can't just kick a man in the testicles when he does that. If you're wondering, put a chair in front of your refrigerator. Bend over the chair and pick up the refrigerator.

Now do it standing on one leg.

Luckily he was a bit out of it; maybe a rock or two had clipped the back of his head on the way down. I turned outward, and he "forgot to let go"—not an uncommon mistake, which is why the trick is old—and as his arm straightened, I braced the elbow with one hand, grasped his wrist with the other, pinned the knife edge of his hand to my body, and turned against his shoulder joint.

His free hand flew around wildly trying to slap me off him, but couldn't reach far enough to do any damage. As I increased the pressure he flipped over onto his side, and I drove his arm up into a hammerlock, taking a grip on the back of his head by the hair and arching his back to prevent him getting any traction.

Something hit me hard from behind.

It was well above the kidneys, so it stung like hell but didn't do any other damage. Then I was being flailed at, not effectively, by long thin arms and soft hands, but for all its weakness the attack was still fierce.

Whatever was slapping me got pulled away from my back. In the confusion Brunreich had gotten his free hand most of the way under him, so I said, "Put that arm out in front of you," and when he didn't obey instantly I started cranking on the hammerlocked elbow. That made him move.

I had some breathing time, finally. I got my grip well set and looked around.

Mrs. Brunreich was sitting in the open door of the pizza van, sobbing. Paula had an arm around her and was saying soothing things.

Robbie, a thin woman with dark crew-cut hair, dressed in backward Pirates' cap, baggy sweatshirt, and parachute pants, was off to my side, Taser in hand, as she was supposed to be.

Brunreich's breathing was loud and labored; he sounded like he'd just run a few miles. I realized I was holding his head up by the hair, arching his back at a painful angle, and that I might not be able to keep that up forever.

I figured I'd enjoy it while I could.

"Where's Porter?" I asked.

"Here in the van," she said. "You said to stay in here no matter what."

I was really beginning to like that kid. She followed instructions, and she was the only member of her family who hadn't hit me yet this morning.

"Well, you can come out," I said. "But I'm afraid I'm going to have to be mean to your dad. And Brunreich, I'd rather not have to do anything uglier to you than I've already done, in front of your daughter. But you know I will."

"Yeah, I know." He sounded sad and tired.

"Right then. You're covered by a Taser. At the moment you're under a citizen's arrest. When I let go of you I'm going to step back and get my Mace out; you can't possibly turn around fast enough to get to me before I'm ready to put that into your face.

"Now, I can keep you in this hold, which I'm sure is

extremely painful, or I can let you up. If you say you will behave, I will let you up. Clear?"

"Clear. I'll behave."

"You know that if you *don't* behave once I release you, you get cut no slack? You'll get the Taser and the Mace right then?"

"I understand. I'll behave."

I let go of him and took a long step back. He brought himself around to where he was half-leaning, half-lying on the grassy bank in the streak of mud he'd made coming down it.

He wasn't looking his best. The front of his shirt and pants were smeared with grass and mud, there were huge dark circles under his eyes, he'd gotten a slight bloody nose somewhere in the process, he was a few days behind in his shaving, and somewhere in the fight with me, or maybe the fight the day before with Payton, he'd torn out one knee of what used to be expensive trousers. He was breathing more easily, but his mouth was still open and gasping like a carp's, and his eyes seemed to wander from thing to thing—Robbie and her Taser, me and the Mace, his sobbing soon-to-be-ex-wife, and then just off into space.

Finally he spoke. "What happens now?"

"Cops happen," I said. "Lots and lots of cops happen. Once the trouble started Robbie called nine-one-one on the cellular. You'd really better just sit tight. If you like, Paula can call your lawyer for you."

"Thank you very much." He gave us the number, and Paula called; at least Brunreich had a guy who did some criminal practice, and knew about getting it together for the client in a hurry, even at a strange time.

It wasn't nine o'clock yet—it had only been five minutes since we'd come out the door—but I was good and tired from the events of the morning so far.

I was a bit worried about the flight time, but the cops got right there and the handover was very smooth. I showed my license, and they agreed that I was indeed a licensed bodyguard in Pennsylvania, as was Robbie, as was Paula. We all three agreed that Mr. Brunreich had assaulted me, and I would be pressing charges, and they agreed that I could come to the station to swear out the complaint later.

At least Mrs. Brunreich was willing to corroborate it. Sometimes in these divorce things they'll suddenly start lying to protect the bastard.

It didn't take more than another ten minutes for them to book Brunreich and take him away. We still had a little slack at the airport, and Paula had phoned ahead anyway and been assured it would all be okay. I was a tiny bit nervous about the lack of security—I thought Brunreich was paying too much attention to the flight number—but I wasn't much worried in that when they released him on bail he'd be restricted to Pittsburgh until his trial, and I figured a lawyer would know enough not to jump bail.

"All right," I said, when the cops said we could go and started to hustle Brunreich into the police cruiser, "you all still have a flight to catch, and my contract's not complete till you're on it. Let's roll."

Everyone piled into the van; I sat in the back with Porter, Paula in the middle seat with Mrs. Brunreich, Robbie driving. Mrs. Brunreich was still sniffling, and Paula was talking to her in a low, soft way that I call her Sensitive Feminist Grandma Voice, which seems to be able to hypnotize even the most spineless or co-dependent people into doing something sensible.

Porter leaned against me, her face on my left sleeve. And said, "Thank you for not shooting him."

"Aw, heck, Porter, it was never even close. Really."

She nodded and kept leaning on my arm. "How do you get to be a bodyguard? Do you go to a special school or something?"

"Well," I said, "it's not the greatest job in the world." The kid seemed to need a hug, so I sort of let her slide under my arm and found myself being held on to like a teddy bear. "But I guess if you really want to, you should start martial arts soon, and maybe learn pistol in a couple of years—that's all competitive sports anyway, and it's fun—and, oh, I don't know, play a lot of sports so you're strong and agile and used to thinking fast on your feet. And it wouldn't hurt to go to college and take some psych and some police science. So you need to make good grades."

At least I didn't know anyone in any field who was actually *harmed* by good grades, and besides, if I was going to be stuck as a role model, it was the kind of things role models said.

"Should I enlist in the Army?"

"Some do, some don't. I didn't, but Robbie did. But don't worry about it too much. You have a lot of time to decide what you're going to be." I was starting to realize, as the adrenaline from the fight wore off, that I was pretty tired, and on top of that I was beginning to sound like Mr. Rogers.

"Yeah, I know," she said, "but how often do I get to talk to a real bodyguard?"

The way she said "real bodyguard" made me feel about ten feet taller, which I suppose is a natural reaction to a cute blonde woman who thinks you're wonderful. Even if she's ten.

"You want to be a bodyguard like me?"

"Well, yeah, but more like Robbie. She's *awesome.*"

I suppose I deserved that. The rest of the drive out to the airport we talked about names for dogs, the *Hardy*

Boys and why real-life crime wasn't much like that, and the riding lessons she was supposed to start soon.

Part of the back of my brain kept figuring that Brunreich was really well-and-truly crazy, and if his lawyer got right over to municipal court, and there was no line in front of him—and on this kind of weekday morning there might not be—

We had at least a forty-minute head start, which should be good enough.

At the airport, I just handed my automatic, holster and all, to Paula (much easier than getting it cleared through security), and Robbie and I took them through. We'd phoned ahead so we could have them preboard during cleaning; it's a routine little trick, since it makes it all but impossible for the client to be physically attacked.

As we walked up the corridor, Porter asked, "Do you believe in ESP?"

"Not me," I said. "But I wouldn't mind having it, in this line of work."

"Me either," Robbie said. "I'm strictly a materialist."

"You ask too many questions," Mrs. Brunreich said.

Porter ignored that last and said, "Uh, I just had like a . . . like a dream but I was awake, this flash of the future, like . . . I'm *always* going to be walking between bodyguards."

That got to Robbie. "Aw, *honey*," she said, "it's not like that. This kind of thing could happen to anybody. It's not necessarily going to happen to you forever."

"It didn't seem like a *bad* dream," Porter said, "just like that was the way it was going to be."

Naturally, at the gate, the airline flunkies had decided they'd never heard of the arrangement, and that we would have to stand around in plain sight while they phoned the universe.

Mrs. Brunreich seemed just as happy, since it let her get another couple of cigarettes in (and with the way her nerves must be by now that was probably a plus). "And could I possibly get in a trip to the ladies' room?"

It didn't seem like there was much danger, even with the annoyance of having to wait around, so Robbie peeled off to escort Mrs. Brunreich in there, and I stuck around with Porter, doing my best to keep us standing where we wouldn't be too visible, behind a couple of outsized plants near a column.

"You're probably just getting those pictures because you want all this to be over," I said to Porter. "When life sucks you think it'll stay that way forever; but it doesn't."

She sighed. It was not a good kind of sound to hear out of a tiny little girl on a bright, sunny spring morning. "Mom's sending me to camp in another few days, as soon as she finds a new camp since she doesn't want to send me anywhere Dad knows about. So it won't be my regular place, and I'll have to get used to all new bunkmates."

"That's rough," I said. "It would be nice to have the friends you're used to."

"Yeah." She said it with a hopeless little shrug. "Anyhow when I'm twelve I get shipped to boarding school, and then I won't be home much after that. So it won't last forever."

All I could think of to say was, "You're a nice kid, and anyone would like to have you around. Your parents have huge problems, but there's *nothing* wrong with you."

She nodded, but I doubted that she believed me.

There was a commotion down the corridor from us, and some instinct made me move Porter in among the plants, whisper "Stay put," and step out to see what it was.

Brunreich burst out of the crowd. He was carrying a ball bat. His eyes looked utterly mad; I suppose whatever grip he'd had on himself, he had none now.

I strode out to face him, doing my best to draw his attention; the corner of my eye showed me Robbie taking a pop glance out of the women's room and jumping right back in.

I walked straight toward him, kept my voice level, and said, "Put down the bat and go away. You're in enough trouble already."

Every now and then some lunatic will really listen to you. Usually not. This time it was the usual thing.

His training might have been good, but it was pretty well gone from his mind by now—he just swung the bat at me, one-handed and overhand, down toward my head, like he was driving a huge nail.

Time slowed down. I was a step out to the side, so I reached up with my right arm—up, up, as if I were swimming in Karo syrup . . . my right hand got there, just barely, just to the left of the bat. It scraped down over all my knuckles and the bulge of my wrist, slapping my arm into a hard flop against my head, skipping the elbow to slam the outer muscles on the upper arm—

Time sped up again. My right arm slammed like a half-full sandbag against my head, and from wrist to armpit I felt the force of the blow.

I planted the ball of my right foot, pivoted, picked up my left in a tight coil, and snap-kicked him in the solar plexus with everything I had. He bent over, clutching his gut, and the bat went bouncing off on its own—he couldn't have held on to it one-handed after hitting the unyielding floor that hard.

Sounds came back then—along with more pain—the bat ringing on the cold, hard floor, people screaming, the crash and bang of people dropping their things and scattering to get away.

I let him have another snap-kick, this time across the face, and when he didn't rear up but didn't go down, I stepped into him. He tried to swing at me, a funny groping little punch like he was doing a Barney the Dinosaur impression, and I slipped inside that and rabbit-punched him.

He hit the floor hard—was probably out before he landed. I backed away.

The airport cops showed up. They knew they were looking for Brunreich, so they didn't have any trouble hauling him off; they let Porter and Mrs. Brunreich get on their flight, but the last hug I got from Porter was a bit strained since they had me in handcuffs.

By the time Robbie and Porter got that one talked out (at least Norm, my lawyer, didn't have to get involved, and I didn't end up with another arrest on my record), I had been up twenty straight hours. My right hand was swelling up into an interesting purple blob, which was going to be a hassle since I don't do much of anything very effective left-handed.

"Relax," Robbie said. "You've never shot anybody, anyway."

"Unless that's the hand you use—well, never mind," Paula said. She was driving.

"Where are we going?" I asked, as we came around onto the Parkway, headed back into Pittsburgh.

"You're going to a doctor and then home to bed, or else home to bed and then to a doctor. No other choices on the menu," Paula said. "In fact why don't you just try to fall asleep back there? We'll get you home."

I started to argue I wasn't sleepy, and we could go someplace to get breakfast, but suddenly the pent-up sleep hit me, and I didn't have the energy. I'd just close my eyes for a few minutes and then maybe I'd wake up before we got back to my place—

For some reason that silly kid's face invaded my dreams. She seemed to be asking, again, *How do you get to be a bodyguard? Do you go to a special school or something?*

As I slid into uneasy dreams, part of me answered that kid: "Yeah, sure. Special school. Shadyside Academy then Yale for undergrad and grad." And I was back into the dream . . . the dream that I always wanted to be interrupted from, where in the middle of things I would wake up and nothing would have gone any farther than that . . .

2

Used to be that I spent many long hours unable to sleep, sitting in Ritter's or the Eat'n'Park, drinking coffee without end, and while I was doing it I would think: people get it all wrong about the trouble with being lucky in your childhood. They have this idea that if there's money and parents who love you, and you've got a lot of natural talent, you get spoiled and weak.

Wrong.

Trouble is you grow up so healthy and strong that when things go really, horribly wrong, you're too stubborn and too strong to just collapse and give up, wind up in a mental hospital or a casket the way sensible people would.

I won't bore you, and a really great childhood is boring to hear about. The worst you could say about it was that Dad pushed us kids pretty hard to do well at everything, and the twins—Jerry and Carrie, two years younger than I—and I did pretty well at things naturally.

My father was at the Center for Studies in Islamic Politics at Carnegie-Mellon, and Mom taught part-time and got grants and edited the *Journal of Formalist Method in Philosophy*, not one page of which I've ever understood. All us kids (except Carrie, the math whiz) really had a handle on was that Mom worked at home, and you weren't supposed to interrupt her, but that every so often she'd just take a day off and we'd all go do something together, like climb a mountain or go down into a cave or all sorts of things the other kids envied us.

Grade school faded into high school, where I was a valedictorian, as was Carrie (poor Jerry got a B in Driver's Ed, leading to a standing joke that he was the "family dunce" and god knows how many times we told him we wouldn't let him drive). Between the three of us we lettered in everything.

Girls were a pretty simple matter to me; not every one I asked said yes, but if the one I asked out didn't, there was sort of a bench waiting, and if I do say so myself, the team had depth in those years.

It stayed the same way at Yale. The first girl I ever really fell hard for was Marie, whom I met because she and Carrie roomed together on gymnastics team road trips, and after that there wasn't anyone else; I married her a month after I graduated, when she had a year to go, and I was going right back into Yale to get a doctorate in art history.

By the time I was twenty-six I was about to start a dissertation and had already had a job offer or two; I had settled into a rhythm of teaching and writing during the school year and going to archaeological digs (taking Marie along) during the summers.

I never really appreciated my wife, I suppose. She was beautiful and highly intelligent, and I appreciated that; she supported everything I did, but having only my parents' very happy marriage to judge by, I didn't realize it wasn't always that way. And I think I didn't pay enough attention in those years, because to this day I wish I remembered more of the things she used to say that made me laugh. Or more moments when the light hit her just right, and I thought what one painter or another might have made out of her . . . or the way she could be on a long day on a dig, the patience with which she would clean one little artifact, the neat way she noted down every one of the tiny facts . . .

No, I never appreciated any of them enough.

I don't know exactly when I figured out there was anything at all dangerous about what Dad did for a living. Not much before I was in junior high, I guess. When he came back from every trip he had a lot of fascinating stories, most of which were about how he got to meet the "real people involved" and get the "real story behind it."

It took me a long time to realize that Dad's specialties were political violence and terror, and that that meant those people he was talking to were top security people, both Communist and Free World, and the people who trained terrorists (East, West, freelance, anybody)—and the terrorists themselves.

I remember realizing that when he described a secret PLO/Mossad prisoner swap, he was talking about going there with the PLO and leaving with the Mossad, not as a prisoner but to get both sides of the story. I have a vague recollection, one night at the dinner table before I went off to a movie with some interchangeable cheerleader, of abruptly realizing that to talk about what he was talking about, he must have spent time inside a ChiCom terror and subversion school, must have interviewed the instructors after observing the classes.

It still didn't really register with me. I suppose everyone with good luck as a kid thinks their family leads a charmed life. Dad went everywhere, alone and unarmed, to talk to everyone; Mom ran the house and had the occasional phone call from a Nobel laureate; I won judo tournaments, Jerry won shotokan tournaments, Carrie competed in women's rifle and gymnastics, and we all excelled at Scrabble. So what?

Marie fit right in—bright, athletic, beautiful, from the same kind of family.

By tradition Dad always got us all together on the Fourth of July. He said he was an old-fashioned patriot and besides, he needed an excuse for homemade ice cream. Usually—a law student like Jerry, a physics grad student like Carrie, and young marrieds like Marie and I didn't have much spare cash—he'd end up springing for the plane tickets, not to mention flying himself back from wherever. It was one of the few predictable things Dad did, and one of the most predictable—every Fourth of July we'd all be there in the big house overlooking Frick Park.

That particular year, the Fourth fell on a Saturday, and we all got there on Friday night in one big laughing and giggling gaggle at the airport. Marie and I had to be back at the dig in Tuscany Tuesday morning, but it was great to be back for these couple of days.

The Fourth itself, we all slept late, and then got up to just walk around the old neighborhood after a pleasant brunch. Jerry leaned close to me at one point, while Marie and Carrie were talking about whoever or whatever Carrie's latest flame was, and said, "Did Dad seem a little strange to you?"

"Yeah, a little. Could be jet lag—he's not saying officially, but you can tell he just came from Teheran—"

"We've seen jet lag on him before, Mark, and all that does is make him sleepy." Jerry stuck his hands in his pockets and looked down at the ground. "This is different. Something's eating him."

"Could be," I admitted. "Figure he'll tell us about it?"

"If he thinks we need to know. Or if he thinks it's not dangerous for us to know . . . and if he thinks we won't worry. But *he's* worried. Do you think we should tackle him about it?"

I watched a couple of kids rolling in somersaults down Sled Hill. "Think we should have Sis and Marie run over and teach those kids to do it right?"

"You're evading the question."

"I'm not on your witness stand, counselor." We walked on a ways; I admired the way the white dress and white pumps showed off the tan Marie had gotten on the dig, and the way the breeze pushed it against her. The Fourth, this year, wasn't hot, but there was no hint of rain. I think, maybe, then, I felt just a little of how lucky my life had been.

After a while I answered, "I think he's old enough to decide for himself, and let's respect that. What he wants to tell us he can tell us."

"Lots of common sense in that, big brother. Wanna see if we can get these debutantes to be seen with us getting a beer someplace?"

"You're on." And that was all we said about it, then.

That evening the problem with Dad was a little more noticeable, but not enough to spoil anything. Mom's homemade ice-cream cake came off as always, but still Dad seemed sort of abstracted and not quite there, and Mom was working pretty hard to keep us all convinced that she didn't notice, that there was nothing to notice.

The oddest part was that Dad had no stories at all to

tell. Tonight—when he wasn't staring at the wall—he wanted to hear about the Etruscan pottery we'd found and what it implied about the connections to the Greeks, about Jerry's candidacy for being a clerk to a Supreme Court justice, and about Carrie's "summer job" at Battelle—it sounded like she was working on Star Wars to us, but she was being a good girl and not dropping hints, not even when Jerry tried to surprise her . . . "So, Sis, would you like another slice of cake, and some more coffee, and are you really building a disintegrator ray?"

"Yes, yes, and I can neither confirm nor deny that."

"Better go into corporate law," I advised Jerry, "or hang around with dumber criminals."

In that sense it was a very strange Fourth—usually Dad dominated dinner table conversations. And why not? It was pretty hard to top a guy whose stories began with, "Yasser Arafat once told me—" or "In Tunis, there's a tiny little bar, hardly more than a hole in the wall divided by a board, with a one-eyed bartender who serves only German beer in bottles from iced coolers, and a lot of old SS men gather there—"

As the light faded into soft grays outside, and the first fireflies were dancing over the wide lawn, we went out on the second-floor back porch to watch the fireworks over the park. I remember the silky tube top Marie was wearing and her soft, deeply tanned skin pressing back against my arm as we sat on the bench next to each other and watched the bursts of flame and listened to the distant roar of explosions.

"The bombs bursting in air," Marie said softly, musing aloud.

Dad glanced over at her. "What I was thinking, too. Phrase from a dangerous time . . . within days of those lines being written the White House was set on fire by a foreign army . . ." He leaned back and stared off into space. There was a long sputtering burst of those very bright, white, loud ones. The light flickered on Dad's face as he looked up at them, and a long second later the distant booms echoed across our house; we could hear the "ooohs" and "aaahs" coming from the park beyond us. "It's not a bad country, really, and most amazing is that it's such a *safe* country."

The finale came then, a whole big string of things blowing up and scattering streams of bright colors into the air.

As we went inside, Mom asked Marie for some help on kitchen cleanup, and the two of them headed down that way, just as Dad asked us three to come into his study "for a nightcap." It had a suspiciously planned feel to it, and after the odd way Dad had been acting all day, Jerry and I glanced at each other; I knew we were both figuring we'd finally find out what was up.

We'd always said our parents' studies were like them; Mom's was obsessively neat and orderly, ringed with blackboards from which she copied her work into lined and numbered bound notebooks; Dad's was a huge untidy heap of books, papers, offprints, journals, videotapes, audiotapes, and crazy-quilt bulletin boards. He heaved a pile of papers off each of three leather chairs onto the floor, then moved his own briefcase off the big old swivel chair next to the mountain of paper that was his desk.

Lifting a crumpled map from the top of the pile on one shelf, he uncovered a bottle of brandy, some little French label I'd never seen before, and a set of snifters beside it. He put a splash in all four glasses, handed them round, took his own glass, and raised it in a toast, "Another year." We drank to that, and then he sat down in the desk chair and added, "The USA—peace, safety, and prosperity." That was good for another sip from all of us.

The light in his study was gold-colored from the warm yellow lampshades and the brass fixtures it reflected from. There were many crevices and cracks, dark corners and crumpled papers, forming patterns of warm yellow light and deep shadow. Not for the first time, I reflected that it would have been a perfect place for one of the Old Masters to paint.

Carrie sat so still that she looked like a painted angel in the warm glow from the lamp; Jerry's face shone with light coming down from above like a martyr's; and Dad was backlit like an old burgher in a crowd scene, or like the way Death was often depicted, with deep, distorting shadows masking most of his appearance.

"It's not easy to admit I may have done something dangerous and stupid," Dad said. "I don't know yet what the consequences of the dangerous, stupid thing I've done will be, or if perhaps I've acted quickly enough to avoid them." He sighed.

Jerry stirred a little, as if to ask a question, and Dad held up a finger for silence. "Let me explain a little. Some years ago I became aware that there was some new force at work in Mideastern terrorism. You all know, I think, that I am not an alarmist. Indeed, with both students and the press, I have always tried to make it clear that there is rarely or never such a thing as 'mindless terrorism.' If you think it's that way, you'll never be able to combat it—"

For the moment he was talking as if he were lecturing his seminar, and just for that long he was his old self, the way he'd always been before. "Terrorism, at least in the planning stages, is the work of men who go about their business as sensibly, deliberately, and rationally as any banker.

"I know you've all heard this before, but bear with me.

"All the same, after all those years of preaching that terrorism happens in a situation where terrorism works, and where there is something to be gained by it—that people do it because it pays off in something they want—all the same, having preached that all these years, I was finding myself confronting the evidence of a terror movement that seemed not to have read that particular book. Moreover, this new group was more shadowy, kept its secrets better . . . and was also better financed, better organized, better equipped— in fact they were so well equipped that I spent months chasing the red herring of superpower involvement, for some of the small amount of captured equipment seemed to be so sophisticated that the source almost had to be an American, European, Soviet, or Japanese laboratory—no one else could do that kind of work on that kind of scale and get the weapon operational."

Carrie caught my eye and winked. I don't think it reassured either of us. She looked too frightened.

Dad coughed and went on. "I could find no rationale for this new group's activities—*none*. Much as I have always stressed that terrorists do things for rational if deplorable reasons—though perhaps not the ones they announce—I had to admit that here was a group whose interest was in outrages, and not merely outrages but huge outrages that were difficult to pull off, and ones with no point at all. When Palestinians attack Israeli settlers, it makes a certain sense, for once that land is settled by Israelis the government of Israel cannot give it back—machine-gunning schoolchildren is evil and disgusting, but *one understands why they do it.* It makes sense for a Shiite fundamentalist to shoot a garrison commander who is Sunni, if uprisings will happen later that year, and the officer next in line is a coward, a sympathizer, or corrupt. It even makes sense to set off bombs in Europe and invite American and European retaliation by aerial bombing, for the population's reaction to the bombing can be used to shore up a leader—nothing makes a man more popular than to have him denounce the Americans and pledge he won't knuckle under to them when the night before American bombers were blasting away at his city.

"All these things are horrible and involve gross harm to innocents, but they can be understood. And I long ago learned that I, at least, could look evil straight in the face as long as I knew *why* it was. But this group—" Dad sighed, almost groaned, and the hand that stuck, pale white like a claw, out of the deep shadow in which he sat, tightened on the brandy snifter. "They call themselves Blade of the Most Merciful. They have staged actions on every continent except Antarctica—and they're so fierce and so fond of outrage that I wouldn't be surprised if they blew up an airliner full of tourists making the trip across the Pole. They have accounted for perhaps five thousand deaths and a billion dollars' worth of property in less than three years. The IRA, Red Army Faction, and PFLP combined have never even come close to such a record.

"And yet because they operate in secret most of the time and in conjunction with other groups—and because they never issue public statements—Blade of the Most Merciful have received very little publicity.

"Their level of activity and the ease with which they have evaded capture suggests Blade must have close to fifteen hundred fighters and a covert logistical tail at least as large, and so far as I can tell none of them ever has to do anything for money, so that the usual tracing through the employment of low-level, part-time members has proved impossible.

"In short they are the kind of organization that cannot have been created or financed by its members. They must surely have been set up by some large, significant power for some large, significant purpose. Yet their purpose does not even seem to be to consistently cause chaos.

"In one African nation they assassinated the dictator, *plus* every significant opposition leader, in or out of the country, in a single night. That same night they blew up the radio station, phone central, national bank, and Ministry of Defense. All this triggered weeks of rioting and something far too chaotic to be called civil war, while the country writhed like a beheaded snake, not even able to find a bad or an incompetent leader. And then the Blade did *nothing* to take advantage of the chaos; anyone could have done anything, and yet they did nothing.

"In Colombia they staged a dozen bank robberies, murdered four judges, had the government teetering— and then suddenly the Blade slaughtered the leadership of the drug cartel they were supposed to be working for and shipped so much solid evidence to the government that it may be a decade before they can even get all the criminal charges filed.

"And in both of these cases, they seemed to be functioning much more like a mercenary army than like an Islamic covert terror group. Yet at the same time, they were competing fiercely for turf in the Mideast. The more established groups seemed to learn quickly to get out of their way.

"Which wasn't always possible." He lifted the rest of the brandy to his lips—it was good stuff—and swallowed it as if it had been cough medicine. "The Blade often literally forced themselves onto other groups. They would demand that the 'host' group they had pinned down act as 'sponsor' and claim responsibility for some Blade crime, sometimes insisting that the group supply arms and men for what amounted to suicide missions. They were thus able to keep every little group on every side in the Mideast hating and distrusting each other . . . not that that ever requires anything like the effort the Blade put into it.

"A senior Mossad official—yes, the Israeli Secret Service itself—told me that their refusal to cooperate with a Blade demand that they butcher one whole refugee camp led to a Blade attack on a secret Mossad safe house in Germany and cost them the lives of six agents. They lost eight more hitting back at a Blade base deep inside Libya—"

I whistled. "Fourteen Mossad agents—"

Dad shook his head. "For what comfort it may be, they aren't supermen. Mossad killed almost fifty of them, between shooting back in Germany and the Libyan raid. One reason they were able to make the Libyan raid is that Qaddafi saw a chance to get rid of Blade and offered Mossad the chance to 'sneak past his radar unseen.' Hell, he even gave them topo maps; the Blade apparently offends Qaddafi."

"Has Blade of the Most Merciful announced any goals at all?" Carrie asked. Her face was drawn and tight, and so was Jerry's; mine must have been, too. Dad had already told us that he had done something he considered dangerous and stupid, and this didn't sound like a group to do that kind of thing around.

Dad shook his head. "None at all. No goals. No purpose. If I had to deduce them from the evidence, I'd say they like to see either complete anarchy or iron-fisted autocracy."

"Maybe they're nihilists," Jerry suggested, "like the old anticzarist terror movement."

Dad shook his head. "Those people were out to create chaos, but only so that the revolution could happen once authority collapsed, and to make sure the revolution was complete. Blade has no such strategy; they don't follow up on it when they create chaos, and they sometimes turn the other way and help repressive regimes. They seem to just want violence to happen."

There was a long silence. Dad stirred slightly in his chair, as if about to speak, but said nothing. Maybe because I was oldest and had usually been first to speak up, I finally said, "And why did you take us aside to tell us all this? Do you think they're after you?"

Dad pulled his single, exposed, white hand in from the light; now only his bony white knees, exposed by his Bermuda shorts, and the shining bald top of his head, were in the light. He might have been a skeleton. "I don't think so. Not anymore. I spent the past three years, you see, trying to get to meet some of them, and working on a book about them. After all, studying terrorism and writing books about it is what I do. And strange as it might seem, it has never seemed very dangerous to me, before now, because most of these groups, you know, have a message to get out, and so they are not going to shoot a potential messenger.

"So long as I took no sides and reported honestly and carefully, I was much more useful alive than dead. To normal terror and antiterror organizations, that is. But Blade is not normal . . .

"Just how not normal took me a long time to realize. For two years I tried to meet anyone, anyone at all, connected with Blade of the Most Merciful. First I tried for the leaders, then for just any spokesman, finally just anyone—couriers, former members, anyone.

"I had no luck. I had to assemble the book from tertiary sources and circumstantial evidence. As sheer detective work it was brilliant. I assembled a very complete picture of the size, scope, resources, activities, and *modi operandi* of Blade—of everything about them—except for one little detail: why they did what they did. On that, there was nothing, nothing, nothing at all. And despite every plea I sent by third parties, I heard nothing back—until this spring.

"The man who came to see me was short and dark, with large muscles under his baggy sweater. He said to call him 'George.' He had a long irregular scar across his nose, and he stepped into my office on the campus as if he had just materialized there.

"He sat down and said he was from Blade of the Most Merciful. To prove that he rattled off sufficient details of every major attempt I had made to contact them. Then he said—I quote him in his entirety—'Do not publish your book. Cancel it with your publisher. We are speaking to them as well. They will understand.' And he left.

"I darted out into the hall to expostulate with the man, and he was as gone as if he had never existed.

"Well, of course I went back into my office a very puzzled man. I had no idea what to do. It almost might have all been a hallucination, but if so it had been the first of my life. I knew they meant what they said, and time was short to cancel—my publisher was bound to be angry. Indeed for all I knew the copies

were already printed and sitting in a warehouse somewhere.

"The phone rang. It was my publisher. The presses
had been bombed, with a man killed, hours before the
print run of my book was to start. Blade of the Most
Merciful had paid a call on the publisher as well."

His sigh was deep and heavy, and he seemed to sink
far into his chair, as if he might recede right through
the black hole of darkness in which he sat and vanish
completely. "And there you have it. The publisher is
the feisty sort and wanted to make a public stink about
it and defy them. But I have a family and a quiet life.
Perhaps back when I started in all this . . . or even if it
were just me and your mother . . . or if anything
assured me that the Blade would concentrate its
vengeance so that only I would be struck . . . well, then
I would have the courage to defy them. Perhaps. I cannot deny there is a deeply romantic part of me that
wants to tell them to go to hell.

"But for all your sakes, and your mother's—and
because I have *seen* men blown to bits and don't want
to end up the same way—I withdrew publication of the
book. The only copy is in safe hands, and I have given
instructions such that whether I am alive or not, it will
not be released to the publisher if there is even the
slightest danger to anyone in my family. As a practical
matter that probably means that no one will see it
within our lifetimes."

He sat perfectly still, and by now the room seemed
very dim. It was all but impossible for me to connect
the things Dad was saying with my own life. Bombs
and irrational vengeance, and for that matter the sup-
pression of a book, seemed like something in the
movies. What was real was Marie's white dresses, and
our little apartment in Italy, and the nice academic

friends we had in New Haven, and the little parties where we drank too much and got profound about art and solved the world's problems. Terrorism was on some other planet entirely.

Finally, as the whole room seemed to be receding into unreality, I said, "Well, I don't see anything wrong in what you did. It won't hurt your career at this point if it's a long time before your next book, and it isn't like you're the only person who knows about the Blade. They sound more like a job for the CIA or the big news organizations anyway."

Jerry mumbled something, Carrie said "yeah," and Dad asked him to repeat it.

Looking down at the floor, the light from the table lamp glowing off the back of his head, Jerry said, "It seems to me like . . . well, I can't criticize your choice but . . . I wish you hadn't made that choice. It's um, well . . . Dad, it's just now how you raised us, and that's all there is to it. And I . . . well, it's water under the bridge anyway, I guess, since you've already done it."

Dad shrugged. "I can finish your opening speech for you, Mr. Prosecutor. It's nothing I haven't said to myself many times at night. The real problem now is that it will be known that I can be threatened. Blade of the Most Merciful will make sure enough of that. And once it is known that I can be threatened, whatever small security I once had is gone. Anyone who wants to slant my scholarly writing can now do so, just by threatening me.

"The fact is that I'm now afraid to go out in the field again. I could not return to Teheran, Islamabad, Baghdad, or Beirut. I would only wonder who would first say to me, 'Don't write this, or thus-and-so will happen.' And from there it's a very short step to 'You must write this, and sign your name to it, and swear publicly that it is so—or thus-and-so will happen.'

"They've broken me already, you see. I am going to take early retirement. Then perhaps I will devote myself to a little study of mine on arms smuggling in the Persian Gulf before World War I. I don't think Fiscus has said the last word on the subject. Perhaps I'll also translate some modern Arabic literature that I think hasn't yet received a fair hearing in the West. But my career as you and I have known it is over."

Carrie shook her head. "Dad, this isn't right. This is America, and a bunch of rag-headed—"

"Carrie, I still do not tolerate racist—"

"When they threaten my father, they're rag-heads." Her eyes were burning with anger; she'd have made a great model for a Joan of Arc right now. "And when he gives in to them, he's a coward. Excuse me. I meant to say a fucking coward." She got up and stormed out. There was a very long awkward silence.

Jerry stood. "She got all the temper, you know, and most of the brains, but . . . she's right, Dad. I'm not mad, but I'm very disappointed. I guess you can't help it, and we're still family and all that, but I'm real disappointed."

He went out with no sound at all.

That left me. After a bit Dad said, "And you think I did right?"

"Well, I'm married, too. And this might not be the time to mention it—I was saving it for breakfast tomorrow so don't let on—but maybe my feelings will be made clearer if I mention—" Deep breath here; how do you tell them these things? "Marie is pregnant—you're going to be a grandfather."

He jumped to his feet and surprised hell out of me by hugging me. "Yes, I guess you do understand."

I don't know what Mom told Marie or said to her about why all of us were off with Dad. Probably just kept her distracted—Mom could babble up a storm of small talk when she needed it—but when I came up to bed Marie asked nothing about what had been up.

We made love slowly and without any noise, with the lights on—she was so beautiful I always preferred it that way—and it took a long, long time. I don't think we knew what was coming; I think we just knew that in a few months we would not be able to do this for a while. It was very gentle and felt wonderful, both during it and after. I remember her whispering, "Mark, Mark, Mark" in my ear at the end as her slim fingers danced along my back and her long, thin thighs held me close.

The next morning our announcement seemed to break the ice at the breakfast table—there was a lot of cheering and whooping, and Jerry and Carrie started an immediate argument about whether a child is better off with a favorite aunt or a favorite uncle.

But Marie and I, knowing the family, had planned this one out carefully—there wasn't much time until we were to take the twins back to the airport, since both of them were flying out that day.

Dad was always a rotten driver—he thought about too many things besides the road—so as always, Mom was to drive the van. She got into the driver's seat, and Marie got in behind her. Jerry, saying something silly about adjusting the child-restraint seat, climbed in next, and then Carrie reached out for the doorframe and stepped onto the running board.

The van exploded.

The bomb under it had been wired to the ignition—Mom must have turned the key, but I never saw that—and was big enough to flip the van over and roll it down the lawn, slamming most of the frame and floor up into the ceiling.

Carrie was flung back against me like a sandbag. I didn't so much catch her as cushion her impact. It was only all those years of training that kept my head up as I hit the pavement on my back, with Carrie on top of me.

Dad, who was farther away than we were, grabbing some last-minute thing, saw more than Carrie or I did. I've always been sorry for that.

As I pushed Carrie to the side and slid out from under her, my ears and nose running with blood from the force of the blast, the first thing I saw was that the stumps where her legs had been were squirting blood like paint from a sprayer running out of pressure.

It was pure instinct—in a case like that you don't think about how much of the limb you can save. I had my belt off in an instant, wrapping it around one of Carrie's legs and passing it through the buckle, hauling it tight with all my strength.

Praise god Sis had skinny legs. There was enough slack left in the belt to reloop around the other stump and come back through the buckle again. It was messy work—her blood was everywhere on me and the pavement, and I was afraid my hands would slip on the makeshift tourniquet, but I had kept it dry enough; I hauled, tugged, used my other hand to straighten things and make the rough figure-eight tourniquet bite deep into her flesh, then tied the anchor knot to keep the free end from going back through the buckle.

The stench of blood was everywhere and when I unconsciously wiped my face I got more of it there. I didn't really realize that until days later, when I was looking at a *Post-Gazette* and there was a "scene of the tragedy" picture. I looked like hell—though I wasn't much hurt. Physically I mean.

I was just telling myself I should have used Carrie's belt to make a second tourniquet when I finally looked up far enough to see that her left arm was also gone, shredded bits of meat and bone hanging from eight inches or so of upper arm. I undid her belt, yanked it through, whipped it around the stump up close to the armpit where the pressure points tend to be—I vaguely remember the next day a doctor bawled me out because if I'd put the tourniquet down lower, or used the pressure points, they might have given her a bigger stump to tie a prosthetic arm to.

The evil spurting and the sickening spat-spat-spat of blood on the flagstone pavement stopped at once.

She was still breathing, and a quick check showed no more wounds and nothing that looked like a hole in her. For all I knew she was hemorrhaging internally, but there was nothing I could do about that.

At last I looked up. Maybe it would be more accurate to say that I had run out of things I could do for Carrie and couldn't stop myself from looking up. It had been maybe twenty seconds since the bomb had gone off. (I was just realizing it must have been a bomb.) A lot had changed in those twenty seconds.

Dad had run by me, moving terribly fast for such a heavy old guy. I turned to get up and follow him, and that was when I fell—looking back I discovered, quite suddenly, that my ankle was broken. That can happen, I guess, with enough adrenaline pumping into the system. But though it could keep me from feeling the pain, it couldn't make me stand up on something that would no longer support me.

So I could do little, as I pushed myself up off the

blood-slick pavement with my hands, except to look toward the van.

It wasn't there, because the blast had flipped it and rolled it down the lawn, but it was easy enough to follow the track. It had rolled several times, smashing a hole through the yew hedge, crushing roses into the soft damp mulch of their beds, tearing deep gouges in the dew-wet sod. There were long strips where the black mud showed through, as if the yard had been raked by giant fingernails.

Now the van lay on its side, flame and smoke pouring from it. The underside was toward me, and I could see how it had been slammed upward, bending into the body everywhere it wasn't tied down, broken at the top of the crude dome it formed.

Dad, forced back by the heat, was dancing around it like an overmatched boxer, trying to find a way to the still-open side door now on the top of the van. From where I lay, I could see it was hopeless—the frame had been bent and jammed up into that space, and even without the fire he couldn't have gotten anything out through there.

He said he saw something or someone moving in there in the long second between when he got there and when the gas tank blew. The coroner said, though, that to judge from the shattering of the bones that remained afterward, there was nothing alive in there at the time; he thought Dad was probably hallucinating, or perhaps had seen a body sliding down a seat or falling over on its side.

Anyway, if the coroner was right, Mom was probably crushed against the ceiling instantly; the brains that people all over the world wanted to talk to were smashed like a pumpkin in the wreck of her skull. Jerry was impaled on a piece of chassis that—again, to judge from where they found him and it—must have ripped up through the seat, moving at bullet velocity, entered his body somewhere near the rectum and exited by way of breaking the collarbone. His whole body cavity must have been torn to jam before the first time the truck rolled, and the sudden pressure loss would have meant he was unconscious before he knew what happened.

The coroner spent quite a bit of time on the question of what had happened to Marie. The skeleton— what was left of it after it burned—was in a horribly distorted, coiled form, and his best guess was that the whole seat had been hurled against the ceiling, fracturing her skull (but the cracks could have been caused by the fire, and people sometimes survive fractured skulls), breaking vertebrae in all three dimensions (I would have tended her for fifty years if she'd been a quadriplegic) and ripping both shattered femurs out through her leg muscles. There were undoubtedly many internal injuries that mere bones could not document . . . the coroner figured the pressures involved must have ruptured many of her internal organs. He assured me, repeatedly, that there wasn't any way at all that she could have been conscious by the time Dad got to the van. Chances were she was dead before the first time the van rolled, dead while it had not yet crushed the roses let alone rolled down the lawn.

Chances were.

She probably never knew.

But Dad saw something moving in there, just before the gas tank blew, and if Mom and Jerry had both received unquestionably instantly fatal wounds . . .

It could have been a hallucination. Dad doesn't hallucinate, but anyone might in the circumstances. Anyway, the door was blocked. Anyway, it could have been a body falling. Anyway, moving someone with a fractured skull and spine would kill the person immediately. Anyway, a severed spinal cord wouldn't transmit pain, not even if the body were on fire.

Anyway anyway anyway.

Dad said he saw something moving in the van. But the van burned all but completely before the fire trucks even got there, burned while he danced around it trying to get in and see and maybe pull something out, burned while I crawled miserably down the lawn, my clothes still drenched in Carrie's blood.

3

There had been a lot of weeks afterward when they just
gave me pills, and a lot of mornings when I would
wake up and try to pretend that at some point or other
it had all become a dream. Sometimes I pretended that
Marie was going to be there next to me when I rolled
over, and we would be back in our house with our new
IKEA furniture and the walls covered with Pre-
Raphaelite prints. Sometimes instead I pretended that I
was waking up in my dorm bed my freshman year, and
that I had dreamed Marie, that Jerry and Carrie were
still in high school and nothing had really changed
my life yet, but there were all sorts of adventures in
front of me. And sometimes I pretended that I was
about ten, that the whole dream of being an adult was
just a nightmare, and I was really still going to grow
up to be an astronaut. Mom and the twins and I were
going to go for a day hike up in the Laurel Caverns
area.

I pretended pretty hard, so it wasn't for lack of effort

that I always opened my eyes on the bleak world I had closed them on.

I stayed that way for months. I rarely was awake for ten hours in a day, and when I was I sat around in a bathrobe, looking at old pictures or just staring out at the yard where the burned and torn scars on the grass were healing, watching as leaves fell and snow began to blow.

Dad, meanwhile, got better. The Center went out and got donors like crazy, and they funded a full set of bodyguards for him. Then he went ahead and published his book about Blade of the Most Merciful, after a revision to make it more readable by laymen—a thing called *Solely for the Kill*.

It was the kind of smart, effective revenge you might expect. The news stories plus Dad's book did the job. Any normal terror outfit tries never to hit in the USA because they know how crazy the public goes and how completely it unleashes the President, who is suddenly trying to look as tough and mean as possible to the voters. Most of the time Americans are merely annoyed by terrorism as "something weird that foreigners do, over there." But let it get "over here," and the sky falls in on whoever brought it. Look at what happened to Libya a few years ago . . .

Blade of the Most Merciful went from something whispered about to front-page news, instantly. Moreover, they were too hot for anyone to touch— they had nowhere to hide and everybody was glad to turn them in. There were strikes by the American Delta Force, by Seals and Green Berets; SAS, Mossad, the West Germans, Egypt, all got into the act. I followed it in a half-interested kind of way, on the news and in things like *Time* and *USA Today*. It seemed like one more branch of the sports news . . . something else to read in

my bathrobe as I ate cold cereal up in Dad's spare bedroom, and fell asleep, and woke up again and again
hoping it hadn't happened.

Once what had happened to our family—plus Dad's
book—made it clear to everyone that this was a mad-
dog outfit, it was cleaned out in a hurry. *Newsweek* did
a front-page profile of Dad, and they used the word
"courage" about every other paragraph, which made
him furious.

They ignored me—one look and I suppose they
decided that was the kindest thing—but they just loved
Carrie. In just a few weeks she was getting around on
her powered wheelchair and doing her physics grad
work mostly over computer modem; it seemed to take
her only a day or so to master the one-handed key-
board. She began to move very quickly toward her
Ph.D.—she said it was a matter of not having sports to
distract her anymore.

There were two Blade of the Most Merciful assaults
on the house, finally; they came when the organization
was on the ropes and desperate and, I suppose, wanted
to show that it had any fight left at all.

The first was the night before Christmas. I'd done no
shopping and barely knew what day it was; I suppose
in my strange, muddled state I was hoping that Santa
would bring me a new life or take back all the bad
things that had happened, or some such. I was asleep,
in the usual restless dreams, when the delivery van
leaped the curb from the alley, crashed through the
wire fence at the back of the yard, and headed straight
for the house.

The men from Steel Curtain Guards were on the
stick. By the time my feet were hitting the floor after
the crash of the fence, the Steel Curtain guy watching
the back had flipped on his infrared spotting scope,

seen the crude armoring of the engine on the oncoming van (strips of Kevlar stretched across it), put his laser designator spot on the biggest gap, and started pumping rounds in. Those nifty little .22s were designed for SWAT teams, and they have practically no kick and a very high rate of fire—once they're sighted in they'll chew whatever is in front of them to hamburger. In an instant he'd cut a hole through the radiator, and he could see a scattering of hot little lights, like crazed fireflies, streaking and pinging around in there.

I was still reaching for my robe when the SCG "utility infielder" on the second floor got to a window, sized up the situation, brought his AK to his shoulder, and started blasting down into the roof of the oncoming van.

The angle was lousy. He might have gotten the driver, but it's hard to say. At least he was able to rake the unarmored roof twice, and if he didn't do any damage, he surely made the driver's last moments a little more nervous.

More likely if the driver was hit it was by something coming through the fire wall from the first sharpshooter. In any case both the riflemen guarding our house agreed that the driver never tried to get out, the door handle never moved, when the van slid to a halt in the good old Pittsburgh mud, thirty yards short of the house, its engine dead—by that point the engine had absorbed most of a magazine, and no doubt plenty of wires, belts, and hoses were severed, or maybe the alternator had gotten zapped. Anyway, the van sat there for three long seconds—meanwhile I was in my robe and running out into the hallway—and then the forty or so pounds of C4 in it, probably placed under a barrel of kerosene, blew up with a deafening roar.

I was running down the stairs screaming like a madman, which I suppose I was at the time. One of the nice strong woman guards from Steel Curtain—their specialist in mental patients—grabbed me and pinned me down just after the bomb went off. Other people were charging upstairs to get Carrie and Dad, and they quickly swept us into the "secure room"—the old laundry room that they'd fortified as a kind of bomb shelter in the middle of the house.

By the time they let us out, the Steel Curtain guys had put out three minor fires on the roof and one blazing curtain inside the house, a repair crew was on its way to board up and reglaze the broken windows, and the house and yard were crawling with cops, FBI, and various guys who never exactly said who they worked for but looked like they were more used to wearing uniforms than the new suits they were in.

It was Christmas morning. I got up, wandered through the house that smelled strangely of smoke, and went to my untouched bedroom. I shrugged off the robe, got out the razor, changed the blade, and carefully shaved, then took a shower. I needed a haircut but I had no idea where I'd find a barber today.

My clothes fit really loose, and I realized that several months of not eating or exercising much had taken a lot off me. Well, the old weight set was down in the basement, and maybe the Steel Curtain people had an idea where I could get a little roadwork in on a track. And certainly I ought to be safe enough at my old dojo—being surrounded by friendly martial artists, with armed guards outside . . .

I went down and asked the cook Dad had hired (the book was rapidly making him rich, which was a good thing considering how much Carrie needed) to fix me a huge breakfast. Carrie stared at me for a long moment, then pulled her wheelchair around next to me to eat her own bagel and coffee.

"What are you going to do today?" she asked.

"I'll start by apologizing," I said. "I'm afraid I haven't gotten a thing for either you or Dad."

Dad came in then, and he said, "Seeing you like this is a pretty good gift as is. We didn't exactly know what you'd like, Mark, so we took some guesses. Want to come and see how we did?"

"Sure." I pushed the now-empty plate away, grabbing a last piece of toast to tuck into my jaws—I needed my strength back quickly—and went out with them to discover that I had gained a few sweaters, a pair of running shoes, and several large collections of prints. I was careful to praise all of them thoroughly.

I spent most of the rest of that day talking to the Steel Curtain people, and then on the phone to the extremely annoying shrink Dad had hired to pester me. Something about giving guns to mental patients bothered the guy, even when the mental patient could explain perfectly coherently that a gun was exactly what he needed.

It was simple. When that bomb went off—even before, when I knew something was happening—I wanted a gun in my hand and a chance to shoot back. I'd never fired a shot at anything but a paper target, nor hit anybody since I was a kid other than in the dojo, but that didn't matter. I'd found a purpose in life—hitting back.

It wasn't exactly the kind of thing a shrink approves of, but Dad and Carrie backed me up, and eventually Doctor Svetlana went for it as well. I think they figured it was just a phase, but a better one than watching me slowly fade away to a ghost. Anyway, it took about three days, and then all of a sudden everyone caved in, and I had the clearance to start getting myself qualified as a bodyguard.

If the shrink wasn't crazy about it, Hal Payton, the head of Steel Curtain, was about as unenthusiastic as you can get. Having the client decide to join the bodyguards was not at all in his recipe for how things ought to work. Once again, though, I wore him down; the fact was that if I'd been an applicant off the street, with my skills, he'd have hired me in an instant. Moreover, he had the testimony of half a dozen people, plus his own eyesight, to tell him that I had found something that I could really take an interest in, and that, irregular as it was, it was making me better.

I passed his qualifiers on pistol and martial arts with no hassle at all, even showing one of his guys a thing or two about the pugil stick. It didn't take long for me to get through the bonding process—there was practically nothing to investigate and it was all out in the open. And the exam for a Pennsylvania PI's license could be passed by a young chimp. By the new year I was a licensed bodyguard, working as a freelance contractor, nominally hired by Dad (for the minimum wage—I could hardly ask him to pay me a "real" salary for something as crazy as this) to work with Steel Curtain.

The other bodyguards seemed a little bemused by it all, but when they found they could rib me about it and that I'd tease back in a friendly way, they accepted me pretty quickly. I realized early on that I would have done better to have a little military experience—you live closer to weapons for a longer time that way—and that maybe I should think about studying for the police exams; a surprising number of rent-a-cops are guys who found the test too tough, but I figured the police exam couldn't be any tougher than the Ph.D. comprehensive exam I had been preparing for.

I especially liked sitting up at night; maybe that was

because I figured that was when it would happen. Maybe because the bomb had gone off in bright daylight. I didn't care—one perk that my strange position carried was that I could pick my own hours, and I was certainly going to exercise that.

The family had always gone to church on Epiphany, January 6, the celebration of the coming of the Wise Men, and although Reverend Hamlin took a little persuading—he thought armed men sitting around in Ninth Presbyterian might disturb the parishioners a bit—he came around after Dad made a big donation to the building fund.

This was partly Dad's idea and partly Doctor Svetlana's—"reestablishing family rituals" was what he called it, meaning it was better to get used to doing things without Jerry, Marie, and Mom than to have the empty time there to prey on our minds.

Epiphany evening service is not one of the biggies among even the most devoted churchgoers, but Reverend Hamlin gave a pretty good sermon, told the old familiar story pretty well, and had just gotten to the point of announcing that we would be taking communion next when the doors at the side of the sanctuary flew open.

The Steel Curtain guy on the other side of Dad pounced on him and brought him down to the floor; the one next to Carrie would have rolled her from her wheelchair to the floor except that she'd already gotten down there herself. Most of the congregation just gaped and gasped, but Reverend Hamlin did a very creditable job of taking cover under the communion table, knocking grape juice and little chunks of Wonder Bread everywhere.

Payton should have tackled me, but he was busy reaching for his sidearm, so I lunged, cleared the pew in front of me, dropped between pews, and had my Colt up and leveled before I was even aware that the top of the pew to my left had suddenly splintered. I saw the men bursting through the door to the right and fired twice, not really aiming so much as just getting shots off to make them keep their heads down, slow them up, and spoil their aim. From around the church, wherever a Steel Curtain guard could get a clear line of fire, pistol shots were cracking out, and the first two Blades to make it through the door made it only a step or two before they were cut down.

If they'd come with a bomb or a grenade, they might have pulled it off, but even then it would have been close. There was a clatter of gunfire outside, and the terrorists bursting into the sanctuary whirled to run back out. Steel Curtain men shot them in the back—I was shooting myself, but later it turned out that the bodies had only .38 slugs and one .357 Magnum in them, and all my shots were found in places like the doorframe or the side of the choir loft. Payton later told me it was buck fever.

Thirty seconds after the attack began, the Blades were all dead or dying on the floor. The firing outside turned out to be the city cops, who had been closing in and had caught the getaway vehicle.

But it took us a while to find that out. First everyone had to get up from behind pews and look around nervously, and the Steel Curtain people made Dad and Carrie stay down and quiet for a long time. There were a few holes in the stained-glass windows—I noted that the Lamb of God seemed to have taken one right between the eyes—and a lot of the older parishioners weren't going to be exactly the same for a while, but the only innocent bystander hit was the Sunday School director, a kind-of cute young thing who had all sorts of "very serious and important raps" with kids; some plaster chips had gotten blown into her thigh, and the blood ruined a good blue wool dress.

Aside from the dress, Dad ended up paying for new carpets by the sanctuary doors (bloodstains don't come out easily), new paneling and woodwork in various places where rounds had hit, plastering to cover pockmarks in the walls, and a new surplice and stole for Reverend Hamlin, his having been ruined in a rain of grape juice. (He looked pretty grim getting up from under the communion table, but I could see where his sense of humor might have gone to hell about that point.)

And though I hadn't hit a thing, I was confirmed in my choice of profession. Three months later the FBI said they were pretty sure Blade of the Most Merciful was out of business, and Dad and Carrie started traveling with just a guard or two each. I opened Mark Strang Bodyguards.

Since then I'd been hit several times, and hit people back, and I found that it was what I lived for. Five years had gone by, and Carrie was Dr. Strang now and doing all sorts of hush-hush stuff for Uncle Sam, Dad had two more books out and was on the talk shows a lot to explain the Mideast—and I was still living over my storefront office.

But hey, with the exception of getting thumped on by nuts like Brunreich, it wasn't such a bad life, and it wasn't like I'd be doing anything else. And I still had two years left on my leave of absence before I would actually have to tell them I was never coming back to settle into the quiet life of art history.

My whole life wasn't exactly flashing by me as I rode

in the back of Robbie and Paula's van, but that was the gist of it. The dreams kept returning to two things . . . the last glimpses I had had of Marie, alive, and the moment when I found out how good it felt to hit people.

Not necessarily to hit them back, either. They didn't have to have done anything to me. What it was, I think, was simply that a part of me had figured out that the whole world was just too damned violent, and people hurt each other much too often. And one way to get people out of the habit of hurting other people was to hit the aggressor with whatever force was to hand.

It was simplistic and dumb. And I believed in it down to the very core of my being.

My face was a little damp from my own slobber when Robbie gently shook me awake; Robbie's a small woman, and it was some effort for her and Paula to get me inside my apartment and dump me on my bed. They knew where the spare key was—they'd done house-sitting for me a time or two—so they just locked the place up behind them. (I was dimly aware of this as I considered whether or not I wanted to get undressed and get under the covers rather than just stay where I was.)

After a while, I slept, and when I woke up, the world looked very slightly better. It was late in the afternoon, and the answering machine downstairs showed that the phone had not rung at all during the day, which made it a typical day. The mail was the phone bill and Ed McMahon; I considered referring them to each other. I was loaded, between Marie's life insurance and the allowance Dad had settled on me, and it was a good thing too, because the business needed infusions of cash pretty regularly.

My right hand was aching where the tip of

Brunreich's bat had grazed me, and though I could flex all the fingers, I suspected I was bruised pretty deeply. This was going to cut into my ability to do anything effective for a while; I'm not much good on the left side in karate, judo, or hapkido, and I don't shoot left at all. Probably I should practice all of that, but I never seem to get around to it.

I wandered back upstairs, fixed myself macaroni and cheese, took off my clothes, and got into a hot tub, with the plate of food on the toilet lid beside me. The warm water and the cold beer seemed to do my hand some good, and the meal helped, too; pretty soon I was quietly drifting, thinking of any old thing. That poor kid Porter had a tough row to hoe . . . she was just about the first client I'd ever cared about much, other than as a source of income and the "prisoner's base" I was supposed to guard in this elaborate game that gave a grown-up man an excuse for violence, or for threatening violence, on public streets.

The other agencies in town didn't like me much. They liked to work by intimidation. I liked to work by preemptive strike. I wondered what Porter might eventually hear about me, and I wondered even more why I cared.

Maybe it was getting time to date somebody again, though that seemed a waste of time and effort, too. I had a couple of alternatives, as it were—I could always get Robbie and Paula, who were always broke, to go to dinner and the movies, with no risk that either of them was going to want a good-night kiss, let alone to get into bed with me. And there was a former client, Melissa, whose ex-pimp I'd roughed up, who didn't mind occasionally giving me some in-kind payment on the bill she still owed me, if I just wanted physical contact.

She was a nice enough girl in her way . . . what if I actually took her out? She said she wasn't a working girl anymore, except for what she was doing for me (she didn't seem to keep books, so I never told her whether she was anywhere near paying off the debt. The truth was, I didn't see any reason to let her stop, and I didn't care enough if she just decided to).

That was kind of an odd thought. Dinner with Melissa. Not a great idea—might lead to conversation. She knew my story well enough, and I knew all about hers, but that didn't mean conversation was safe. I wasn't quite ready to have opinions about anything.

So what did I want next year to be like? Maybe I just wanted to have an opinion about something, living versus dying, say, or liking some client or other.

Well, I had liked Porter. There. Smart quiet ten-year-olds were nicer than their crazy parents. I had an opinion about something. And heck, by the time I was thinking about dating anybody again, Porter would probably be looking for her second husband, the way things work these days.

Having an opinion didn't seem to require any action, which was fine with me. I finished off the mac and cheese, looked at my hand—it was still swelling a little further, but I was sure now it was just bruised—and opened another beer for dessert.

I had just about finished beer number two and once again reached the conclusion that I wasn't going to change anything about my life right away when the buzzer from downstairs went off. I jumped out of the tub, spilling the last of the beer into the gray suds, wrapped a towel around myself, went into the single large room that's the rest of my apartment, and flipped on the video camera for the peephole.

He was a big, square-built guy, standing there

patiently in the late-afternoon spring sunshine, and at first glance I would have figured he had a job lifting boxes somewhere, but the way he moved, sort of leading with his head as he looked around the street, suggested that he did some kind of brain work, might even be a scholar, and just happened to keep himself in shape. His hair was salt-and-pepper gray, thick, and overdue for a haircut; his nose spread across his face like someone had used a chisel to reshape it into a triangle. If he had students, they probably thought he looked like Fred Flintstone.

I pushed down the talk button on the intercom. "Can I help you?"

"I need to engage your services—or someone's—as soon as possible." His voice had that "educated American" accent that my dad's does, the one that professors cultivate.

"Are you being followed right now?" I asked.

"It's entirely possible."

"Then come inside. I'll be down to let you into the office part in a couple of minutes." I pushed the door release button, and the buzzer went off; he turned the doorknob and came into the front room of my office, quickly closing the door behind himself. I flipped the video camera control over so that I could keep an eye on him there, though there wasn't much to worry about—the desk, file cabinets, and safe were all behind a dead-bolted solid-core door in the inner office. I suppose he could have torn up the old copies of *Architecture Today*, *Reader's Digest,* and *Art Collector* that I keep there, or stolen one of the plastic chairs.

This made it a little more intriguing. He had two cases with him, one about big enough for a few changes of clothes and maybe some books and papers, the other about the size for an outsized briefcase.

Usually if someone is being followed when they come to my office, it's a woman with a crazy husband or boyfriend, or a couple of times it's been a woman who was being stalked by one of those strange characters who decide they're in love with a pretty face on the street.

Well, maybe he was in a love triangle or something.

I threw clothes on and hurried downstairs. When I opened the door from the inner office, he had set his cases down but he was keeping his hands close to the handles, not making a big thing of it but obviously ready to grab and run if he had to.

I said, "Come on in and have a seat." He did, and I dead-bolted the door again behind us, then took my own seat behind my desk.

The first thing he did was lift the smaller case up, thump it down on the desk on its side, and open it. He took out a small bound stack of bills, the kind you get from the bank, and handed it to me; it was a set of fifty one-hundred-dollar bills.

I looked at it and said, "I don't work for the mob, religious cults, or governments-in-exile."

"Neither do I," he said. "You may find this hard to believe, but I'm just a plain old professor of sociology at Pitt; the cash is from my savings. My name is Harry Skena. I'm only hiring a bodyguard because I can't get the police or FBI to believe me."

I nodded. "Who's after you, and what do they want?"

"What they want is easy enough to explain. They want to kill me in order to silence me. As for who they are—well, that's where I'm getting into trouble, getting the police and FBI to take me seriously. Have you read—"

He happened to glance up at the wooden plaque

Robbie had made for me, over the desk, the one that said "Mark Strang, Licensed Professional Bodyguard." His eyes got wide, and he said, "You are not, by any chance, related to *Gus* Strang?"

This made me believe him a little more; his academic colleagues all call him Gus, family and old friends call him Augie. "He's my father."

There was a long silence, while he licked his lips and seemed to think. "Well, then you're either going to think this is a strange practical joke, or you're the best man for the job.

"Let me start at the beginning. As a scholar, I'm afraid I am not in your father's league; I'm not an original theorist and I don't do anything very groundbreaking. My area of study is the formation of organized crime in immigrant communities. It's not really a hot area because there haven't been many new ideas in it for a long time, and my research isn't exactly hot either, because I end up confirming what everyone knows already, but it's the sort of thing that has to be done, making sure that what 'everyone knows' has some correspondence to the truth.

"What I do is hang around with an immigrant group for a while, talk with them, get to know them, establish trust so they'll tell me things, and then find out what I can about organized crime, if any, among them. And normally what I find is that if the job ladder is blocked for them, their businesses aren't succeeding in reaching a wider market than their own community, and they're frozen out of city politics, there's an organized crime syndicate pretty soon. If the doors are open to them, for whatever reason, usually there's not. And if they're the kind of ethnic group that makes a big deal about family loyalty, then it will tend to be a bigger and more systematic crime syndicate, because the hoods have more brothers and cousins to go into business with.

"None of that's very new, and it really just confirms what everyone knows. And I've been doing that kind of study for fifteen years." He raised both his hands and made a funny little flipping gesture, as if shooing away his work, showing how unimportant it was.

"It's dull and it's routine and I do it because it's my job. As soon as the crooks find out I'm not a reporter or a cop, they don't really care about what I'm doing, so it's not even dangerous.

"Or it wasn't till just recently. About three months ago, I got interested in a new organized crime mob that seemed to be showing up everywhere across the country all at once, and that seemed to target practically all Islamic American communities. Now, that was strange enough—there are many different kinds of Islamic immigrants and, for that matter, many different kinds of Islam in the United States, and they don't have a lot in common with each other. Some of them don't even like each other much.

"And this mob was a really bad-ass outfit, too. They seemed to *prefer* threats and extortion—often they didn't really give the first people in a community that they threatened time enough to give in, they just did something to scare hell out of everyone else. The kind of mob that kills just to prove they'll do it, like some of the really nasty crack mobs, or the bad old days of the Colombian cowboys, or going back farther, like the early days of the Capone mob or the Bronx Irish gangs.

"And most of the Islamic groups have been very resistant to organized crime anyway; too many successful businessmen and kids going to college in the first generation for them to get interested in crime.

"Sociologically speaking, this new mob was the

wrong kind of criminal in the wrong kind of community at the wrong time. It made no sense for them to be there according to all the orthodox theory. So naturally they got my attention." He sighed and stared into space a moment. "After all, if you're not brilliant, but you're pretty good at documenting things, your best ticket is to find something interesting to document.

"Anyway, in no time at all, in the Turkish, Pakistani, Algerian, Syrian, and Iranian neighborhoods around the country, there was just plain *terror* of these guys, and small wonder."

I felt my throat tightening, and I wasn't sure whether I was hoping for or frightened of what I might hear, so I made myself ask, "And who are they?"

He looked down at the floor. "I think they're the remnants of Blade of the Most Merciful."

4

There was a long silence, and when I didn't laugh or throw him out, he went on. "The leadership of Blade of the Most Merciful was never caught, you must know, and only about half of them are accounted for by the raids that put it out of business. And the only ones in prison were the few whose lives were saved medically— did you know about those?"

"Yeah," I said, my mouth completely dry. "Yeah, I know. Nine captured, wounded members. Four died in the hospitals they were in, a couple of them probably with help. The rest died in prison within a year of going in, all of them ruled suicide, though I think a couple of them also had help. Not one of them ever said a thing, not even the simplest political statement to the world."

Harry Skena nodded, tugged at his ear gently. "In the other case I have the evidence I could show you that these are Blade people."

"If they are—why are they doing it? And what's a

terror organization doing turning into organized crime?"

He shrugged. "Maybe they're broke and they need the money, and they've got a lot of practice at violence. The Soviet Union recently went out of business, and though I don't think they were behind Blade, maybe Blade was getting money from them for contract jobs. Or maybe they were never really a terrorist outfit—maybe they were always just a plain old criminal enterprise, that found a way to make cash in the terrorist biz. Or maybe what they really are is something totally different, and organized crime and political terrorism are both means to the same end, which is something different from either politics or profit. I have no idea. The trouble is, I have good reason to think that at about the same time that I was figuring out who they had to be, they were also noticing me, and figuring out what I knew.

"They aren't the type of outfit that gives warnings, but I didn't want to run until I had to. So I got kind of a habit of not being at home, keeping irregular hours, making myself unpredictable. Not hard to do, I'm a bachelor, and I've lived by myself for years. This afternoon I came by my apartment to get a change of clothes for after handball. My side of my building—the Park Plaza, up on Craig Street—was caved in. Cops and fire trucks were running in all directions. I called the newsline and learned that it had been a bomb blast—there were a bunch of people hurt in Duranti's, but luckily very few tenants were home. Best guess was that a maintenance man had accidentally set off the bomb.

"Maintenance was coming to my place to set mousetraps this afternoon. They left me a note to that effect.

"I walked back to Pitt—just a few blocks to my office in Forbes Quad—picked up these two cases, which I already had packed, and took a cab here. One car stayed with us for four blocks, so I asked the driver to do some evading. He thought he had lost them."

I nodded. "Mind if I make a phone call?"

"I'd *expect* you to."

I picked up the phone. I had a secure line—they're a necessity in my line of business—and so did Dad, because with the ever-present danger he'd decided he had to have one, too. We'd never used them to talk about anything other than where to meet for lunch (and come to think of it we usually met at Duranti's— that would have to change). The phone rang twice, then Dad picked it up and said hello.

I told him what was up, in a few short sentences.

"Well, yes, I know Harry Skena slightly," Dad said. "Tallish, big, square-shouldered, graying hair, clean-shaven . . . looks sort of like—maybe I shouldn't say this, but one of my grad students is a former student of Harry's and always said Harry looked like Fred Flintstone."

"That's the guy," I said. "Is what he's saying plausible?"

Dad sighed. "Well, Blade has to have gone somewhere. I suppose organized crime might suit them as well as anything. They really had nowhere to run once the world started hunting them down, so there's nothing too wildly implausible about that part of the story. As for why—well, Harry's absolutely right. You remember that's what baffled me about it—why on Earth they were doing the strange, pointless violence they were doing. So in a way the parts that don't make any sense are exactly the parts that are really consistent with their known character."

"Okay, but then why haven't the FBI and the cops believed him?" I glanced up from the phone and saw that he was sitting there, his hands folded in his lap, listening patiently. If what Harry Skena was telling me was true, then he was sitting there watching me decide whether or not to help, which might be literally life and death for him, but he looked no more alarmed than he would waiting for a dog license or for a restaurant to approve his credit card. I liked that about him at once, so I wanted him to be telling me the truth.

Dad sighed. "Well, you and I both got to know them—and I was a consultant while they were hunting down Blade. Mark, we both know the official cops are good, but they're also file-closers by nature. They like to have things officially over with and they don't like to reopen investigations. So somebody you've barely heard of—a nothing-special professor at a second-rate university—comes to you with a story like that . . . and you can either reopen the file and trigger all kinds of hard work for yourself . . . or you can pat him on his head, note him down as a nut, and most likely it will turn out fine. And if it doesn't—well, Harry Skena may be dead, but then they'll really *know*, won't they? As long as the evidence isn't ironclad, and it's not their neck on the line, it's awfully easy to leave that file closed, and pretty hard to decide to open it. That's what I would say is going on."

"It makes sense," I admitted. "Uh, in present circumstances I'm going to have to get Harry to a safe house somewhere and do it right away. If you like, once I have him somewhere safe with a secure phone line, I'll fax you his evidence."

"I'd appreciate that. If Blade is back, I've got another book to write. Besides, maybe I can get some official action on this—I think the FBI would listen to me, especially after this bombing attack. Give them a call, too, once you're dug in somewhere. Tell Harry hi from me. And Mark?"

"Yeah."

"Be careful. I wish like hell you'd get out of that stupid line of work and start using that good brain of yours again, but if you're going to do it, at least stay sharp and tough. And if you do find you're shooting at Blade bastards . . . shoot me a couple too, okay?"

"Deal, Dad. Love to Carrie. You guys get careful, too. Might be worth having Payton put more guards on for a few days."

"I'd already thought of it."

We said "bye" and hung up. I nodded to Skena. "You check out okay. So we're leaving right away—my car's in a secure area a block away, and we need to get walking before anyone turns up. We'll head out of town and work out where we're going as we go—if we take 79 North we can go either way on the pike or just keep heading north, or backtrack and bypass the town. It's about the fastest way there is to make our tracks hard to follow."

"Fine," he said. "Er—on the matter of payment and expenses—"

"What you've given me is good for a while," I said, "and if it really is Blade that's after you, for purely personal reasons I'd be willing to do this as a *pro bono* case."

"Good, then. I shall pay you every cent I'm able, but I'm afraid my case still won't be much of a money-maker for you."

He stood up and extended his hand; we shook on the deal.

Then there was a terrifying roar as the front door of the storefront was blown down with a small shaped charge. Skena grabbed his cases; I yanked a drawer open and grabbed the .45 in there, leaped over the desk, ran to the office door. I could hear the heavy footsteps and the rush of deep breathing, and then the doorknob turned uselessly as they tried it before blowing this door as well.

I put a shot straight through the door—it was solid-core, but at point-blank range a .45 slug will get through the wood, and even if the slug itself doesn't have the energy left to kill, the spray of splinters into the guy's chest and face ought to distract him a moment. There was a howl of pain and, as I stepped aside, two answering rounds punched holes in the door, spraying splinters all over the back wall.

"This way," I said to Skena, keeping my voice a lot calmer than I felt. One thing I had learned from Payton was to have a back way out; you never knew when you might have to move a client through undercover. Mine was a steel fire door behind a fake bookcase; I opened it and gestured him through. A shot rang off the dead-bolt, but the office door held; as I closed the bookcase door it was still holding. "Down," I said. "This takes us to the place next door's basement."

The place next door was Berto's pizza joint. Jim Berto, the owner, was an old beer buddy. I paid him a retainer every month for these occasions. I'd only had to use this twice before, in five years of business, and it was worth every penny.

The basement was his garage, and I had keys to every delivery car. I had Skena get down in the back-seat of one, jumped into the driver's seat, and we were off through the back alley. From my office I could hear shouting and running, and there was a swarthy type standing by my back Dumpster, but he didn't look at the pizza car departing—or not right away.

As we were just turning the corner out of the alley, I

saw men run out of Berto's garage, and the Dumpster leaner suddenly looked a lot more excited. Damn—if I'd had a few seconds more they'd have had no idea where we were headed. I couldn't make an effective run for it in the pizza car—aside from being bright red and white and easy to spot anywhere, it also had less than a quarter tank of gas. And if they knew I was rolling, they'd be headed for my private garage as fast as they could.

If you're given the choice between impossible and difficult, take difficult. I laid rubber right through the alley stop sign, scaring the hell out of one of Berto's real pizza drivers, and roared right up Beacon Street toward my office, with its plume of smoke pouring from its shattered door and front window. A crowd was already starting to gather to see what was going on, and I decided more diversion would be a good idea.

I held down the horn and sped up. Sure enough, that had to be their car pulled up on the sidewalk—I guess terrorists don't worry much about parking tickets—so I took a chance, pushed the electric window down button, pulled my .45 from its shoulder holster, slowed just a little, and leaned over to the passenger side, putting a round into one rear tire and one front tire on their van, and then one into the startled driver. I had just an instant of seeing his shocked face and the hole torn in his neck before I had to get control of the car again and floor it up the steep, winding street.

I'd finally shot someone, and it was a Blade terrorist. My life was made—from here on out anything good that happened was going to be pure profit.

A shot screamed off a phone pole on one side of me, and the back window of a car shattered—whoever was shooting wasn't being very effective just yet—then we were around the corner and headed down Murray Avenue. With luck they might split up forces and lose me, trying to cover the parking garage and both directions on the parkway all at once. "You okay back there, Dr. Skena?"

"Fine so far. Should I stay down?"

"Might as well. Do you have a gun?"

"Yes, but it hasn't been fired in twenty years, and it's been longer than that for me—"

It figured, somehow. "Okay, then just stay down and let me do the shooting."

I whipped the pizza wagon into the entry of the parking garage I use without signaling or slowing down; it fishtailed pretty badly, knocking a traffic post a little, but it minimized the time to react in case anyone was following or watching. At least there was no line, so I rolled up to the ticket booth, grabbed the ticket, and the pizza car was through the gate before it was entirely raised.

You're really not supposed to drive up the down ramps in a parking garage at forty miles per hour, but it was still a bit before rush hour, and I figured the more chaos I created the better, at the moment. What I hoped for happened; two exiting cars pulled over to get away from me and ended up in fender-bender situations on the ramp. One ramp partially blocked, and I knew which one . . .

The high-security area was on the top floor of the parking garage; I had the electronic key in my hand as we pulled up to it, and the Mercedes 510 SL "woke up" for me in its stall, the engine running smoothly and the lights coming on, before I had fully stopped the now-battered Berto's pizza wagon. It occurred to me that if I'd seen the way I was driving, and not known who I was, I'd have ordered all my pizzas from Berto's from then on—it sure looked like the most determined delivery driver I'd ever seen.

I yanked the car to a stop just short of the gate. "Out, and bring your cases," I said to Skena, and jumped to push my combination into the gate lock's buttons. The gate opened smoothly, and Skena and I ran to the Mercedes; another press of the electronic key opened my trunk, and we heaved his cases next to the packed suitcase, spare pistol case, and spare ammo I always keep in there. Then we were inside the car, and I pulled it sharply out and headed outward.

"You've blocked yourself in with that—" Skena was saying, but before he could get out "pizza car," I had slowed briefly, bumped it hard, and, since I had left it in neutral, rolled the pizza car backward onto the down ramp, its doors still hanging open. It gathered speed and headed downward to jam someplace or other, making one more barrier, but I was already on my way—down the up ramp, this time, to balance out the way I had come in.

We damned near made it. Would have made it, too, except for a vanload of Little Leaguers coming up the other way, and Mom who insisted on straddling the center of the ramp instead of moving to the side. It only took about thirty seconds for me to pull out of her way and let her through, but that was enough.

The Mercedes was just zooming out of the last turn when the first shot made a dent in the bulletproof windshield. I yanked it hard in the basic 180 maneuver—wrapping and unwrapping my arms to make it jump briefly sideways—and that got us past them with just two more hits on the glass and armor, one of which broke a back window—

But then luck really ran out. They had an old pickup and they backed it straight into the path of the Mercedes as I tried to go through the apparent hole. We must have been doing thirty-five when we hit the truck, hard enough to knock it sideways against the concrete retaining wall.

It was up too high for bumpers to meet, and the truck slid up the hood, its weight crushing downward, the undercarriage peeling away metal from my hood like a can opener. Something or other got the engine, and, anyway, I could hardly have backed out and run away with a truck jammed halfway onto my hood.

They tossed a grenade in the open back window; I saw it for just the instant before Skena flipped it back out, and it blew only a few feet from us, making my car echo like the inside of the bass drum in a hard-rock band. They had all dived clear of it; they were back in an instant, pumping rounds into the Mercedes's armor and glass.

"Bulletproof" doesn't mean it stops every round forever; it just means it doesn't shatter easily, and it takes a lot of punishment. In a second or so the back window had taken twenty rounds, and it was starting to crumble. I was down behind the seat, glad I'd put a Kevlar sheet into the back of each seat, gladder still I'd been belted in when we hit because right now I needed all the coordination I had—

I grabbed for the .45, and a funny thing happened. My hand wouldn't close around it.

I looked down to see that my hand was an amusing shade of deepest purple. It figured; I'd had that bad injury from the ball bat this morning, and then I'd used that hand twice in a few minutes to fire a .45. Normally no problem—my arm and hand muscles are well developed—but with the injury I'd probably started a major hemorrhage in the muscles, and while I'd been driving here it had been enough to put my right hand out of commission.

All this flashed into my head in one moment of awareness, along with two other facts:

I am, and have always been, a lousy shot left-handed.

And anyway, I didn't dare roll down a window to get a clear shot, and when the back window caved in as it was going to do any second, it would be too late to do much shooting back.

Through the maze of cracks, holes, and shattered glass, I dimly saw a figure running for the car, and realized we were probably about to get a satchel charge tossed underneath us. I had just time to realize we couldn't do a thing about it, and to remember Blade's tendency to overdo it with explosives.

I figured it was going to be quick.

Then suddenly there were bright lights everywhere, and the refraction in the shredded window made things invisible for every practical purpose. Some kind of gun I'd never heard before was firing; it made a sort of whoosh noise, like the miniguns on helicopters, those little high-speed Gatling guns, but it was deeper in pitch and loud enough to make the Mercedes vibrate. It fired three bursts; then there was a huge, booming explosion that echoed throughout the parking garage. The rear window gave way and flew into the compartment in a thousand pieces; bits of it rattled off the windshield and sprayed my back, stinging me but not penetrating my heavy shirt.

I popped up, the automatic in my left hand, and saw that there was nobody shooting back at me anymore; every Blader was scattered on the ground. As I reared a little higher, I saw there was something odd about them—and then I realized they all looked like their heads had been blown up from the inside.

In training films I'd seen what slugs do to human flesh—the way a modern pistol round goes in through a hole you could cover with your thumb, but takes out a chunk of flesh bigger than your fist on its way out. This was a lot worse than that; it was more as if their heads had simply ceased to be, turning into the thin red jam that was smeared all over the parking-lot walls, leaving them with stringy flesh sticking up from the abrupt ends of their necks.

The bomb blast had raked over the already fallen bodies, and dust, dirt, and smoke were stuck on the bloody walls, but nothing obscured the strange way they'd been killed.

I climbed a little higher in the seat, looked around a little more. Still there was no sound.

I looked down at Skena; he had a strange grin. "There's a fire in the past of most things," he said, very loudly. I was about to hush him since I had no idea who or what might be around, when the who or what answered.

A soft, low-pitched female voice—one I liked immediately—said, "And where there's fire, there's light, and where there's light, truth."

Harry Skena sat up abruptly; obviously he felt perfectly safe. "There's something you haven't been telling me," I said, partly because I really was irritated and partly because I was doing my best to hide my shock.

"We're taking the whole vehicle," the voice outside said, "so brace yourselves."

The whole vehicle? Brace—?

It got very dark. The world fell away the way it does in a plane that has suddenly gone into a dive to let gravity have its way. There was a silence that was like being struck deaf, and another part of me noted how like a dream it all was, how I didn't exactly seem to be in touch with my body, and I wasn't precisely where I seemed to be.

Then a kind of gray light came through, and a low

humming that was about an octave lower than the sixty-cycle hum you sometimes hear on stereo systems, and the world started to take shape again.

I was pretty sure I was not in a parking garage in Squirrel Hill anymore. First of all, the land around me seemed to stretch out for quite a ways, and though there was a wall in the distance, it wasn't nearly as close as the one in the parking garage had been. Then after a bit I realized that there was no wall at all, we were in something like a great big parking lot, with no other cars on it, and the pavement seemed to be metal.

I sat up farther, tried using the power switch to lower the windows; it didn't work, so I cranked mine down. The metal parking lot, in very bright sunshine, stretched out in all directions, and then more of the gray fog lifted, and sound came back, and I suddenly realized that the metal parking lot was trough-shaped, with the car at the bottom of the trough.

Hesitantly, I opened the door and stepped out. Far to either side of me, immense buildings, like giant high-rises or apartment complexes, rose up into the sky; we seemed to be right between two rows of them, and they looked to be about a mile apart.

I looked on up the side of one of the huge buildings, and it just kept going up—it seemed to be bigger than the World Trade Center is when you're standing on the sidewalk in front of it—and then . . .

I saw the sky. You can't have grown up a kid in America and not recognize that sky.

The Earth hung overhead, a little to the side of the building tops, eighty times wider than the full moon. And cutting across it was a wide dark line that swung around across the sky and converged with the building tops over my head.

I was on some huge, ring-shaped space station, the

kind of thing you ran into when you were a kid reading science fiction.

The bright sunlight, I realized, was coming from thousands of overhead lights; as I watched, the Earth "set" over one end of the "street" in which I stood, and the Sun and Moon rolled by. A couple of spaceships—at least that seemed like what flying assemblages of metal like that had to be—whizzed right into the ring, and, strangely enough, a silvery airplane, not much different from the old DC-3 "Gooney Birds," flew by overhead.

I could do nothing but stand and gape; while I was doing that, very dimly a part of my consciousness was aware that some kind of conversation was happening beside me, and that Skena was answering a lot of questions.

The Earth rolled back into the sky. It had been less than ten minutes, I figured, so this space station must be spinning pretty fast. I figured it probably had to since the gravity under my feet felt normal.

The most likely explanation was that I was dying on the pavement back in the parking garage, and this was a hallucination borrowed from my childhood reading. The second most likely thing was that I was already clinically dead, and this was the last hallucination before the lights went out. Then after that there came that I'd had a breakdown earlier in the day—say maybe Brunreich really got me with that bat—and had hallucinated everything since, including Harry Skena.

There was also the extremely unlikely possibility that this was really happening. I did my best to dismiss that thought, but the metal deck under my feet seemed disturbingly real.

I looked back at the Mercedes—it was a thorough mess. The armoring I'd had put in was all internal, so the body had a bunch of nasty-looking holes all over it.

The rear window, of course, was gone pretty completely. There were still bits of the underside of the pickup truck jammed onto and through its hood, and a mix of engine fluids was dripping underneath it.

"Naturally we'll fully restore it," Harry Skena said. "Good as new, or actually, given the relative state of technology, better than new. Better grab our things from the trunk—the pickup will be here in a minute or so."

My feet started moving, probably because whatever was left of my mind had just heard a program of action, and even if it didn't make any sense, at least it was something to do.

I unlocked the trunk—had to use my left hand, as my right would not now close to grip the keys—and raised it. The armoring had kept bullets out of any of our stuff, and I sort of mechanically unloaded everything to a few steps away from the car, not sure what a "pickup" was—I doubted he meant a pickup truck—and therefore not knowing how much room it might require.

As I moved the last of the cases and laid the spare pistol and supplies on top, it got sort of dark. I looked up to see something huge and round descending, and decided that as hallucinations go, this one was pretty amazing, and, moreover, that I had a lot more of an imagination than I ever had thought I did.

It was a strange angle, but I finally decided that, yes, it really was a big, silvery blimp coming down over us.

The soft, female voice from before spoke. "The airship will take us around to the other side of the station, where you can get medical treatment, and then it will drop your vehicle off for repair."

I looked around to see that she was standing there next to Harry Skena, and saw what she looked like for the first time. She was tall—I'm six-two and she was just about exactly my height—and built like a female bodybuilder. (I'm not sure whether I'd have bet on her or on Paula in an arm-wrestling contest.) Her face wasn't so much pretty as handsome—her features were very strong, cheekbones high but thick, jaw a little square—and her eyes were a cold, piercing blue. Her hair was jet black and very thick and wavy.

She was wearing a set of coveralls that looked more like clothing for fixing a car or painting an apartment than anything else, and under that some kind of thin clingy stuff. It looked sort of college-girl dress-down cute, except for the wide brown belt, from which hung a weird-looking polished metal thing that resembled nothing so much as one of those high-powered squirt guns—but which pretty clearly was the gun she'd used in settling the Bladers before she brought us here.

Wherever here was.

If there was any such place, I reminded myself.

"Where . . . am . . . I?" I asked very slowly. It felt very much as if I were in some kind of dream.

"You're at Hyper Athens," she said. "Specifically you're at the Crux Operations Rescue Landing Field here; we're taking you around to another part of Crux Ops in a few minutes. Meanwhile, you'll get to look over the city a little."

"Hyper Athens . . ." I said. "Athens . . . Georgia? Athens, Ohio?"

"Athens," she said. "In this history there's only one."

The Earth rolled back overhead as the huge space station continued to turn.

Harry Skena came forward to steady me a little.

"My name is Ariadne Lao," the woman said, gently, "and I'm a Crux Op. None of this is familiar to you, and you shouldn't expect it to be for a while."

Her eyes were very kind; her features, I realized, were sort of Eurasian.

I groped for a question to ask and came up with a stupid one. "Your last name is . . . Chinese?"

"Of course. The Chinese have been Athenian in this history for . . . oh, a thousand years or so, give or take." She smiled at me very warmly. "We don't really look different from any other Athenians."

Well, that cleared that up. I shook my head to clear it, and she gestured to the long tube which had descended from the blimp. "This is a . . ." she seemed to think for a moment " . . . your word might be 'lift' or 'dumbwaiter'—"

"An elevator?" I suggested. I've always been good at crosswords.

She nodded briskly. "Thank you, yes, that's the English word I was looking for. For some silly reason they gave me East Atlantic English instead of West Atlantic English in the translator, and only updated to about fifty years before your time. It will all become clearer once we get onto the airship and get you to a physician."

Pretty clearly this bizarre dream was not going to go away, so I let her and Skena herd me into the small, soft, baggy thing that hung at the end of a translucent hose from the blimp. As soon as we were inside, it hugged us all close—very gently, and it didn't feel frightening—and we shot up into the belly of the dirigible, coming out in what looked for all the world like an Art Deco cocktail lounge overlooking the area. I looked down through one glass-bottomed port in the floor to see what looked like a lot of spiderwebs wrapping up my car, then the car was on its way up to the bowels of the blimp. I was about to say "our bags" when a door in the wall opened, and there they were.

Ariadne was already at the bar, and she said, "I'm afraid this is a history that's never learned to like distilled liquor much, or tobacco, but I can offer you strong wine, beer, coffee, tea, hemp, or chocolate. I'm afraid we're rather prudes about opium and cocaine."

"Um, it's okay, so am I," I said. "Coffee would be great, I guess."

With everything picked up from the landing field, the blimp rose quickly into the air, and as it did I felt my weight dropping down toward nothing. By the time she floated over to me, extending a little squeeze bulb of strong coffee, we had cleared the tops of the buildings, and I could see that the whole space station formed one giant ring, with its open ends roofed over in glass or some such; we were flying through the weightless middle of it, and all around us dozens of other blimps and airplanes were doing the same. Through the spidery steel girderwork and the occasional reflections from the transparent windows far below, I could see the stars, the moon, and the shining edge of the Earth. Overhead was more of the city-in-a-ring that was Hyper Athens, and as I watched the city below me fell away and the city above me grew.

In a moment the blimp rolled slowly over, while we were completely weightless. We had passed through the center of the station, and now we were slowly descending toward the other side of the ring.

"You haven't tried your coffee," Ariadne said.

"Sorry, uh, Ariadne? Miss Lao?"

"Citizen Lao would be customary here."

"Thank you, Citizen Lao." I took a swallow of the coffee; here it was served with honey, clove, and cardamom, as far as I could tell. My hallucination was being very clever about what the differences were going to be, I decided.

"Er, if I may ask . . . *when* am I? I must be somewhere in the future?" Weight was returning rapidly, and I made my way to a sofa to sit. It was quite comfortable, but I still felt pretty weird.

"Well," she said, very gently (she really did seem like a very kind person and I was glad I had made her up that way) "er, Citizen Skena, you know, um . . . "

"Mark Strang," I said. "I'm a citizen of the USA, but I bet that doesn't count."

"Mister Strang, I think we'll call you," she said. "Citizen Skena, you know Mister Strang's world far better than I do. Perhaps you'll know how to answer his question."

"The truth will do," I said. I felt a little grouchy at being handled like a kid, and, besides, my hand was beginning to really hurt me.

"It's more a question of telling you the truth in a way that lets you believe it," Skena explained. "Er, let me think—it takes me a moment to convert. Locally we would say the year is 3157. But that actually corresponds to your year of 2726."

"I'm . . . eight hundred years in the future?" I began to feel a little weak and woozy, and I slid down the couch cushions a bit.

"Not in *your* future," Skena said.

Things rolled around once more and beneath the vast city street stretching through space and arcing up around us, I saw the great sphere of the Earth, the Horn of Africa plain as day to my right, the edge of South America far off to my left. Another silver Gooney Bird flew by, and as I watched a complex trusswork of metal beams—some kind of spaceship I supposed that never came down into the atmosphere—passed by the glass far below us. "Not in *my* future?" I think I asked—just before I fainted.

5

The first thought I had as I woke up was that the game I had been playing with myself since the bomb killed Jerry, Marie, and Mom had somehow finally worked, because I knew I wasn't in my own bed in my apartment, nor in my old bed at home.

Then I started to wonder about what I remembered. I still had not opened my eyes, and it didn't quite seem like I should yet. The bed had that kind of comfortable feel that your own bed doesn't, but it was somehow— too clean? too impersonal? Like it was designed to really fit my body, but my body hadn't quite worn it into shape.

All right. The Brunreich case. Porter Brunreich had talked to me quite a bit. Mrs. Brunreich jumping me while I was fighting her crazy husband the first time. Another fight with Brunreich in the airport, and getting my hand hurt. Robbie and Paula getting me home to bed. Yep, all there. So now I should be waking up and deciding to get a shower and some chow and a beer—

Wrong. Then the buzzer would go off and Harry Skena would be standing outside my office door.

Unfortunately all the memories I had connected with Harry Skena were every bit as vivid as the ones I had connected with the goofy Brunreich family. Right down to the call to Dad. No, if I was having a hallucination, I couldn't find the point where I had slipped over into it. So chances were that when I opened my eyes I'd be somewhere I'd never seen before.

I was right. The room was a pleasant soft blue color, very clean, obsessively cheerful, and bare. I knew I was in a hospital right away.

I sat up in bed and looked at my right hand. It was perfectly fine, though the nails were kind of long—which is odd in a guy who bites his nails as much as I do. Then I checked the other hand, and those nails were pretty much as always.

Getting out of bed to look for a toilet, I decided if this was the future, it was amazing that they still hadn't invented hospital gowns that fastened in the back. I also noted that there wasn't the funny twinge a cold floor always gave me in the ankle that got broken in the bomb attack, five years back; in fact the long white scar where the surgeons had gone in to fix it was gone, too.

"If you need a toilet," a pleasant, friendly voice from nowhere said, "put your hand on the black bar on the wall to the right."

I looked, saw what looked like a strip of black duct tape sticking to the blue wallpaper, and put my hand on it. A door slid open, and there was a small, comfortable-looking seat, very low to the ground. "Push the red button to dilate the seat," the voice said. It didn't seem to be in my ears; more like in my head.

I pushed the button and a hole formed in the seat; I

used the thing more or less the way I would at home, and a voice said, "Push the blue button for a wash," so I did and what happened was startling but not unpleasant, and no different really from a bidet . . . when I stood up the hole in the toilet closed, and I heard a gurgling noise that I assumed was the flush. Well, clearly, in this part of the future no one was ever going to complain about men leaving the seat up.

The voice told me that if I pushed another black strip, I'd find temporary clothing "while yours is being repaired," so I did, and sure enough there was a soft unitard-like thing that the voice assured me was underwear (it turned out to have a built-in jock), a comfortable coverall to put on over it, and a pair of perfectly fitting slippers that were shaped a bit like high-top sneakers and automatically contracted to grasp my feet and ankles when I put them on. It told me to go back to the bathroom and push the red button for the toilet again; I put the hospital gown in there, and it closed up and gurgled.

I had a question, and experimentally I tried just thinking it. Who was this voice?

"I am a module installed in your brain temporarily, to allow you to understand our language and to explain customs and situations to you as they come up. I am physically located in a small socket just below your right ear. If you pluck me out, you will stop hearing me, but the local language will become unintelligible."

It made a certain amount of sense—enough for the moment anyway—and I wondered what I was supposed to do now. It turned out that the chip in my head didn't know either, so probably someone was coming to tell me. Or us. I wasn't sure I knew what to make of this "passenger," though as a way of acquiring a language it beat the hell out of memorizing verb conjugations.

There was a knock at the door, and I said, "Come in," realizing my mouth was forming some other words entirely. A door opened where there had just been blank wall, and Harry Skena came in, which confirmed one part of my memories, followed by Ariadne Lao, which confirmed another part. "The hospital said you were up and getting dressed, Mister Strang," Ariadne explained. I noticed I really wanted to be invited to call her by first name, but the voice in my head said that even in the best of circumstances that was going to take a long time—this was a polite society.

The chip also told me it wasn't anywhere near time to ask her to call me by my first name. "I seem to be a lot better," I said. "And, um—my hand, I thought, was—"

"That was the major thing we had you in here for. You're young, healthy, and resilient enough to be able to deal with a slightly unbelievable situation—or rather with one you've never had to believe before. We injected you with nanos, Mr. Strang—that's a word your culture has just coined, and you won't actually have the thing the name goes with for a while yet, but what they are is tiny machines that can duplicate the work of cells in your body. In this particular case they swam around in your hand marking the damaged tissue to be destroyed and causing the healthy tissue to grow in to replace it. They also have a tendency to get loose in the body and fix anything else that looks like damage, so if you've lost any old scars or badly healed injuries, it's with our compliments, but if you've lost any tattoos, piercing, or scars you were proud of, do let us know, and we can restore them."

"Oh, I'm pretty happy with the quality of work," I said.

She smiled slightly. "You'd be surprised how many people are upset when they find their pierced ears and noses have been completely healed—or that a tattoo that took months has vanished overnight." Then she turned to Skena. "You're the one who knows both cultures, Citizen Skena. What do you suggest?"

Skena chuckled a little. "Well, let me think a bit . . . it's been a long cultural leap for me, too. But if you didn't find the view of space too disorienting, Mr. Strang, then perhaps we could go out on one of the terraces, have something to drink, and have a long talk. First question—do you accept, for the moment, that this place is real, and you are really here?"

The question took me a bit aback because I had been doing my best to ignore it for quite a while. There was the remarkable fact that everything stayed consistent—in my dreams, places and people usually flowed into each other. And how often do you meet strangers in a dream? And also, although this place was obviously a century or so advanced beyond my own time, it was *consistently* advanced and in ways I believed. It made sense that when a space station got big enough, since you'd only have "artificial gravity" at the rim, you'd use airplanes and blimps to get around inside. The little translator voice was like something out of the *Time* magazine article about cyberpunk. And maybe the most convincing thing of all was that toilet, which seemed like something you might find in a Neiman-Marcus catalog in ten years or so. And the fact was too that my experience was continuous—I fell asleep and I woke up, but that was the only interruption, and even that was normal, right down to the normal-for-me waking up wishing that I were somewhere else at some other time.

I could go on thinking of this as a hallucination if I tried, but I couldn't make myself *feel* that it was a hallucination. I suppose I could have thought Pittsburgh to be a hallucination, too, but the reality of the concrete and brick, wind and rain, traffic noise and strangers would have convinced me pretty fast.

"I think this place is real," I said, "and I think that I'm not crazy. Or at least not crazy in seeing this place; I reserve the right to be crazy independently."

Ariadne Lao snickered, and said, "Good enough." A smile from her was worth a lot at that point. Harry Skena opened the door—I noticed that now that it had been opened from the outside, it had somehow grown one of those black "door-open buttons"—and we walked out onto a pleasant, rambling gallery that overlooked a big, parklike commons a few stories below.

"This is a beautiful place," I said.

"Oh, yeah," Harry Skena hadn't lost his Pittsburgh accent yet. "I'm always glad to get back. Unfortunately they don't rotate us very often." We walked along the long gallery, looking out over the parklike malls and terraces below. Many people seemed to be out just enjoying the day.

"Is this all a hospital?" I asked.

Ariadne made a strange face. I realized the word "hospital" had not passed through the automatic processor, or had been left alone, so that it came out in English. It had somehow felt funny in my mouth, after some hours of speaking—what did they say? Attic?

The little gadget embedded in my skull explained that there was no such word in Attic.

Harry Skena shook his head. "We don't exactly have hospitals." I could hear the gadget in my ear hesitate before deciding not to translate; it was a pretty smart little box but didn't have much of a memory. "Since medicine is all done by nanos and robots, we just have spare rooms here and there in every city. If you get sick or hurt, they put you in the nearest room available—usually a private home."

"How do people feel about having strangers in their houses?"

"For us, having a guest is an honor. Not to mention we get a large tax break for it, since most of us feel it's an absolute duty to take good care of one's guests, and the state has no right to tax money you need for such a sacred purpose." Skena was explaining it very slowly, really, as if to a small kid, and then I realized this was something so basic that if I was to get around at all in this culture, I would have to know it. "Those who can't afford or don't want a guest room pay a tax that goes to cover medical equipment."

"So whose guest was I? And is some form of thanks due to the host?"

"You were ATN's guest," Harry explained. "The people we work for. ATN stands for Allied Timelines for Nondeterminism . . . and that will get a lot clearer over lunch."

Just as he said "lunch," we came around the bend to a place where the gallery widened into something that looked like a streetcorner café. "And here *is* lunch," Skena said. "To give you advance warning, our custom is that there's one dinner served at any given place, and you eat what that is. So if you don't like lamb, speak up, because that's what there is today."

"Suits me fine," I said, and we sat.

We started out with a mixture of fruit and vegetables that didn't taste very much like anything else I'd ever had; the thin syrup poured over it wasn't exactly salad dressing but wasn't exactly not salad dressing either. I was all set to find out what was actually happening, but Ariadne said the place was secure and we could stay as long as we wanted, and that I might as well enjoy the meal before we got down to business.

I still had not exactly figured out just which of

them was the other's boss; maybe they were both colleagues?

The not-exactly-a-salad was followed by plain boiled noodles in butter; copying my hosts, I didn't eat much of them. It seemed to be some kind of ritual. Then the roast lamb came out, and it was pretty much like spicy roast lamb anywhere—that got my undivided attention. At first I figured I was just hungry after missing some meals, but Skena mentioned that the nanos got power directly from blood sugar, so I had a lot of replacing to do anyway.

That was followed by some more plain boiled noodles with butter, and a little dish of honey and vanilla; following their leads, I sprinkled that on my noodles, too, and ate more of them this time.

As I ate, I found myself deciding I was going to have to believe in pretty nearly everything they told me, at least at first; it was clear we were in some culture I'd never heard of, from a dozen things. The seasonings on the food were peculiar but consistently peculiar, the way you'd expect; dinner was eaten with spoons, chopsticks, and a little set of tongs; that odd little bit with the noodles, too, was the kind of thing that a society develops naturally without thinking.

When we'd eaten, I finally swallowed hard and said, "So . . . um, from what I understand of what you said yesterday before I went to sleep—I would guess that this must be a society descended from Periklean Athens?"

They glanced at each other, and Skena said, "Well, I told you the data we had indicated he was sharp."

"Sort of," she said, answering my question. "Perikles existed in our timeline, but there were a couple of important figures who actually took over from him in . . . er—"

"What you'd call the 430s B.C.," Skena finished for her. "Look, in your timeline, who won the Peloponnesian War, and how long did it last?"

Anybody in any branch of history at least knows that. "Sparta. And it lasted about thirty years."

"Well, in this timeline Athens won, very early in the war, and all but bloodlessly. And then a couple of people you didn't have in your timeline—Thukydides the Younger and Kleophrastes were the important ones— created a new Athenian Empire, with a very generous citizenship policy, structured as a sort of federation. That federation went on to win control of the Mediterranean, and then to conquer Asia east to Burma, all of Europe to the Urals, and all of Africa. A couple of thousand years later, they fought a long war with China over control of the New World—and at the end of that, Athens ruled the Earth, which meant one generation later, everyone was Athenian."

"Everyone male was Athenian," Ariadne corrected him.

Skena blushed a little; I realized this society was obviously just about where mine was in terms of equality of women—not terrible but not yet perfect. At least it was something that I would be able to relate to.

"And you found a way to visit other timelines?" I asked.

They both made a funny chopping motion with their hands; then Skena laughed, and said, "Uh, that's the same thing as shaking our heads. No, definitely not. What happened is that about a hundred years ago—in fact, just when there was a lot of discussion of ending the five years required military service for everyone, on grounds that we hadn't actually had anyone to fight in centuries—we were hit with a Closer invasion. It was a very near thing, but we beat it back by the skin of our teeth—"

"The first timeline ever to do that—" Ariadne added, and there was so much pride in her voice I swallowed my questions for a moment.

"And we got their technology for crossing timelines. So ever since, we've been locked in a war between the Closer timelines and ourselves, and our many allies, of course."

"Uh, this is still a bit fast for me," I said. "The Closers are . . . I don't know, a bunch of antinudists?"

Harry Skena laughed, and Ariadne Lao scratched at her ear where the translator must be. "The gadgets don't deal well with puns," he said. "No, Closers, like 'one who closes.' That's not what they call themselves. They call themselves Masters. We call them Closers because they close off all but one possibility for every timeline—you could call them very aggressive imperialists; what they try to establish in every timeline is totalitarian rule. Then one small family of Closers moves in and rules the Earth, or the solar system, or sometimes even the solar system plus some of the nearer stars, as the hereditary top of the hierarchy. As near as I can tell every Closer we ever deal with is the slave of some other Closer; presumably somewhere back in their home timeline there's just one Closer that owns everyone."

"And, uh, your side—you said ATN—"

"It's a translated expression—the abbreviation for Allied Timelines for Nondeterminism. We're everybody that is trying to fight off the Closers, ganged up for mutual defense. We have members of all sorts—there's a couple in which humans never left the Stone Age, there's one that has starships. The only general principle is that we want to go our own way in our own timelines—though we don't have many slave societies, or global police states. Those tend to join up with the other side."

"I see. So, uh . . . what were you doing back in my timeline?"

"Oh, strangely enough, just what I said I was doing. Investigating Blade of the Most Merciful."

"Investigating them for what? Are they going to be more important in the future of my timeline?"

"Not if we can help it," Skena said, and his voice was grim. "They're a Closer front. Part of their usual strategy. They destroy all the alternatives between police state and anarchy—because most people will pick the police state—and then take over the police state. They get you to destroy your own freedom and then they just knock over the local masters and take over the operation themselves."

I nodded slowly. "So what were you supposed to do to them?"

Skena shrugged. "Timelines are sticky. They tend to fall back into each other one way or another. If you shoot somebody in one, the world where he exists and the world where he doesn't will tend to drift back together and merge. That's part of why there's so much contradictory data in history, you know. You said you were in art history at Yale—"

"I didn't," I said. "But obviously you knew it anyway. So you had looked up things about me before coming to my office? What are you up to?"

Ariadne seemed to be fighting down a smile. "I do believe you said he was sharp."

Skena seemed to have the beginnings of a blush forming, but then he shrugged and said, "Well, it's like this, then. You were on my list of people to look up eventually, and I'd been keeping a tab or two on you for some years. Then when it turned out that your family was targeted by Blade . . . well, it was the kind of thing that sometimes falls into place."

"How did I get on your list?"

He shrugged. "In timelines who join the Alliance, sometimes we find records of our agents. You've turned up in several. That means we must have recruited you at one time or another, or that you got involved in this. Always assuming that you are the Mark Strang—it's always possible that some other version of yourself is the one who ends up working for us."

"So if you offer me a job—"

"Well, that's just it," Skena said. "I was playing a hunch when I came to your office. I had just gotten a threatening visit from Blade of the Most Merciful. I decided I had better run for it while the running was good. And since you were on my list for eventual investigation and contact, and you work as a bodyguard—"

"I see." I took a sip of their strangely flavored coffee and decided that I might just get to like it. "Am I the only person in my timeline you're tracking?"

"Oh, no," he said. "There are eight others. Six of them were with Blade of the Most Merciful—they're the ones I think are ringers from another timeline—and the other's in Pittsburgh, but you wouldn't have any reason to know her, at least not yet."

"All right, and what happened after we got rescued?"

Ariadne Lao smiled, and that's very impressive and pleasant. "Well, Mr. Strang, it so happens that we were able to fix things up pretty well. Your vehicle was repaired while you were asleep, and I've taken the liberty of returning it to its locked parking space—a few seconds after you left it. I moved the damaged delivery vehicle down to where yours had been, so now the witnesses will be in hopeless contradiction . . . moreover, when you're feeling ready for it, I'm going to have you visit the police station on some small matter of business at just the right time to give yourself a complete set of alibis."

I thought about that for a bit and shuddered. "So I'm going to be within a few miles of myself . . . "

She looked very sympathetic. "It takes getting used to. Yes."

"And—er, about my being an agent for you—"

"Well, that's the odd part," Skena said. "We aren't supposed to recruit agents from a timeline until at least the leadership knows about us . . . and you don't even have a unified leadership, you know. So clearly you're supposed to come to us irregularly . . . "

"Can't you just *look?*" I asked.

They explained a lot more to me that day; in later years I was to realize just how much I hated briefings, which are never brief. They couldn't just look because timelines are braided and twisted through the past, and different ones are close to different others at different times. And although it's cheap to jump crosstime, it's terribly expensive to jump back in time along one of those lines. So to find a critical incident would require an agent leaping back to about when it should have happened, staying in the field long enough to find out if it had yet or not, and if it hadn't, jumping forward till it had . . . and then once the incident was finally found (kind of like running down a runner between bases), observing it. By that point, apparently, they'd have expended enough juice, or whatever it is that time machines run on, to power a small planet for several days.

What Harry Skena was doing was nudging our timeline toward the ATN path. That meant in general he was working for personal freedom and against dictatorships, but other than that he had very little in the way of a program; mostly he just tracked the people he was supposed to track and kept an eye on things. I got a distinct feeling our timeline was a backwater, but

Ariadne said no, several important timelines were descended from it, and if it had really been a backwater, they wouldn't have had an agent on station.

That was Skena's title, Special Agent. A Special Agent was "our man in that timeline" and in charge of either keeping it headed for the ATN or turning it that way. "I had an assignment when I was younger in a timeline that was headed the Closer way," he said. "One where Stalin got the nuclear bomb way ahead of everyone else, and then lived clear till 1975. The Closers hadn't found that timeline yet . . . and the job was to get it loosened up before they found it. Scary job, and I had to do a lot of things I'm not very proud of. That's why I got sent to your timeline—because it was an important one, headed our way, that the Closers didn't know about."

"But they do," I said. "Didn't you say Blade—"

"Oh, yeah," Skena said. "They do now. And worse than that, they're better equipped than we are in that time—because they've got a crosstime gate installed in a world they control. That's why they can hide so effectively and have so many resources—because their bases are in a world where Hitler won World War II. At least a lot of their gear looks like souped-up descendants of German stuff . . . "

"Can't you do anything about it?"

"All kinds of things, if we could find the timeline they're coming out of," Harry said.

"You just said it was the one where Hitler won World War II."

Ariadne coughed. "It takes some getting used to, Mr. Strang. There are just over eight hundred timelines in which Hitler won."

I whistled. "That seems like a lot."

"It's not, relatively speaking. There are about eighty

thousand in which he lost. And then there are just over a million where he never existed or never amounted to anything."

I thought about that for a little bit . . . and then for a little bit more. It seemed like a huge number . . . that was all I seemed to be able to think about. "And that's how many timelines there are?"

"That's how many we know about. The Closers probably know about more, since they've been at it longer. They don't talk to us, exactly, they just send people over to demand that we surrender."

"I'm familiar with the style," I said.

"Our best guess is there might be around a billion timelines with human beings in them. And then of course there's all the lifeless ones, all the ones with no intelligent life, all the ones with alternate intelligent life . . . but it's the ones near you that are easiest to find, and so we've only made a couple of sampling probes and small expeditions. Despite the comforts of this place, Mr. Strang, we *are* at war. The first attack of the Closers leveled the Acropolis; one way you can spot our agents in any timeline, I'm afraid, is we always find an excuse to go see the Parthenon."

"Ours is damaged," I said, I guess to have something to say, but Harry Skena sighed and nodded significantly. "I've still been there four times," he said.

Ariadne made a face. "Wretched security practice. I would bet that the Closers set up somebody to watch the Acropolis within half an hour of arriving in a new timeline."

"Have you ever gotten to see it?" I asked.

"No, and I'd crawl through fire to. But seeing the Acropolis is not likely to come up—unless the next time Citizen Skena gets into trouble he has the good taste to do it in Greece somewhere."

I looked back and forth between them. "Uh, I'd figured you must be his supervisor?"

Harry Skena shook his head. "She's my Den Mother."

She looked as puzzled as I felt, so I figured the translator had not picked that one up either.

"I'm a Crux Op," she said. "Crux Operations Recovery Specialist. A 'crux' is one of those places where events are being manipulated to form a new timeline; manipulating the events is called 'special operations.' Every so often we stop getting messages from a Special Agent like Citizen Skena, or we get a distress call like the one he sent us. We know our agents well enough to know they don't cry wolf—so if we get such a call, a Crux Op jumps in to get the agent out, and if possible to make sure the original mission gets accomplished."

"Search and Rescue," I said.

"Exactly. Now, as far as I can tell, I've straightened it out; while you were asleep I raided every Blade HQ Citizen Skena had identified, and staged a bunch of very nice massacres if I do say so myself—leaving evidence pointing to other Blade groups. Your FBI and CIA, at the least, will be all over them during the few weeks after you return—they'll think an internal war broke out in the outfit. So if I return you and Citizen Skena, I'm probably done—unless I've missed a loose end somewhere."

"I don't think you have," Skena said. "And as much as you've stirred them up, maybe there's a better chance now of finding their crosstime gate. Especially since I've now got a much better native guide." He looked at me significantly. "Could you stand to have a secret client for a few months, one who pays you a lot, in cash?"

"With a big risk of getting killed," Ariadne Lao pointed out.

"And a good shot at Blade of the Most Merciful? Maybe even tracking them back to where they came from?" I grinned at them. "Not to mention my ankle feels better than it has in years. Oh, yeah, I'm in. Just try to keep me out."

From the way they laughed—and the glint I saw in both their eyes—I knew I had finally found my own kind of people.

6

It *didn't take long* for me to get reequipped; they'd
cleaned and pressed my clothes and in fact repaired
some spots that I'd been careless about. I suspected
nanos had had a hand in that, and knew it for sure
when I noticed that all the bills in my wallet had
become crisp and new.

Going back wasn't quite so dramatic; I knew what
was happening. It got dark, and quiet, and then gray,
and then sound and sight came back. Harry Skena and
I were standing by Panther Hollow Lake, a scum-
covered pond in Schenley Park that hardly anyone goes
to, especially in the middle of a warm day. We had half
an hour to go establish my alibi. Right now I was opening my second beer in the tub . . . but that was a week
ago to me.

Time travel won't be popular till it's reasonably easy
to find your way around, I decided.

Skena was just going to lay low in some hideout or
other for a few hours, someplace where he knew Blade

wouldn't find him; if he just didn't poke his head up where they saw it until tomorrow, things should be fine—they'd be on the run, not him.

I had a perfectly great excuse to go down to the police station—I had to swear out a complaint against Brunreich, as I explained to Skena.

He got a very strange expression. "Brunreich."

"Yeah, Roland Brunreich."

"You were guarding—"

"His wife Angelica Brunreich. And their daughter Porter. If you get an offer of a double date, pick Angela for sex and Porter for conversation."

"I'll bear that in mind." He grinned at me. "By the way, now that we're in this timeline, I would consider it normal for you to call me Harry—I noticed you were having to remember to address us as 'Citizen.'"

"Just not used to it. And you know how we Americans are. Every damned receptionist and car rental guy and mechanic addresses you by your first name. So I didn't want to give offense—"

"Not wanting to give offense is one of the more charming characteristics your people have," Skena said, "along with apologizing for what in fact is generally fairly polite behavior and a lot of willingness to learn other people's customs. You should see what the Frenchmen are like in the timelines where Napoleon's heirs went on to rule the world."

I had the odd thought, climbing up the path to the bridge that would take me out of the park, that he'd made me just a bit proud to be an American. It seemed only fair; he was certainly proud to be Athenian . . .

Visited the Acropolis four times. And just glowed when I mentioned it.

It was the same nice spring day it had been, but now I was rested and my hand was healed. It occurred to me that I wasn't going to have much of a civil case for medical expenses, but I didn't let that bother me much.

I figured I'd just walk across the Pitt campus and catch a bus downtown. The area right around the library and the Cathedral of Learning is sort of nice, except they tore down Forbes Field, where the Pirates belong, and the last place in which Babe Ruth ever played professional ball, to build a butt-ugly classroom building that looks like something Albert Speer rejected for one of his Nazi-era city centers. I always take a moment to spit on it as I go by.

Another thought that occurred to me, crossing the street, was that there were a lot of short skirts and bare midriffs around. Either I needed to give Melissa a call, or . . . well, hell, who would I ask?

"Mark! Hey, Mark!" It was Robbie—she's in some kind of part-time program at Pitt, one that seems set up so that you can get your law degree just before you die.

"Hi! How are you doing?" Aside from the fact that she's a friend, and I'm always glad to see her, there was also the strength to be added to the alibi.

"I didn't expect to see you awake quite this early. How's your hand? Did you have a doctor look at it? I know it's too much to hope that you'd have a natural healer look into it—"

"Whoa. Yeah, the doctor checked it out, and it's fine—here, look, see? Moves in every direction it's supposed to. Good as new. So I don't need anybody to wave a feather rattle over it—"

"You're incorrigible. Got time for coffee or something?"

"Well, unfortunately, I'm supposed to be heading downtown to swear out the complaint against Brunreich. Assault, battery, being a weenie . . ."

"At least twenty counts of being a weenie. I can give you a ride if you like—"

"Deal."

Her van was parked nearby, and traffic was fairly light with rush hour not yet started. Mostly we talked about old jobs, scrapes we'd been through together, that sort of thing.

In five years there can get to be a lot to talk about, especially because old friends have a way of sharing stuff. "You know," she mentioned, "there are some detective agencies that won't hire us because me and Paula are, um, together?"

"Their loss," I said. "Are you not getting enough business?"

"It's tight. Real tight."

"I've got a new heavy client that just came aboard this afternoon," I said, "and I can throw you some business I'm sure. Maybe not before next week. And I'll pay you as soon as the Brunreich check clears."

"That's what I was hinting around about," she said, smiling a little. "Stupid business, eh, boss-man, where we have to get paid in cash and all? Takes the fun out of being a paladin."

I grinned back at her. "You see yourself as a paladin? When there really were knights-errant and all that, you'd have been flat on your back under some fat drunken lord, getting pumped full of babies."

"Boss-man talks nasty. Kids would be okay. I'd just have to talk His Obesity into taking off on a crusade . . . and staff the castle with some buxom serving wenches. So what about you? I know either of us could get a better job than this; hell, you could be Professor Strang someplace in no time. Why do you stick with a moron job?"

"It's not a moron job," I said, a little defensively. "It's just not a book-smart kind of job. And you know how I—"

"I know how you got in. I've heard Hal Payton tell that story many times. But why the hell do you stay in? I mean, for your own good, Mark, this is a business where you mostly get bashed up when you aren't being bored."

I shrugged and told her the truth. "Well, in the first place, I like to beat people up. But in the second place, the client I'm going to be covering is . . . um, well, dealing with outside terrorists coming into the USA, let's say. I don't think he'd want me to tell you his business. But suffice it to say what I'm going to be beating up, or shooting, is people a lot like the ones who killed my family. So for this job, anyway, I know exactly why I'm doing it. Okay?"

Robbie made the turn by the back of the City County Building and said, "Well, sorry if Aunt Robbie has been tough on you. And it sounds like your new client is going to be interesting."

Inside it was the usual routine; fill out forms, talk with cops, get papers in order. Norman, my lawyer, has a "kit" for all this that I use—sort of a checklist to make sure I'm giving the prosecutor enough to work with in the unlikely event it ever comes to trial. The purpose of pressing charges isn't usually to put these guys in jail— most of the people clients are afraid of are their "loved ones," and they don't want them imprisoned—it's to have a bargaining chip so they can't sue *me*, and in the case of a few very dangerous aggressors, to give the prosecutor something to crack them open with, make them confess to the more serious crimes that would otherwise be merely their word against the client's.

About an hour into the process, I felt a hand on my shoulder, and a voice behind me said, "I think I've got bad news for you."

I turned around and found myself facing Lieutenant

DeJohn Johnston, a guy who looks more like an all-pro linebacker than anything else. I should say I was facing his chest.

DeJohn's an old friend, so I looked up to make sure this wasn't a joke, and saw right away it wasn't—he was making the kind of "sorry to tell you about this" face that meant bad news.

My first thought was that Blade was on the loose again, and they'd attacked Dad or Carrie—I have night-mares about them getting Sis at home alone, Payton's guards drawn off or knocked out, with her trapped in her wheelchair and with just the little 9 mm she keeps strapped beside her to fight back with.

DeJohn said, "I think your car has been stolen and used in a major felony. At least the garage where you park it is where there was some kind of shoot-out, and we have a description from a Mrs. Goldfarb and her four children that matches your Mercedes, so—"

I wanted to laugh with relief, not to mention the thought that Mrs. Goldfarb was going to look pretty stupid when they found the Mercedes where it belonged and a Berto's pizza wagon shot up in its place. But I still had adrenaline pumping from when I had thought it was my family, so I was able to let my jaw drop, and say, "Somebody stole a car out of the locked area? And a big obvious red 510SL, instead of something that would blend into traffic?"

"Unhhunh. Sounds like. I'm real sorry to tell you about it, buddy."

"Shit." I did my best to look disgusted.

"I'll drop an unofficial request to the squad car at the scene so that they'll check it out, but it sure sounds like yours. Wish I had better news for you . . . you going to make the softball game this year?"

It's a standing joke; every spring there's an "ops versus

cops" game at South Park, a bunch of private investiga-
tors and bodyguards from around town playing ball
with a bunch of policemen. It has to be one of the
greatest places ever developed for picking up rumors.

"If I'm in town, you know I won't miss it."

"Well, try not to hit so many straight into the
ground by third base this year. My arm gets tired."

I did a big mock wince; it was true, unfortunately,
that something about my not-quite-healed right ankle
had always made me hit just a little funny, right
toward DeJohn. Of course he's tall enough to play third
and second at the same time . . .

"Oh, I'm in better shape these days. Might surprise
you. Anyway, I have to run—meeting a client soon—
but thanks for letting me know about the car. I'll call
the garage in an hour or so and see if they can tell me
anything. If they can't, I imagine I'll need your help
again."

"You got it. Say, did your client get through the
Seattle airport okay this morning? That is where they
were headed, isn't it?"

"Yeah—what do you mean, get through okay—"

"Well, you put 'em on the plane early in the morning, and it's about a six-hour flight, so I was just thinking that when the hostage situation developed there it
must have been about when your client was landing."

"*Hostage situation?!* I haven't had the radio on all
day. When was this—"

"Middle of this afternoon—still morning their
time," DeJohn said. His face got sort of soft and concerned, and I realized I must look pretty bad.

"Who's doing it?"

He blew out his breath like a man who has just realized he has to do something tough. "Ah, shit. Mark,
buddy, I really shouldn't have mentioned it. It's the old

enemy, Blade of the Most Merciful. Looks like they're back, and some kind of gang warfare seems to have erupted around them—they've been running the crime in the Islamic communities in a dozen cities around here. In fact a CMU prof was working on documenting that, and now he's disappeared, guy name of Harry Skena, and—"

"Damn, damn, damn," I said, more to shut him up so I could get away than anything else. "Skena was supposed to be my client starting tomorrow! He's turned up missing?"

"Didn't show up for class, and the dean's office at Pitt got a call—"

I knew Harry was okay, of course—this was leftover information from earlier—but it was a good way to get DeJohn out of the way while I ran to see what was up about Seattle. I didn't exactly know what powers an ATN Special Agent had, but maybe he was kind of like a US Marshal in the Old West, or a freelance superhero, and if I could get him to hit Blade I wanted to watch him do it. I hadn't forgotten how effective that little silvery gadget Ariadne had used to waste a dozen Bladers had been.

"We had a private hideout for something like this— sorry but I'll have to grab a cab and go there. I'll call you if he's okay, all right, DeJohn? And save a few strikes for me."

"Will do, buddy, and 'preciate it."

He went back toward his desk, the bag of McDonald's lunch still under his arm, and I bolted out the door and down the steps.

I was just dashing out to look for a cab—in Pittsburgh hailing a cab is nearly impossible, but I didn't want to run all the way to the next cab stand— when a hand caught my elbow. "You heard the news from Seattle?"

It was Skena. "Yeah, I heard," I said.

"Come on with me," Skena said. "I've already notified base, and we will be expected there—they'll have weapon packs for both of us. We just need to get down to my van in the garage, here."

We got on the elevator, and it dropped quickly. "I might have a former client on the site."

Skena grunted. "Of course you do. That's why I was so surprised earlier. She's the one I thought you couldn't possibly know, that I'm keeping an eye on in this timeline."

"Mrs. Brunreich?"

"The daughter, Porter."

I gaped at him. "She's just a ten-year-old kid—"

"Yeah? Well in more than fifty timelines descended from this one, she gets a *lot* more important, pal. So far we don't think any of those timelines have been found by the Closers, but maybe one has, or one in which she's important has, whether we know about it or not. Doesn't matter much; the point is, it's quite possible their whole reason for coming here, aside from capturing this timeline, was to find her and kill her." The elevator door opened and Skena ran through, pretty fast for such a big guy.

He unlocked the back of his van, and, just as he opened the door, a window shattered. I turned, saw the man with the pistol, and had my .45 out instantly, giving him a couple of rounds to pin him down.

"Inside!" Skena shouted. I wasn't sure why it was urgent, but I could tell it was, so I jumped in—

It got dark, and silent, then gray, then vision returned, then sound returned. I was getting used to this.

We were standing in a little white room with two of those silvery "super squirt guns" on holster belts lying on a table. He put one on and handed me the other.

"Sorry to rush, but we're in real time, Mark. It's only the big machines up at ATN that can go forward and backward. These little gadgets just take us short distances crosstime. But it's still the fastest way to SeaTac."

"Well, if we're in real time, then let's go," I said, buckling mine on. "How do I use this gadget?"

"It's called a SHAKK. Seeking Hypersonic Ammunition Kinetic Kill. Point it and squeeze the trigger. It hits whatever is in its sights at the time you pull the trigger, out to about six miles, so be sure you aim—hip shots are a real bad idea. Don't lead anything—it homes in on what it's pointed at, and anyway at Mach 10, you don't need much of a lead. You have two thousand rounds in the magazine. Move the switch back, here, for semiauto. Middle position is six-round bursts that hit in a hex pattern about a meter on a side. Far position is full auto, about 400 rpm, and you'd use it against a whole army—won't need it this time. Better stick to semiauto. Got that?"

"How much recoil?"

"Zip. Ammo is self-propelling, like a rocket. Any other questions?"

"Nope. Let's go grease some Bladers."

He grinned at me. "Knew I could count on you for a fun time. All right, god knows what we're going to find. I'm bouncing us right into one of the airline frequent flyer clubs, which with a little luck won't have anyone in it at the time. Use your common sense. Radio traffic that the artificial intelligence is analyzing says there's no good guys inside—just the hostages, us, and Blade. Remember the goal is wipe out the Bladers, then get back out—soon as we've got 'em all we've got to run back to the club. I don't want to have to shoot my way through your local police just to avoid having to explain these gadgets."

"With you all the way," I said. I made sure my SHAKK was set for semiauto, and Skena said, "Delivery system, attention, activate please destination specified *now*."

When he said "now" it got dark, silent, gray—

Luck was not with us, or maybe it was. We popped into the clubroom that Blade of the Most Merciful was obviously using as a headquarters. There were about ten of them standing around, and when something went poof in their midst, being the sort of guys they were, they were pointing guns before they knew what it was.

Moreover, at that HQ level, figure a few of them had seen Closers pop in and out, and had a good idea what was going on. The only thing that saved us, I think, was that they didn't know the Closers had enemies with the same technology.

I saw nothing but men with guns in front of me, so I brought my SHAKK to bear, squeezed the trigger, popped it from man to man doing that. They were grabbing for their guns, but I'd gotten most of them before one of them did get an AK swung around—

There was a deep whirring noise beside me and the rest of the enemy fell over. "Wha—?"

"Never say never. I used full auto. Your authorities are really going to wonder about all the little holes in the walls, but the ammo has already self-destructed in there. Let's go."

When we came out the door, there was a Blade guy coming in the other way. I popped him, and that was the first time I had time to see what the SHAKK actually did. A long time later it was explained to me that when you point a SHAKK at a human being, the round not only homes in on him, it finds his head and then, after penetrating his brain pan, "slows down" by spiraling through his head. Since it starts out at Mach 10, by the time it comes to a stop it's pretty much converted the head to puree.

What I saw was that I squeezed the trigger and his head bulged for an instant, there was a sort of pink spray from his ears, nose, and mouth, and then his head fell inward like a deflating water balloon, which in a sense was what it was. I took a moment to heave, but I ran after Skena all the same; next time I wouldn't be freaked out, but this first one was a surprise.

We were suddenly out in the common area, and the Blade guys were everywhere, standing with their AK's over the hundred or so hostages lying prone on the floor. They'd tied their hands and made them lie down close together so that when the time came to kill them they need only spray the floor with full auto, and I found out later that when we burst in on them, the hostages had been in that position, with no bathroom breaks, for seven hours. Quite a few of them had ended up pissing themselves, and one diabetic had gone into a coma and quietly died during that time . . . but I don't suppose any of that bothered Blade of the Most Merciful.

Skena belly-flopped onto the hard concourse floor, and I followed his lead, flipping my own SHAKK to full auto. From the angle I was at, anything live and standing was a Blader, so I swung the SHAKK back and forth twice, holding the trigger down. It made that deep bass whoosh that I realized must be the sonic booms of its tiny ammunition. (Later, again, I learned a SHAKK round was about a third the volume of a BB shot and almost entirely propulsion and guidance system. It was the sheer energy of impact that did all the damage with those things.)

Skena had been spraying, too. As soon as we'd hit every target we could see, we leaped up again. A shot rang off a pillar, giving away the Blader just coming out of the men's room—a lesson in taking the time to aim. I sent a shot after him, and it nailed him as he turned to run.

Skena pointed his SHAKK at a hand slowly reaching up over a sofa and fired a shot at the hand (a little crack! noise like popcorn popping hard); an instant later we saw the pink spray from behind the couch. "Neat gadget, hunh?" he whispered to me.

I didn't answer—I'd seen a flicker of movement near the women's room, and I was running toward it while I tried to think what it might be. Maybe just a female Blader deciding to hide in the toilet—

I charged in anyway. As I rounded the corner a shot bounced off the tile beside me, spraying me with the fine gravel of the wall, and the boom of the pistol echoed through the bathroom. I dove in in a headfirst slide, the SHAKK in front of me, had just an instant to see three men and Porter, pointed at the first man and squeezed the trigger—

The second man leveled a pistol at me, the third jammed his gun into Porter's neck, lifting her head, and as time slowed down I saw his finger start to move down onto the trigger.

I was already squeezing the trigger on the SHAKK, and I brought it to bear on the gun thrust into Porter's throat. There was no time to think of aiming, I just hoped I was pointed right—or did I even have time to think that? Remembering it now, anyway, I always hope it was pointed right—

It was. The SHAKK round recognized explosives at the bottom of metal tubes as dangerous, so first it looped around, smashing the inside of the barrel into a thick mess of metal fragments, blocking it, then it smashed the bullet backward. The gun blew through at the hammer end. I imagine it would have hurt like hell, since it tore most of his hand into pieces and sprayed them up his sleeve, but I was squeezing off my second round, and this one went right into him; his head did the inflate/deflate routine.

A round had screamed off the floor in my face, and I brought the SHAKK around, got it pointed at the surviving Blader's foot, squeezed the trigger, and made his head do that funny pulse, too.

Then it was quiet with a ring. I was about three-quarters deaf from the effect of all those shots in a bathroom, and so it took me a moment to realize I was hearing something besides the high-pitched scream of my own tortured ears.

It was Porter, and she was starting to sob. I stepped forward and scooped her up into my arms—

"Mr. Strang?"

"Yeah, kid, it's me. Never mind how I happen to be here. And listen, you've got to *not* tell anyone it was me, you got that?"

She pulled back and nodded solemnly. "Are you— you must be working for some very important organization or something. Like the CIA or something?"

"Like that, yeah."

"That gun is some kind of special equipment, isn't it?"

"You bet," I said. "Just trust me, I'm working for the good guys, okay? Where's your mother?"

Porter's face folded up like it was being sucked inward, and I knew before she gasped it out. "They, they, they . . . they said they were going to show us what they'd do and they . . . they said they'd show us . . . they—"

"Oh, Porter." I held her tight; I knew, god I knew, from the way I'd lost Mom and Jerry and Marie to the same bunch, but what consolation could that be to her?

Later when I got the full story, it was what I would have expected if I'd been thinking at all. They "decided" to kill someone right off to "let the other hostages know they were serious." (Of course it was really what they were there to do right along.) They announced they were going to kill Porter Brunreich, who they pretended was just a random name from a passenger manifest. So Harry Skena had their number right.

But they hadn't bet on Angelica Brunreich. She might have been crazy as hell, and sometimes she was pretty unpleasant, but she was more of a hero than I'll ever be; she switched tickets with her daughter and volunteered herself to spare everyone else's life. Poor Porter had been so stunned she had no idea what was happening until it was too late—a big Blader just grabbed her mother by the hair, slapped her, shouted "open your mouth," and when she did, jammed a short pistol on full auto between her jaws, hard enough to break her front teeth, deep enough to gag her, and pulled the trigger, emptying the clip.

She probably died too fast to feel much pain. That's what I've always told Porter since.

They forced a couple of people to clean up the hideous mess; Porter sat and watched them drag her mother's bloody body away. Then, somehow, she thought after they got a phone call of some kind, all of a sudden they had figured out that perhaps they hadn't executed who they had meant to. It gave their game away, of course, to admit that "Porter Brunreich" wasn't a random name but in fact their real target—but by then they must have been desperate, for the FBI was within an hour of storming the place (a process that was to scare the living daylights out of most of the hostages, who were still lying tied on the floor, unable to get up).

So they had just grabbed all the kids between about eight and twelve—clearly they had some idea of what age person they were looking for—and started interrogating them. "Porter" could be a name for either sex, and anyway most kids carry no ID, so it took them a while.

They had just grabbed Porter and figured out that the ticket they had seen her trying to throw away must be her mother's. Blade of the Most Merciful were about to execute her when they heard Harry Skena and me making our fast, rude entrance and decided that she might be more useful to them alive, as a hostage; they had just reached that decision when I burst in.

She couldn't tell me any of that—I learned all of it later. All she could do at the time was sob into my shoulder, and all I could do was hold her. I wanted to tell her it was okay, it was going to be all right, but I remembered my own experience. It wasn't okay, and it was never going to be all right again.

"I'll take care of you," I whispered. "I promise. I'll make sure you're taken care of." It was all I could think of.

As I carried her out of that blood-spattered public toilet, Harry Skena came in. "All secured, and—oh, god, then you know."

"Yeah," I said. "What can we do—?"

"I've got someone coming over from HQ, one timeline over, to take care of things. She'll be all right—or as all right as you can be, I guess—and we'll make sure she's taken care of. You and I have something else we have to do right now. We've got a chance to get at the Closers themselves if we rush."

I hesitated. Porter was hanging on to me like she'd never let go, and I couldn't bear to pry the poor kid off me.

"She really will be well taken care of—my word of

honor on that," Harry Skena said, "and what we've got is a chance to shut down the Closer bridge into your world. That means possibly years of peace before you have to fight them again—"

"Go do it," Porter whispered into my neck.

"Do what, honey?"

"Your friend says you can go beat the bad guys and make them go away for good, right?"

"Pretty much, yeah."

"So do whatever you have to do. If he's sending someone to take care of me, I'll be okay. But you *have* to shut down the bad guys. It's *important*."

She pushed away from me just a little and looked me in the eye. Her blue eyes were red-rimmed from crying, and there was a dribble of snot at the end of her nose, but I have never seen a more serious or dignified human being. "Go shut them down," she said. "Nobody will be safe until you do."

"Aw, Porter," I said, and gently set her down. "Now be good and do whatever the people Harry sends tell you to do, okay? And I'll do my best to get in touch just as soon as I can."

She nodded firmly, and said, "I'm old enough to behave myself, Mr. Strang. But please go do whatever you're supposed to do about that base. I won't stop being afraid till those people are wiped out."

"It's a deal, kid," I said, and kissed her on her forehead. I turned to Skena, and said, "Okay, Harry, let's go get them."

We went out via a bathroom; Porter was running down the hall, when last I saw her, to call the police outside and get people untied if she could. God only knew what they were going to think when they found all the Blade of the Most Merciful dead with exploded heads, and nobody in there but the hostages. Especially because I knew Porter was smart enough to dummy up and not tell them anything.

It would keep some guys in Langley, Virginia, busy for a good long while, I figured.

As we stepped into the bathroom I said, "So they'd take over the world here, under some kind of dictatorship, and then put Closers in at the top of the hierarchy? Is that what they're after?"

He shook his head. "Basically this is a timeline they'd strip-mine, Mark. You guys are 'unclean.'"

He had been fiddling with a gadget on his belt; he grunted with satisfaction. "All right, good, they'll pop us from here in two. Stand close to me, in the center of the room. There we go. Now, to continue . . . Closers are nuke phobes. Their language is akin to Phoenician, and we think what they are is Carthaginians. Probably in their timeline Hannibal took Rome and won the Second Punic War, and then they went on to conquer all of Europe and the world. And our guess is they fought a lot of nuclear wars in the process; so the only place a Closer will settle is in a timeline where no nuclear bomb has ever gone off. In the ones where nukes have happened, trusted Closer slaves run things, and they basically steal everything nonorganic for export back to the Closer timelines. We think it's a superstition, that maybe they had nukes a long time before they had genetics and that as a result they have some kind of visceral terror of nukes that we don't understand."

I nodded. "You don't know much about them?"

"After a hundred years of war, no. We'd love to find their home timeline—it's a disaster that they know ours, but at least we have many allies they haven't found yet. There's no way we know of to track a time invasion back to its source—but it does give off a special kind of radio pulse that we can easily detect. That's how I know that a whole bunch of things just crossed over in the Bellevue area near here, and if we had a car, we'd just drive but—"

It got dark and silent. I was beginning to feel like I was riding an elevator or subway—if you can remember the first time, when you were a child, it was pretty scary, all sorts of fascinating things happened, but by the time you'd lost count of how many times you'd done it, you were barely aware of it at all. I found myself waiting slightly impatiently for the gray . . . which came, and then the sounds came. We were back in the white room.

"Better reload—this may be heavy duty," Harry said. "Push on this stud."

I did, following his example, and little drawers like the drawers on a coffee grinder slid out of the sides of both our weapons. He grabbed an open can from a sideboard—it was filled with a heavy gray powder—filled the drawer full, and shoved it closed. There was a "beep" noise from his SHAKK. I followed his example.

"Is this some kind of gunpowder—?" I asked, but then it got dark and silent, again. The question went right out of my mind.

I've been to Seattle a few times, and it's hard to find a less appealing area (unless you're a computer dork) than Bellevue. The buildings all look like movie sets from B-grade science-fiction flicks, except for the ones that look like concrete building blocks used by a giant child who just happened to be a complete idiot.

What we were facing, just off the freeway, from a drugstore parking lot, was an immense blue cube. It was all glass on the outside, with just the fine tracery of metal wires holding the glass in place. The blue was very deep, like ink in water. Harry Skena laughed bitterly. "Jeez, they must have worked to keep this one out of the news. This is absolutely typical Closer architecture. They build buildings like this wherever they go. They must really have had substantial plans for this world, though god knows what. With Closers you never quite know."

"What do we do now?" I asked, dubiously.

"We start by walking toward it," Skena said. "The instruments I've got here—passive radiation gadgets, so there's no signal they can detect, I hope—show it's pretty much hollow inside. Nothing that looks like gun emplacements. But notice something about this parking lot?"

I looked around, and then the thought hit me. I ran to check and then came back. "There's nothing in any of the cars. Any of them. They're all different ages like a real population of cars, but nobody has any old McDonald's wrappers, or a shirt hanging in the window, or anything like that."

Skena nodded. "Yep. And I bet what happens every night is a bunch of low-level flunkies from their base come out in ties and jackets, drive the cars away, take a bunch of different routes to some hidden garage someplace . . . and then all park and transport back to where they came from. And do it in reverse the next morning."

I grunted. "A pity we don't have enough time."

"For what?"

"Ever driven in Seattle? The idea that someone is putting thousands of extra cars into the traffic for no reason . . . well, if you let word of that get around town, there'd be an angry mob here in no time, and they'd burn the thing to the ground."

Skena laughed. "It's a charming image. But, no, I'm afraid it's just you and me, and we'll have to do it the old-fashioned way; right now it's clear they're . . ." he glanced down at his gadget on his belt, and then started to trot toward the building.

"What—" I asked, matching his strides.

"They're powering up their transmitter in a big way. And there are a lot of human bodies in there. Probably they're taking the remnants of Blade of the Most Merciful back to wherever they stored them before. If we hit 'em now, we can kill most of Blade, and some Closers, and maybe toss a couple of bombs through the portal when it opens."

He said that last as he broke into a dead run. Any doubts I might have had about the kind of facility it was were erased when three men with rifles ran out of the building and started to level them at us; I fired a one-second burst of auto at them, and they went over with shredded heads.

But I could see a steel door sliding down over the entryway—the place was turning into a fortress before our eyes—and under my feet I could feel the rumble and vibration of immense engines, or maybe the generators, powering up to move great masses across time.

"How do we get in?" I shouted at Skena, as we rushed on, now only a few dozen steps from the steel-shuttered entryway.

"The good old-fashioned way," he said, pulling up. "Set for bursts." I did, and as I looked up he was opening up on the door.

I followed suit. The little slugs did nothing fancy, but they carried a huge load of kinetic energy, and six of them in a hex pattern were hitting a space no bigger than an ordinary double window with each burst. Visible ripples formed in the steel, and the door shuddered under the impact. Then, as we pumped burst after burst into it, one of the ripples snapped and cracked, and a few more bursts made a hole more than big enough to get in through.

I ran on ahead, and then an idea hit me, and I sprayed a dozen bursts at the huge blue glass wall that towered around the gate. Windows shattered everywhere.

Harry Skena followed suit, and as he caught up with me—glass was still plunging to the pavement all around—he said, "Great idea, for diversion?"

"Naw. I'm an art scholar. I've just always wanted to do that to a modern building."

He laughed, and I liked the sound of it. It was great to have a friend to do these things with.

We charged on through the gap we'd blown in the steel door, past the deserted reception desk, and down a corridor. All around us we could hear alarms going off. Skena dropped a few little tennis ball–sized objects behind us—"PRAMIACs," he said, "set to go off whenever we're both out of the building or dead, whichever comes first."

I was going to ask what a PRAMIAC was, but there was no time; we were turning the bend, and suddenly we were in the heart of the building, on a high platform overlooking a huge room that stretched to the top of the building ten stories over our heads, and at least that far underground. At its center there was a black column, beginning to glow a faint blue.

"That's a full-fledged gate," Skena said. "They could bring an army through there."

Machine guns chattered on the other side, and we dove for the deck. I crawled over next to him, squeezing off SHAKK rounds toward the gunners—stray rounds were doing things like knocking down pieces of guardrail and fluorescent lights, unfortunately, because my angle was so bad I couldn't really aim straight at the gunner—

I concentrated and put one into the machine gun, which blew to pieces with a gratifying roar. Then I rolled over next to Harry, some question half-formed in my mind.

But I didn't get to ask it. He was gasping for air and blood was puddling under him; he'd taken a round in the chest, and you didn't have to be a doctor to know he'd be gone in seconds.

"Harry!"

"Take a PRAMIAC from the hall. Leave blue knob as it is. Turn red knob to position *eight*—no farther! Get it close to the base of the column."

"Red to eight, base of the column, got it—Harry, can I—"

But I couldn't do anything for him, at least not anything except what he'd just asked me. His chest had stopped heaving, the blood that ran from under him was no longer gushing, and in the long second before I tore my eyes away from his, his eyes filmed over just a bit as they started to dry out.

For the first time, I had lost a client. More than that, I had lost a friend. And though I didn't know what exactly I was doing, I had a feeling if I followed his instructions, I could probably avenge him.

7

I scooted backward, ran down the hall, grabbed a PRAMIAC from the floor, shot the door off where it was marked EXIT, and ran down the stairwell.

As I ran I noted that the PRAMIAC was marked with symbols I couldn't read. I stopped and stared at it, and then the little symbols swam before my eyes and I saw which one the eight was, by the red knob. How did I—

A familiar voice in my head said, "Remember, they didn't remove me. I am still here to translate as needed—if I know the language."

"Thanks," I said, to the empty air, then the building started to buzz and shake like it might just come apart even before the PRAMIACs went off—I figured they were bombs of some kind.

The bottom door was locked, too, so I set for burst and fired five, experimenting with rotating the SHAKK. Sure enough, the bursts at angles to each other cut through the steel and concrete like a Sawzall, and the door fell into pieces in front of me.

I charged through, ducking low and rolling; bullets rang randomly around. I was about eighty feet from the base of the column, which was now that strange shade of deep purple that a working black light turns, and there was a whole gang of Bladers rushing around the other side. I could hear someone yelling at them, probably to come back, to judge from the way a couple of the more alert-seeming whirled and headed back.

I set the SHAKK on auto and sprayed the room in front of me; the last Blade of the Most Merciful went down like tenpins. I love my old .45, and I've won a lot of contests with it, but in a real fight you want high-tech, I decided.

I ran right up to the column and placed the PRAMIAC directly against the glowing base, which gave me an odd tingle but didn't seem to be hot or electrically charged. Two more Bladers popped out—that column was a good forty feet in diameter, so it was plenty to hide behind— and I SHAKKed them without a thought—except the thought that clearly most of them were on the other side of the column.

Which meant if I ran around there—

I flung myself around the column; something made me not quite want to touch it, especially since it now towered twenty stories over my head, all with that fierce blue glow. A few feet and I saw that the other side seemed to be bathed in red light; I pulled the SHAKK around to ready, but the gunfire I expected didn't come, and as I ran on around the corner—

I shot the last two as they entered the red, glowing door of the column. Faintly, through the door, I could see shapes moving—Harry had called this a "gate," and I realized it must be exactly that, some kind of open doorway that they could move big groups of people through. And to judge from the scream of the machinery in the background, this was about the limit of what it could move.

But the main thought that ran through my head at that moment was pathetically simple—

Blade of the Most Merciful was getting away! They were about to leave our timeline forever—before I was done settling the score!

So I know perfectly well what I did next was bone stupid. If you tell me that, I won't even try to argue with you. What's more, I know perfectly well that I would do it again.

Vengeance will move a man to all kinds of things.

Having shot the last two in line, I dove through the gate in their place; I hoped to open up on the backs of the crowd as they entered whatever Closer base they were going to, and then either jump back, get shot to death, or—

Or what? I hadn't thought that far ahead. Jumping back or getting shot seemed like the only likely options.

I hit the deck in a *tsugari* roll and came up with my SHAKK ready, but everybody in front of me was bent over on the floor in a deep bow.

Then the most amazing pain I'd ever felt tore across my back. I looked up to see a man with a flexible little metallic whip that looked like nothing so much as a plumber's snake. When I stared he lashed me across the forehead and pointed to the crowd that was all bent over.

The corner of my watering eyes told me there were hundreds of guards with whips all around, and every one of them was also carrying a sidearm. I wouldn't get half a shot out before they gunned me down. But clearly they'd mistaken me for—

The whip lashed my cheek. Shit, I got the idea; I ran and joined the ranks of Blade of the Most Merciful, bent over on the floor, kneeling with our faces to the ground and our hands locked behind our butts.

Guards walked around lashing the men and kicking them. If I hadn't been scared to death that the same was going to happen to me, I'd have enjoyed the spectacle.

I noticed that the whips drew no blood; probably they acted on the nervous system directly somehow. After the man on one side of me was whipped until he began to gibber and scream and sob, and the man on the other side was abruptly turned over, his pants cut away, and the whip applied to his genitals and anus until he fainted, I decided it was having a real effect on my nervous system, too.

I don't mind admitting I was ready to piss my pants with fear, and I had no idea how I was going to get out of that one. It was abundantly clear that these guards did not speak English, or possibly any other language from my timeline, and my translator wasn't volunteering anything about the strange grunting barks they made at each other.

It was also clear that they were just indulging in petty sadism—there was no point to the beatings and humiliations they were administering, they were just doing them to show they could, but the men who were obviously their officers made no attempt to stop it. In fact, when the guards tortured the man beside me, one young officer came over and laughed at the screams. When they threw him, still half-naked, to the floor, unconscious, so hard that I thought they might well have fractured his skull, the officer cheerfully flipped him over on his back, opened his fly, and urinated on the unconscious man's face.

Then they whipped the man on the other side of him into licking it off. The poor bastard threw up, and they beat him unconscious, this time with their fists.

Meanwhile, behind me, I could hear work crews going in and out, and tons of stuff rolled by. I figured it was loot from our world, and wondered how many art heists were going to go unsolved forever . . .

That woke a spark of anger in me. I'd spent years of training to conserve humanity's heritage of culture, and here a bunch of barbarians with a sadistic child's idea of entertainment were carrying stuff off as trophies. I still couldn't work up any sympathy for Blade—they were only getting what they deserved, and it was almost worth the risk of getting the same to be here while it happened—but that didn't make me like these guards any better.

One Blader just ahead of me was being tormented by their touching him with turned-off whips; I could tell when they turned them on by the way he jumped. They played with him in a way crueler than I've ever seen any cat be to a mouse.

Finally, the Blader couldn't take it any longer, and jumped to his feet to run.

I don't exactly know what they used on him. The Closers, I was to learn, have an all but infinite number of ways and tricks for inflicting pain. I think it was something that locked his legs and spine and paralyzed him from the neck down, because after they zapped him with it, leaving him a sort of frozen statue like a running cartoon character hit with a garden hose on a cold day, three of the guards carried him up to the front of the space.

Then they whipped us and kicked us till we were all sitting up straight.

We all watched the poor bastard as his face filled with terror; tears ran all over him, and he was screaming and gibbering for mercy like a madman.

He was about to discover that even if Allah was the Most Merciful, Allah's creations were anything but.

The Closers slowly wet him down with something. The smell permeated the room, and though none of us dared to make a sound, or to move, you could feel the silent shudder run through us all.

Gasoline. Or something enough like it as to make no difference.

He knew what was coming, and now he was raving, shrieking, blood running from his mouth because he'd torn his lips and tongue, but all that did was make the Closers laugh harder. Then they spent a long while teasing him with little torches, bringing the flame close, moving it back; twice they lit his pants and then squirted them immediately with something to put the blaze out, and then wet him down with the flammable liquid again.

Two thoughts ran through my head. One was how much I hated the Closers for being the kind of people who would do this.

The other thought was that I hoped to god this was the one who'd put the bomb under the van. I'd never been able to get over the feeling in my gut that Marie had been conscious when it burned. And if this happened to be him, I was finally seeing my number one fantasy, and as horrible as it was, as little as I liked the Closers for being the sort of people who would do it, if it had to happen, I wanted to be there.

They didn't stop their nasty little game until he finally gave up in despair. When he just stood there hanging his head and neither their whips nor threatening him with the little flames was doing anything to him anymore, they set him on fire.

It's amazing how long a human being can scream after you'd think he'd have nothing to scream with.

Vengeful satisfaction and nausea were fighting it out in me; I knew in a deep sense that this was the end of my fight with Blade of the Most Merciful, not just because they were all going to be dead, but because they were going to die in ways that I would have wished on them in my darkest fury, and because so many of them had died by my hand, and more because I'd helped to foil them.

Still, he was human. The screams tore at my heart, and however much my head might say he had it coming, I couldn't entirely feel that anything or anyone deserved this. And the smell—surprisingly like a barbecue—was making a lot of the men vomit. I felt a little like it myself.

All the while this was going on, the unconcerned workmen were passing by with their loads of loot. I saw crate after crate of stuff, some of it perhaps bought with stolen funds, other parts of it taken outright . . .

They will strip-mine your timeline, Harry Skena had told me, and now I knew what he meant.

The burning man had died, I think; the nervous system no longer held him locked upright, and he fell in a heap. They brought out a little contraption that was obviously a refuse-sweeper of some kind, swept him in, and took him away, without bothering to extinguish him.

Just after a large load of material went by, there was a change in the tone behind me; something was different about the machinery. They were just coming around to whip and beat us back into the position of kneeling with our faces on the floor, when quite suddenly I heard the machinery stop. They must be closing the gate.

Whatever a PRAMIAC was, it was sensing my presence through that gate, and not going off—until the gate started to close. That's what I think happened, and I've been told since it almost certainly is what happened.

I also didn't know at the time that a setting of "6"—what Harry had set his PRAMIACs to—is equivalent, roughly, to a World War II blockbuster, a one-ton TNT bomb. And the scale on it is base-10 logarithmic—going up by 2 means going up 100 x—so what blew up next to the base of the column was equivalent to 100 tons of TNT.

The gate was partly closed, but what that did was cause the force to take on strange properties as it moved through warped space and time. The shock wave that swept through the huge room in which we knelt twisted and broke everything more than a yard or so off the floor, and sheared the pieces off in a dozen directions. The guards were torn apart.

But we prisoners, kneeling on the floor, felt nothing, except the warm splashes of the guards' blood.

The blast had one other beneficent effect—for a long two minutes, it knocked out all the lights.

I crawled away in that time, looking for anything large enough to hide behind, getting the noise of the now-babbling Bladers on the other side of me, away from them, figuring that before they got it together they would again be targets. If I could put some room between them and me . . .

On the way I had a nasty turn as I realized I had put my hand down on a severed human hand. I gasped and moaned but kept crawling . . . too important to keep moving, and besides any noise I made was being drowned out in the general babble. It sounded, from the way they were calling to each other, as if they were trying to form up into their cadres, perhaps with the idea of going down fighting.

I finally got myself behind the remnants of what had obviously been a big crate, big enough to hold a full-sized car at least, and severed at about four feet off the floor in a mass of splinters and torn wire. They were still hollering at each other out there, and the racket was considerable.

It occurred to me to wonder how the homing system on the SHAKK ammunition worked, exactly. If it was entirely visible-light, it probably wouldn't do much, here in the dark, but if it was infrared, or radar—and my guess was it was, several different things . . .

Only one way to find out. I moved the switch to full auto and stood up in the pitch-blackness, then sprayed in the direction of Blade of the Most Merciful. The deep whoosh boomed through the huge room, and then there was a wonderful silence.

I had quite possibly bagged the lot of them, and if not, the survivors were probably good and scared. I crept along the wall, creeping from behind one wheeled cart and crate to another, until finally I found I was at a doorway, where a cart had become wedged, with the dilating door partly closed around it.

Just then the emergency lights—at least that's what I figured dim lights in such a situation had to be—came on, and I ducked, then peeked out. The heap of sprawled bodies told me that I had gotten the rest of Blade of the Most Merciful . . . my revenge, and Dad and Carrie's, and Porter's, too. It didn't bring anyone back, but it sure as hell made me feel better. I just wished there was a way for the folks back home to know what had become of Blade. I thought it might be a salutary example for a lot of terrorist groups.

Come to think of it . . . about "back home" . . . there was an obvious problem here. The gate was wrecked, and I had less ability to work any of the cross-timeline technology than a Stone Age tribesman in New Guinea had to fly a 747. A lot less—he'd probably at least figure out what the controls were, if not what they did. I hadn't seen anyone pull a lever or turn a wheel to do all this.

Well, now that I could see, I could also see that the door the carts had been going out through was bent and broken, and there was a hole I could squeeze through. I was just debating it when I heard the voices and saw the guards bursting into the place. It didn't seem like it would be wise to be there to discuss it with them, so I slipped into that hole and was into the space beyond before I had time to think about frying pans, fires, and all that.

Several of the carts in this hallway had also been wrecked by the whatever-it-was that had rolled out of the blown-up, collapsing gate. It looked like it was some kind of fold in space that just twisted everything as it passed; a picture in my mind developed of one guard whose skull had been wrenched into a bent oblong. I shuddered a little; whatever such things might be I would have to stay out of the way of them.

I wasn't sure whether I wished I knew some physics, so I could figure out what it had done, or was glad I didn't, so that I wasn't totally mystified.

As I went farther down the long cargo corridor, the carts grew less and less distorted and damaged, and the occasional body less horribly mangled though just as dead. I suppose it doesn't take much of a twist in the heart to make it nonfunctional.

Finally, when I had walked more than half a mile along the corridor with no sign of life other than a certain amount of shouting back behind me in the big room, I came to a cart that seemed to be undamaged, just abandoned, and a place where the scratching and scarring on the wall converged down to a triangular point. Within a few yards, the regular lights instead of the dim emergencies were on.

This meant a chance of running into living people; I went back to skulking along, hoping that anything that popped up would either not see me or not have time to sound the alarm.

I was in luck, for once, and when the corridor finally ended in what looked like a giant warehouse, I had still seen no one. I crept among the immense racks and the many crates, looking for anything at all to give me an idea on what I should do next. I was getting hungry, and I would be tired soon; there didn't seem to be much of anything I could do about the hunger, and I had no idea where I could safely sleep—I snore, for one thing.

Finally I just made my way out of the place, figuring that it might be a safe place to hide, but it could do me no good otherwise. I followed any corridor till it crossed a larger one, then followed the larger one, and sure enough in about twenty minutes I was facing a door with a sign over it in characters I'd never seen before, and that the translator implanted in my head was not equipped to deal with. I hoped they said "Exit"—there were just six of them, but for all I knew they were ideograms like Chinese, in which case they might well say "Door is alarmed," "Warning, hard vacuum on other side," or "Police Station."

No way to know unless I opened it, so I did. No alarm sounded where I could hear it, and I slipped out into a bigger space.

A cart rolled by, and the women running it appeared to have escaped from a dirty magazine, wearing high heels, bathing suit bottoms, and no tops. They looked bored to tears.

A moment later a cart going the other way was staffed by two guys with beards down to their waists.

Well, if I'd understood Harry Skena right, maybe the

Closers didn't worry much about what their slaves looked like, or maybe there was a dress code for slaves. This would be one great time for me to discover that a tough "police sport coat" (it only looks like a sport jacket if you do all of your shopping at Kmart; what it is, really, is just a heavy vest made out of polyester, as padding and protection in the event of rough stuff) was perfect inconspicuous slave gear . . .

I walked farther up the corridor, and thought about it. This place seemed to be huge, and so far everyone I'd seen had been moving a cargo of one kind or another. My guess was that I'd found a major base here, probably a sort of Grand Central for shipping supplies to all their different wars.

Something big was coming up behind me. I looked for somewhere to hide, and there was nowhere. Then a bunch of men in guard uniforms came up behind me.

I had no idea whether it would work, but I just didn't think I could shoot my way out and run successfully, so instead I dropped into the bowed-over position on the floor, on my knees with my face near the floor and my hands over my butt. They ran by me without paying any attention, except that one of them sort of patted my head as he went by.

Another half hour of walking, and I'd seen another patrol go by and the same thing had happened; moreover, another group of slaves had been visible at the time, and they'd gotten into the same position. I must have guessed right.

It was clear that all I'd found was a bigger traffic corridor. I'd been passing doors and had slowly learned that there were about four different sets of characters that appeared on them; one was the set that had appeared on the warehouse door, which didn't seem promising, and the other three could mean anything from "Ladies" to "Darkroom—No Light!" to "Large Room" for all I knew.

If you're trying to be inconspicuous, unfortunately, you don't have many options in the way of nosing around. A slave opening doors at random would be pretty conspicuous; walking rapidly and firmly in one direction, just as if I knew where I was going, seemed to be the only hope until I decided to open one door, just as if I belonged there.

Something caught my eye—on a cart rolling by, crewed by three brown-skinned men who were all wearing what looked like short skirts, vests without shirts, and gigantic lace neckties. They were interesting enough, but what caught my eye was the eagle-and-swastika on every crate on the cart.

I'm not sure what made it add up for me. Maybe it was just that it was the first familiar symbol I'd seen in hours, even if it was that one; maybe I was remembering that Harry Skena had been pretty sure Blade's supplies were coming from a world where Hitler won. Anyway, I trotted up and jumped on the back of the cart.

They not only didn't seem to mind, they didn't seem to notice. I suppose it wasn't their cart or their crate, and there wasn't a lot of point in investigating. Whatever the case, they ignored me, and I rode on with them. We were clipping along at about five miles per hour, I estimated, and it was twenty minutes or so before they turned off, through a giant double door that had a set of symbols I hadn't seen before on it.

After some more rolling along, we came to a bend in the corridor, then into a wide area. There was a familiar blue glow, and when we came around the corner I saw that it was coming from a column that stretched several stories up into a covered space, like a missile in a silo; this was clearly a gate.

I got off and walked casually past. No one looked at me.

Then I crept quietly back and watched. The gate glowed red; out of it came many large, swastika-marked boxes, to be loaded on carts and driven swiftly away. Then a couple of small boxes of stuff were sent through the other way, and they powered it down and left it glowing blue.

Interesting. And to judge from the casual way of handling freight, with not all the outbound boxes thrown in this time and with many of the inbound sitting around until a cart came for them, it seemed a safe enough bet that this was always the gate to Nazi-land. It wasn't exactly where I'd have picked to go, but it beat staying here and starving, or getting caught in the open by a big gang of these bozos.

If nothing happened, I'd be caught and either dead or enslaved sooner or later. And nothing was just what was going to happen unless I made something happen.

All of which was the rationale I was mumbling into my own mind's ear as I crept forward, got in among the crates that seemed to be outbound, and saw if there were any I could lift the lid on.

Sure enough, there was one, and what was inside it looked like—it was. Small transistor television sets. At least that was what the picture on the box showed. All the way up to the top . . . but plenty of room for me if I could find somewhere to hide the top layer.

I sneaked over to the "inbound" group and discovered that two of the open crates were only about half-full, with all kinds of junk that looked a lot like stray merchandise, some of it obviously broken . . .

Aha. Got it. Luxury goods they were either selling to

the Nazis or maybe distributing to the Closers over there. Which meant the crate I had opened first was probably going to a civilian warehouse. Perfect!

I hastily stripped off the top layer of TVs, still wishing I could read Closer characters—but what else was a cardboard box with a picture of a box with an oval screen and knobs likely to be? And if I was wrong, I was sure I'd know soon enough.

Anyway, with eight perfectly good sets going back to the factory (some poor slave would probably have to spend hours figuring out what was not wrong with them), there was now lots of room for me in the outbound crate.

I took a moment to quietly take a leak into the inbound crate—I had to go, I needed somewhere to hide it, and besides I had no desire to make life among the Closers any more pleasant—and then got into the outbound. Not having anything else to do, I tried to take a nap.

I must have dozed a little, because I only woke when the crate started to move. They were jacking the pallet up with a little gadget I had seen that was a bit like a hand-operated forklift, and then there was a thud as they slid me and the TVs onto a powered cart. After a moment or two, the cart started to roll forward, and feetfirst and flat on my back, I entered another world.

Going through a gate is not nearly as nice as blinking in and out; I discovered why ATN used blink transmitters rather than gates. My first time, jumping through, I hadn't had time to notice the hard lurch in my stomach or the disorienting dizziness, let alone the strange, enervating tingle that ran up my body in a long slow wave. It felt like my leg going to sleep and the sensation spreading all over my body, and it seemed to last for hours, though really I think it was only seconds.

There was a series of hard bumps that I realized must be the crate being off-loaded. I suddenly had a terrible fear that every other crate would end up stacked on top, and that this crate wouldn't be needed for weeks, but no such thing happened. There were more thuds and crashes all around as other crates were laid in beside mine, then the sound of electric motors whirring, and a truck engine started somewhere and drove away.

After that it was silent for a long while. I figured my resting heart rate was around eighty; it had been the last time I gave blood, so I started counting beats . . . twelve hundred beats should be about fifteen minutes. I wanted to pop out when there was nobody there, but I also wanted to give myself as much time as possible before anybody came back.

Finally, I cautiously raised the lid and sat up. I was tired, hungry, and getting pretty discouraged; from what the ATN people had told me, there wasn't much chance of getting a ride home from here.

The warehouse, if that's what it was, was still brightly lit, but there was nothing moving around in it. I jumped down from the crate to get moving.

I suppose I could have died right there. I don't know what told me to look up, or how exactly I managed to point the SHAKK and pull the trigger before I knew what I was dealing with—

But the Doberman went to pieces as the round zinged around inside him, and fell to the floor in front of me, a bag of smashed protoplasm. I got the Dobe behind him, too.

There were shouts inside the warehouse—somebody yelling for Sieg and Frieda, which I suspected were the two Dobermans. I ran like hell from the direction of the voice, weaving in and out among the crates, hoping for a little bit of luck.

At first I seemed to be having it—it sounded like there was just one guy, who had noticed the dogs going into "attack" mode, coming in to make sure they were just after a rat or something. Probably I could get around behind him and find an exit.

I was thinking that right at the moment when I rounded a corridor turn and suddenly instead of dividers and shelves, I was looking out into an open space. The first thought I had was that this sure as hell wasn't the civilian warehouse I had hoped it would be, because the gadget in front of me was unquestionably a tank, and a pretty high-tech one at that.

It looked sort of like your basic idea of a flying saucer, silvery and clam-shaped, except that it had a long, slim gun sticking out of the side near the top; a crack below that showed where the gun rotated. There were many treads, on short little posts underneath the thing, some up and some down; I suspect it had something like ground-following radar and extended three legs at any one time so that it was always stable and at the same time able to move in any direction quickly.

Right now the part of the upper "clam plate" behind the gun had two big openings, both created by gull-wing doors like the doors on a DeLorean, and there was a big crew of men climbing around on it, a couple of them poking around in the thing's guts, and there were at least ten armed guards as well. Moreover, one of the men was looking straight at me, and he bellowed "look—over there" and pointed.

I turned and ran; I didn't like the way all those submachine guns were coming out. At least back among the goods there might be something too valuable for them to use as a backstop for bullets.

These guys were in shape, too, they weren't some stray garrison guard, gone to fat and sloth. I could hear them running out around and ahead, blocking the different ways. One popped into a corridor before me, and I gave him a round from the SHAKK; he fell dead and I leaped over him and kept going, hoping I had at least put myself on the outside of the net.

A burst of submachine gun fire chewed up the crate behind me and I dove to the floor, wriggling hard to back out of the corner I had run into. A moment later a head popped in, and I hit him with a SHAKK round; two down and god knew how many to go. There was a lot of shouting, and the occasional words I could hear (they seemed to be speaking English, which didn't make much sense to me, but maybe my translator was able to cover German? But why would it be?).

"It's English," the translator said in my mind.

Thanks, I thought back at it.

Sorting out I realized that first of all there was one guy who was upset by the condition Sieg and Frieda were in; later I learned that the ammo for a SHAKK isn't all that smart. It knows where to find the head on a human being, but on any other living creature it zings around everywhere, just staying inside the body. On a really big animal—an elephant, say—if you hit far enough away from a vital organ, the animal might even survive because the pathway through the body didn't happen to pass close enough to a vital organ, and so much energy would be expended in just getting through hide and surface fat. But on something the size of a Doberman—a lot smaller than a man—it had plenty of room to run, and it turned the insides of those dogs into sort of a nasty red jam that dribbled out of them all over the floor, leaving them as drained skins in the middle of a huge blood slick.

I could see why the fellow was a bit upset.

Yet another guard burst in on me, and this guy was shooting as he came around the corner. I felt something hot tag my calf muscle, and then I SHAKKed him like the others. He fell over with his finger convulsing on the trigger, the recoil driving him backward, and consequently knocked out about half the light fixtures in the immediate area and started a bunch of stuff that had been stored up in the rafters to slide and fall around.

It was a nearly perfect diversion, and, despite the stinging pain in my calf, I was up and running. By now I'd figured a set of directions and had decided that the side of the building farthest from me was the one that had the best chance of having an exit to the outside, which meant I'd have to find a way across the area where the tank was parked. Well, I'd think of something.

More shots chewed into crates beside me, and I zagged down an aisle, took the first right I could, turned again—and burst into the wide-open area.

The unarmed workmen there turned and stared, and I ran right into their midst, hoping the guards behind me would have at least a little compunction about firing into a crowd that was mostly unarmed civilians.

I should have figured differently, but I didn't know Closers or Nazis nearly as well then as I was to know them later. Think of a Nazi whose family has been rabid Nazis for twenty generations, think of a guy who would toss a woman's baby on the fire because he likes the way she screams while he rapes her, think of children raised to execute their slave playmates so that they won't become too "emotional," and you've got Closers.

There was a Closer among these guys, and the way I could tell was that for one instant they refused to shoot into the crowd, and I got away into the racks of stuff on the other side, ducking rapidly to the left and jumping a low spot in the stored stuff, hitting in a roll and getting myself back under cover. God, I was glad they hadn't laid this out in nice neat rows, or I'd have been dead—

The voice had an unpleasantly sibilant accent; no big surprise. Most Closers can't quite manage sh's or th's.

"You incompetent s-s-slaves, I'll have you s'ot! So you won't s'oot because zair are s-slaves in ze way! S-s-s'oot zem all now! S-soot zem, or I'll s'oot you!"

And to my amazement, I heard the chatter of submachine guns.

It made me sick and disgusted; I was alive because those innocent workmen had been in the wrong place at the wrong time. All thought of escape left my mind; I turned and crawled back toward them.

"Now form a ssssskirmis'ing line and move forward!" There was a whiny quality to the voice too; later I learned that Closers who are running operations of this kind are often young teenagers, getting extra training in ruthlessness.

I got a look at what they were doing, popped up with the SHAKK set on full auto, and sprayed down the line, the deep whoosh of SHAKK rounds going out into them, half the line falling over and the high-tech tank suddenly flashing from a dozen places and bursting into flames.

Half the line.

The SHAKK had stopped making a whoosh noise, and there were four of them left. I glanced down and saw the readout on the top was flashing "RELOAD

BEFORE FIRING AGAIN," or at least that was what the translator said it said.

I was out of ammo, and the only thing keeping me alive right now was that the four surviving guards and their Closer leader were too busy diving for the floor and trying to get their weapons pulled around to get a shot off at me.

8

At least I had the advantage that I knew something was wrong a split second before they did.

I grabbed for my .45, and time slowed down as I found the deep concentration I needed. Pistol shooting is like any other martial art—once you're good at it, what you want is a clear, cool head.

I also had the advantage of a lot of backlight. Some stray SHAKK rounds must have decided to go into the engine compartment (if that was what it was) of the tank, and had made hash of a lot of things. Smoke was pouring out of the tank, and there was a strong flickering backlight from sheets of white plasma that skittered and ran over the silvery surface. The bright flashes nicely silhouetted the men in front of me, though since they were on the floor, the angle was bad.

I bagged the Closer on the first shot—he was just getting down to the floor, maybe because he didn't want to get his clothes dirty and, like most of them, wasn't so much an officer as a slavemaster.

It had taken one shot to dispose of the Closer; I got two more off, and I think might have wounded one of the guards, before the guy on the far right let off a burst with the submachine gun. I hit the ground rolling and running, and behind me I could hear them getting up.

I just hoped there wasn't another guy at the door.

There was a deafening roar, and the tank blew up. It flung me to the floor in a facefirst skid so hard that I barely kept from banging my head, and all around me the stacked crates, racks, and dividers were tipping over in all directions. I don't know what happened to the last few guards, but I would guess they had their backs to it and weren't quite among the stored goods yet. Probably they were just flung forward into the mess, and I would guess one or two of them were killed by what they hit.

Much of the stuff in the rafters had been stored on plywood sheets running rafter to rafter, and when the blast went off a lot of it went straight up, lifting those sheets and dumping their contents; all kinds of heavy junk rained down inside the warehouse, and if I hadn't been busy running for the door for all I was worth, jumping fallen objects and climbing over collapsed piles of stuff, I'd have been terrified enough to keep my head down. All around me the building groaned as the loads shifted abruptly; in other parts of the storage area, things that were supposed to be kept apart were apparently finding each other, for there were explosions and bursts of fire everywhere.

There was one confused-looking guard at the door, and when I burst out at him he went for his gun. I slammed my feet to a stop in the approved two-handed position and put a slug into his face; he fell backward. After all the exploding heads the SHAKK caused, it was almost a relief just to see a smear of blood, hair, and brains hit the back wall.

As I stepped over him I thought I saw an American-flag patch on his arm; oh, well, if he was working for these clowns, he wasn't part of the America I was. Just because you've got the uniform doesn't mean you play on the team . . .

At last—five minutes, ten or more deaths, and a lot of nervousness after getting out of the crate—I pushed through the door and out into the sunny deserted street, dashed across without checking for traffic, and ran down an alley. There was another alley at a cross angle and I took that route, then swung around one more corner, pressed myself into an inconspicuous corner of a doorway, and let my breath come down to calm and regular while I listened for signs of pursuit.

There was a thundering, ground-shaking roar. Given the variety of stuff that had been in that place, and how mixed together it was getting, I suppose it should have been no surprise. I saw a flicker of flame in the sky through the little opening of the alley above me; I suspected any need to get rid of witnesses or evidence had just been taken care of.

I drew a long, deep breath and took stock. I didn't exactly know where I was, other than I was in a timeline where Hitler won, and a timeline the Closers felt secure enough about to use as a base. There were probably not more than two hundred or so Closers on the planet, of whom I figured I'd just eliminated one, but there were untold Nazis, and not just German ones either. I sure hadn't felt like I could have turned to those guards and said, "See here, I'm an American, too."

I was tired, hungry, without friends or money, two rounds left in the magazine and no reloads, and the SHAKK was useless. I wondered why I hadn't taken along a few pocketfuls of that sand they were loaded with. And about ten extra magazines, two ham sandwiches, and a cold Pepsi.

Worse yet, the alley in which I sat seemed to back up on an Italian restaurant, because there was a wonderful smell of red sauce. Not an easy place to do your planning when you were hungry.

Chances that they would take the money in my billfold—zip. I doubted my credit cards would do much good either. Besides that I had . . . well, I suppose I could stick someplace up if I really had to. But totalitarian states are bad places to take up crime. They're not awfully careful about the rights of the accused, and there aren't a whole lot of situations in which you can just hide among people.

There were sirens wailing—fire crews headed for the warehouse, no doubt, and if there were any survivors there, I'd have cops after me within half an hour. Time to get it moving. I didn't know which way to go or where I was, but "away from the warehouse" seemed like a good plan. I got the SHAKK tucked under my shirt (for all I knew there were reloads for it here) and the .45 to where it wasn't completely conspicuous, in the big inside pocket of the jacket. I just hoped my clothes weren't going to be screaming "arrest me" when I ran into people again.

I rounded two more corners in the tangle of alleys, popped across a street—well, the people on it didn't look weird to me, maybe I didn't look weird to them. I ducked into another block of alleys, and repeated the process. Wherever I was, there was some resemblance to Pittsburgh—I hadn't seen a bit of level ground yet.

All right, I could see plenty of daylight up ahead, and sooner or later I'd have to stick my head out; I gritted my teeth for a moment, listened to the explosions still going off back at the warehouse, figured I hadn't heard a siren close by in a while . . . time to take a walk down a real street and see what happened to me.

I popped out of an alley, looked quietly around. Most of the people seemed to be dressed from a fifties movie, the men in blue or gray suits and the women in calf-length dresses. Everything looked a little cheap but whether that was the way the country was or the way the neighborhood was, who could say.

I decided to walk uphill because there was a slightly better chance of finding a landmark that way. As I walked I did a little more study of the people; some of them seemed not to like me. Clearly there was something about me . . .

Probably that all the men were crew-cut, and all the women in tight little perms. My hair was pretty short, by the standards of where I came from, but I had it. Most of these guys looked like they'd just come from delousing.

On the other hand they felt free to glare at a stranger on the street. This version of America was not *that* totalitarian, then.

I also realized the crowd wasn't just men and women. It was just that anybody from puberty on up was either in a suit or in one of the three permitted dress styles. It occurred to me, too, that I had no necktie. Looked like everyone was wearing clip-ons. I wondered how they'd react if I asked to bum a spare tie from someone.

Well, the next thing to check out, then, was—

I came over the hill and one problem got solved right away. I saw the Golden Gate Bridge in the distance—or rather, about two-thirds of the Golden Gate Bridge. The center part of the span was torn out, and as I looked more closely I saw that there were many cables hanging loose from it; at this distance the reddish color on much of it suggested that it was rusting.

All right, so this was San Francisco.

"Hey, buddy, have a heart, will you, don't walk around like that over here!"

The man approaching me was paunchy, shave-headed, and dressed in something that looked more like a brown-shirt uniform than anything else, but it had American-flag patches on the shoulders and a big white strip over the pocket.

It didn't look like this was a bust, and something about him didn't give off the flavor of cop, so I peered at him for a long moment, reading "Good Neighbor Patrol" on the strip. It sounded like the kind of thing McGruff the Crime Dog would be involved in, but the closer look had also assured me that the American flag now had a white swastika instead of stars in the blue field.

"Come on, buddy, you've seen this uniform before, especially if you've been walking around like that. Let me at least put a tie on you, and if you need the price of a haircut . . . "

So I had been right.

He got closer, then said, "You don't seem very, uh, connected to things, there, pal."

If he started looking at me closer, instead of just hassling me like the street bum he thought I was, I was going to be in deep, quick. So I made myself focus and said, "Sorry—I—geez, where am I?"

"You wandered over from Berkeley somehow," the guy said, shaking his head. "And if you just wander back quick, I won't have to do anything about you, and you won't have to have anything done about you. I know you all walk around like that over there all the time, but there ain't no chick houses or thump clubs here, fella, and you're sticking out like a sore thumb."

He leaned in close—it took me a moment to realize he was sniffing my breath. "Well, you're not drunk, and I don't smell any burning rope. So I don't know what you're on, but"—he shrugged—"it's none off mine. I just happen to have a perfect record for these blocks, and I want to keep it. So—if you'll do me the favor—"

He reached out, buttoned my top button, and clipped a shoddy little rayon tie to it. "And I got a barber right around the corner. Listen, if I get you trimmed, put you on a streetcar—" A thought seemed to hit him. "You got any dough? You didn't come over here to panhandle?"

"Oh, no, not to panhandle," I said, since obviously that would be the wrong answer. "I uh . . . this will sound stupid."

"Try me."

"Well, I put on the jacket and my good pants," I said, thinking frantically, "to look a little more presentable because—you're right, I don't have any dough—but I, um, was over here hoping to find someplace I could apply for work."

His lips pursed, and he quietly whispered, "Vet, hunh?"

I wasn't sure what the significance was, except that pretty obviously it was going to change things drastically, so I hesitated and then he whispered, "That's right, don't talk here. Come on."

And he promptly led me around to a barbershop, but we went in by the back door and he plopped me down in a chair in the back. I could hear the barbers—there seemed to be two of them—cutting hair in the front, then a couple of low whispers near the cash register. I sat and waited.

About ten minutes went by. I was at least fairly safe here, and the guy had not acted like a cop about to make a bust. The trouble was, he'd assumed I was a veteran, and in this context I couldn't even be sure that I knew what war it was going to be. Not to mention that I'd never actually served a day in my life, and if anyone started quizzing me about military slang, I was going to have to rely on old movies . . .

Well, time enough for that when it came up. Meanwhile I could enjoy breathing calmly and safely.

The "Good Neighbor Patrol" guy brought a barber back with him, who said, "Okay, pal, we're gonna make you presentable on some of Bob's discretionary cash. Some system for suppressing vagrants you've got, Bob—dress 'em up to be respectable vagrants."

Bob, the Good Neighbor guy, grinned good-naturedly. "You know why I'm doing it, and it's the same reason you are." He looked at me closely and said, "You wouldn't have been Home Defense—you must have been Regular Army. Wim and me, we got captured halfway across Kansas and spent a long time moving rocks out by New *York* City." He punched the *York* pretty hard, and I realized there must be something different now. "Who'd you serve with?"

I didn't have a clue, but I figured what I'd do is tell him the only thing I could remember offhand, what was in fact where my father had been. I just wished Dad had been more inclined to tell war stories . . . "I was . . ." I swallowed hard. "I was with General Patton. Third Army. Spent a while in a Stalag—"

They stared at me, and I thought for one long instant that I'd blown it; then suddenly they were taking turns shaking my hand. "Then—you were at Gettysburg?"

Maybe I had just taken a hard hit on the head in that parking garage . . . but I played along. "Captured just after."

"Damn! Then you almost . . ." and his voice dropped to a whisper . . . "you almost made the boat."

I shrugged.

"You don't talk much, do you? You do stay over in Berkeley, it's all vets and poets and baxters, isn't it? Feel more at home there?"

I nodded. I suspected that if my hair and lack of tie had made that kind of difference, then I probably would have felt more at home in Berkeley.

"Well, we'll get you back there. Jeez, if the regular cops got you, they'd spend an hour kicking you just to stay in practice. No wonder he can't get work, Wim. His permit must be stamped that he's only employable as a last resort . . . and the last I knew the Black Mark guys were getting two cups of dry oatmeal, a cup of beans, and a vitamin pill per day from the Dole. When was the last time you had meat, son?"

"Couple days ago," I said, which was true, subjectively anyway. "Somebody gave me dinner."

They glanced at each other. "Well, you're getting a haircut, a hamburger, and bus fare back to Berkeley," Bob said. "And after that, *don't* come this way again. Your best bet, no kidding—I've known one or two this worked for—get a freight out of town and get out to the fields. Lose your papers and get another freight. Walk into a forced labor camp and act shell-shocked. It's three hard years, but they'll feed you, and at the end you'll come out as a John Doe, and you can get a job as a janitor or something. Beat the hell out of the way you're living now. And it works as long as you don't get caught."

I nodded. "Thank you."

"Repeat it back to me."

I did. He nodded, satisfied. "There's a train out of Oakland with a lot of empty boxcars most mornings, about four A.M. Catch it soon, pal. If you'd been one block over, you'd have found yourself a real Nazi for a Good Neighbor, and you'd be spitting out your teeth right now. Maybe on your way back to be extradited and put in another Stalag. There's plenty of folks over here who'd love to give you work and food, but they got to keep their heads down; most of 'em are like me, we never miss the VOA, but we sure don't take any chances about it. Maybe it'll all be different when the ship comes in."

Wim grinned. "When the ship comes in, Bob, I'm going to have to lock you up."

"Sure, if you let me shoot my boss first. I swear that's what keeps a lot of us hoping, is the thought that we can dispose of all these petty weiners that Reconstruction left in place."

It was all gibberish to me, but the point was that they were going to help me get to somewhere where I could be less conspicuous. And though I wasn't ready to give up the fight, I'd at least learned from them how I could make myself fit into this world if I needed to, and that was good to know—because I just might need to.

So without much further ado, Wim shaved my head, and Bob went out and came back a bit later with a hamburger, a huge basket of fries, a big slice of apple pie, and a thermos of coffee. He said it was compliments of a "guy up the street that was at the Azores," which at least gave me another battle to refer to.

I'm not bad at geography. The Azores are eight hundred miles west of Portugal; the Axis got nowhere near them in the World War II I knew. And I had about figured out why they were referring to Gettysburg . . . battles tend to happen in the same places over and over. The pass of Megiddo (or Armageddon) is up in the mountains of northern Israel, and the author of Revelations picked it as the site of the final battle because, probably, it had already been the site of so many battles. The same passes, river crossings, roads, and forests are attacked and defended again and again.

The reason Americans are less aware of this is because most of our continent has been at peace most of the time . . . but armies move on pathways dictated by terrain, and they run into each other in the same places century after century. Gettysburg is where an army moving north out of Virginia or the Chesapeake is apt to collide with one coming south from New York or Philly, or one coming east from the Ohio Valley. Pretty clearly Patton had made some kind of last-ditch stand there . . . and obviously, whether he'd won or not, it hadn't worked out.

All these thoughts were hitting me as I stuffed the food in; the other thought crossing my mind was that in an occupied nation—were they still occupied? It didn't quite sound like it—like the United States of this world, I would have to try not to get into any firefights. There were probably a substantial number of good guys like Bob and Wim around, and I didn't want to kill any of that kind.

The burger was great, the fries were great, the pie was great. Appetite is the best sauce, and so forth. I wish I could say the same for the coffee, but it was cut so heavily with chicory that I could taste no coffee at all in it. I realized, somewhere in my second cup, that the "chick houses" of Berkeley were pretty clearly not the massage parlors one might have thought.

Raw chicory . . . a guy would have to spend a while getting used to it.

Finally Bob took me down to the end of the street

and handed me fare for a bus; he showed me one coming along that had a long list of destinations, Berkeley among them. "Just stay quiet till you get home," he said, and turned and went. I didn't get a chance to thank him.

And a good thing, too. When I got on the bus, the driver said, "where to?" and pointed to a schedule of rates when I seemed puzzled. I said "Berkeley Main," figuring that whatever that was it had to be somewhere reasonably close.

"You can take this bus all that way, but why don't you take the direct route? About six blocks and that way—half the fare and a third of the time."

The direction he pointed in was downhill, away from Bob's block . . . something seemed slightly funny. "I don't know the bus system at all well," I admitted.

There were about six riders on this one and they all looked pretty bored; the driver shrugged. "This is a featherbed route, bud. They have me driving long distances just so's I can finish out my time before retiring. The bus runs empty for most of the route, and I got no schedule to make. I get most of the way down to San Jose before I turn around and head the other way; the only regular riders I get are the cops coming off duty at the National Security station down by Moffet Field. I generally pull up there empty . . . and then it's a long time till I get back to Berkeley."

A bell went off in the back of my head. "Six blocks that way—"

"Is a bus that'll get you there in less than an hour. Pay one price. This thing ain't even good sight-seeing."

I thanked him, got off the bus, watched him pull away, then moved quickly and quietly into an alley across the street. San Francisco is kind of a tangle, but anyone who's learned to get around in Pittsburgh is hard to confuse about directions from then on. I got to the place he was talking about without poking my head out much, except occasionally to cross a busy street.

It occurred to me that good old Bob and Wim had learned a fair amount about me, that the food had delayed me a long time, that Bob had had plenty of time to make a phone call. And I found myself thinking . . . if a vet was discriminated against, how did one end up as a Home Guard? There was a sort of obvious answer.

Whether Wim was in on it or not, I couldn't say. I never did find out. But I would bet he was . . . it's pretty hard to avoid knowing that your friend is a fink.

But there was a news broadcast on continuously on that bus, and just as it pulled up to Berkeley Main (which turned out to be one of the buildings on the old campus—now a set of office buildings and small shops, kind of a giant mall—)I heard that the police were looking for a man in a red-and-blue-striped tie and a navy blue jacket who had somehow escaped from a bus on its way to the National Security facility. There was a brief congratulations to Robert Christian, an alert Good Neighbor, for having spotted the man, and the news that the driver was being detained for questioning.

The red-and-blue tie went from my neck into the shopping bag of a lady getting off. I couldn't take off the jacket without making my personal arsenal a bit more obvious, but there were plenty of blue jackets around. And despite the impression I'd gotten as I got off the bus at Berkeley Main, I noted most of the crowd was shaveheads like me.

If I could find someplace to lie low for a bit, things might blow over.

Good old Bob. He'd seemed like every regular guy

you met back home. He probably *was*—but this place wasn't anything like back home.

Checking menus in restaurant windows I figured out that I had the cash for two or three meals left over from that bus fare. If the ratio was what it was like back home, I could probably get things like bread and canned soup and so forth at groceries and stretch it out a few days.

I also had done a little more thinking and realized that if there were people looking for it, there was probably an underground to be looked for. The fact that they talked about my "just missing the boat" was extremely promising, too. There might even be somewhere to catch a boat *to*.

I needed to know a lot more, and the trouble was, I wasn't sure where to look for the additional knowledge.

Berkeley was different—everywhere was different, but Berkeley more so. I realized there had probably been a lot of fighting down here, because so much of the area had been razed; the kind of charm that it had had was about two-thirds gone, with most of it replaced with big ugly block apartment buildings.

Still, there were signs that Berkeley was still Berkeley. I passed three chick houses, and all of them had notes for "poetry reading" and "American folk culture nights." There was some odd graffiti on the walls; "1789!" was popular (I figured that was the year the Bill of Rights passed . . .) along with "BWRY—AA!" with the A's intertwined. That took me a long time to figure out, till I saw another bit of graffiti with the intertwined A's attached to the phrase "All American" and the word NO and a swastika below—so the AA meant "all American" and was a subversive slogan. Another anagram appeared on another building:

Y
RED
BLACK
L
O
WHITE!

Got it. The abbreviation was "Black White Red Yellow—All American!" Pretty clearly there was not only an underground around here, but one that was almost out in the open, at least a little bit. Moreover there was an enclosing arrowhead drawn around the top words, and that explained the little "bent arrow" shapes I'd seen in several spots.

That made me feel a little better, though no safer. There was an anti-Nazi underground, and one they weren't suppressing very successfully. But I hadn't found it yet, and I still had nowhere to sleep.

The other thing I noticed down here was that there were substantial numbers of men without ties, a few even wearing blue jeans, and some women with straight hair down to their shoulders and no makeup. There were also practically no cars on the street . . . probably nobody here could afford one.

A girl of maybe twenty-five walking by, hair to her shoulders, baggy sweater, dress not ironed, and sneakers, gave me a little smile, and I smiled back. At least she didn't look like the robot people over on the other side of the Bay. She looked like she might speak to me—

Then an old school bus came around the corner, and people started giving shrill shepherd's whistles and running into alleys. The girl turned and ran; I stayed for a second longer and saw the bus pull up.

It was a Boy Scout troop bus. On its side was a troop number, and what I guessed must now be the Boy Scout emblem—an American eagle on a trefoil, just as it was in my timeline, but here the American eagle gripped the twin lightning bolts of the SS.

The kids piling out of the bus looked like any other Boy Scouts, but they carried wooden sticks, what looked like pieces of inch-and-a-half dowel rod about two feet long. They were yelling at everyone as they came out, and they headed right for the stragglers— though not for me, it was pretty clear they were mostly after women and old people.

I froze for a second—I really didn't want to get mixed up in anything, with no valid papers, and anyway I suspected what they were doing wasn't illegal, but stopping them might be.

I turned as they went by me. The girl who had smiled at me had tripped over a curb, and before she could get to her feet, five of the boys jumped her, beating her buttocks with their sticks, whooping and hollering, grabbing at her to pull up her skirt.

Without thinking I waded in. None of them could have been older than thirteen; I noticed in an abstract way that they and all the other kids were screaming "Jooger, jooger, jooger!" at the people they were beating.

I grabbed the first one by the back of his shirt and the second by his scrawny neck, and slammed their heads together hard. They both fell down yelling with pain; the others jumped up in shock, and I treated myself to a trick roundhouse kick, getting all three kids in the face. All five of them ran screaming back toward the bus; apparently people hitting back was not in the script.

The girl jumped to her feet, glanced behind me, shouted something. I turned.

The bus driver—a guy who had "Scoutmaster" written all over him, one of those big hale-and-hearty types that you find with car dealerships or as school board members in small towns, was coming out of the bus with an electric cattle prod. Apparently he was the reinforcements.

He did not seem pleased with me. All around, the Boy Scouts were stopping to watch, and the people they had been beating on were getting away, so I guess I had accomplished something useful.

Mr. Scoutmaster Sir was striding along toward me, the prod half-extended, and I could tell he figured I'd break and run. Of course, I knew I had the .45, and he didn't.

But I didn't want to waste a round, and the way he was coming on I didn't have to. When he reached out with the prod, I had already lunged inside his guard, and I slapped the prod to the side. He had just time to look surprised before I kicked him in the balls, giving it everything I had. He dropped the prod and fell groaning to his knees; I brought both hands up over my head, clenched together in a fist, and whipped them overhead and down to the back of his head as I brought my knee up, trapping his head in the smashing blow and shattering his nose and teeth.

That seemed to be a signal; the streets were suddenly boiling with angry people, all closing in on the Scouts. If I hadn't seen the little bastards in action before, I might have felt sorry for them—but I had, and I enjoyed the spectacle of their being cornered and kicked bloody. Apparently these little defenders of public order and the New American Way had never found out about people hitting back.

The girl was at my elbow. "You've got to run. Come with me."

She was obviously right, so I followed her down several streets, zigging, zagging, and backtracking till we were far enough away so that we didn't see anyone else running or acting like anything was unusual. Then she took my hand and said, "Try to look like you're in love."

We walked slowly up the street together, then made an abrupt left into a small, older cottage that had a sign on the door: "Berkeley Free Library."

The inside of the front room was lined with books, with shelves visible through the doorways to the other rooms, and there was a big wraparound desk in the middle. The chairs and tables didn't even come close to matching each other, and there was just one person in there, a short, slightly built guy, shaveheaded but not wearing a tie, in a pink shirt and baggy gray pants. He looked to be about thirty; he could have been a mildly eccentric professor back home.

"Anybody been in while I've been gone?" the girl asked.

"Nope, Sandy, nobody. As usual, nobody wants to read what you have. But I see you've found yet another partner for your life of sleazy abandon."

"Glad to hear there was nobody—this time. Then we were never gone, and my friend here was with me the whole time."

The little guy whistled. His glasses were pretty thick, and they slid down to the tip of his big nose easily, revealing large dark eyes, so he looked sort of like a bewildered owl. "Yeah, what did he do? And what did you do?"

"Oh, the Boy Scouts were pogging Berkeley again. This guy decked the Scoutmaster, maybe hard enough to kill him. Started this medium-level riot . . . probably there'll be reprisals. Thought we better get him under wraps."

The little guy scratched his head vigorously. "Easier said than done, kid. Buddy, you wouldn't by any chance be the guy that escaped off a bus a while back this afternoon?"

"My name is Mark," I said. I'd gotten tired of being called buddy and pal; it was too much like hanging out with my father's friends. "And yep, I probably am. While I'm at it I had something to do with the warehouse fire over on the other side, too."

"You mean the one that all the cops went to, and there was a denial on the radio that there had been a fire, or in fact that there had ever been a building there? Anyone ever tell you you cause trouble wherever you go?"

I liked his voice—it was a little nasal, maybe, but there was something in it that told you he was tough underneath—he could look at anything and report it honesty, could be killed but not intimidated, didn't know how to see with any eyes but his own.

"I've heard that," I said. "What's our next step?"

He sighed. "Well, I'd like to make you wait three hours while I keep working here. I have a pile of notes I should make about Walt Whitman, if I'm ever going to get my little book about him done. Somebody's got to keep the torch of American scholarship alight . . . but then of course somebody's also got to keep the American resistance going. If I didn't have Sandy to run the library, I'd collapse under the load entirely."

Sandy made a funny noise like a horse that's smelled something it doesn't like. "Have you eaten lately?" she asked.

"Fairly recently," I said. "Actually the idea of just sitting down and reading is pretty attractive; if I can hide my coat someplace, I'll probably look less conspicuous, and I can sit somewhere well to the back."

"Good a plan as any," the small man said. He got up and walked toward me, extending his hand; his grip was firm and strong, for such a small guy. "Any man who can upset that many cops is a friend of mine. My name's Al."

We stashed my coat, and it gave me a chance to hide the SHAKK and the .45; then I went into a back corner. The first thing I did was pick up the day's newspaper, to discover that it was August 17, 1961. There were a bunch of notes about the new president being off to a great start; from the look of the editorial page, it had actually been a contested election, the first since Reconstruction was withdrawn. Reconstruction, I had figured out, was the Nazi occupation, and since they kept referring to "the fifteen years of Reconstruction," that seemed to imply that the Germans had occupied the US from roughly 1945 to 1960.

The current president was a Nazi; his opponent in the 1960 election had been Strom Thurmond, and the paper seemed to be in hysterics about Thurmond the "sore loser" having the temerity to criticize the government that had won the election. Their reference to him as an "ultra-liberal crazy" came very close to making me laugh out loud . . . I suppose context is everything.

I tried finding a history book—when you've worked in academia as long as I have, you know Dewey Decimal and Library of Congress pretty well, and it doesn't take much time to find a thing—but those shelves were all but bare of material that covered anything since 1940. I figured that was probably a political statement in its own right. The number of basic authors who were missing from the shelves was a long list, though I did note there was more poetry and literature than one would expect.

Most of the paper was propaganda. I noted that rents were low—ever see a thirty-five-dollar-per-month rental in San Francisco?—and roughly commensurate with the restaurant meal prices. There were several pages about how to establish "normalcy" in your household, community, and church. Normalcy seemed mostly to mean getting people to be very alike and have a positive attitude about it.

There was an ad for the Boy Scouts . . . "IS YOUR SON A SCOUT? IF HE'S NOT, WON'T YOUR NEIGHBORS WONDER WHY?" The picture showed a blond boy giving a Hitler salute, and down at the bottom of the page was the Scout Law. Having been an Eagle Scout myself, I knew that one by heart . . . and I noted they had added three laws to it: "A Scout is white," "A Scout scorns weakness," and "A Scout is normal."

I liked it better the old way.

Department-store ads featured about three styles of dress and did not mention anything about underwear. Suits came in four styles, one of which was "The Latest From New Nuremberg." It took me a little while to figure out that that must be New York.

I got bored or disgusted, I'm not sure which, put my feet up, and went to sleep. It was wonderful to be able to do that at all.

When Sandy woke me it was getting dark outside. "You looked too comfortable to move" she said. "Come with me down to the basement—it's where Al and I have our apartment."

We walked down the long flight of steps with her behind me, and when I came to the bottom or the stairs, she said, "Go left." I turned left and went into the living room.

Al was there, a gun leveled on me. There were four guys wearing hoods sitting around him. I heard the safety slip off and a hammer cock behind me, and I knew Sandy had me covered.

On the table there was my Colt Model 1911A1 .45 automatic, and the SHAKK.

"You've got a lot of explaining to do," Al said, "and we might as well hear the first part in comfort. Sandy will give you some bread and soup, but I'm afraid we'll have to shackle your legs to the table. If you'd like to use the bathroom first, that can be arranged. We aren't out to hurt you or scare you, but we do need to know the truth."

9

I took him up on the offer of using the bathroom, and then let them shackle me and put the food in front of me. "Eat first if you like," Al said. "And if you're thinking of anything other than telling us the truth, think some more while you eat."

I did think. Probably they hadn't made that pistol since about 1945—everything I'd seen on the guards had been some sort of German make. And it's trivial to check a serial number—this one would be absolutely, totally wrong.

All that I suppose I could explain. The SHAKK, on the other hand, was utterly inexplicable. Worse yet, it had that digital readout, and it suddenly occurred to me that I hadn't seen a digital *anything* since I got here; 1960 was too early for calculators and electronic watches to begin with, but I was realizing that everything looked vaguely old-fashioned; either the high-tech was back in Germany, or it wasn't in existence at all.

I seriously doubted I could convince them that the SHAKK was a toy.

There was the possibility that, somewhere out there, there might be a hidden base. Patton's troops had apparently made it there, or some of them had, if I had understood Bob's hinting around correctly, and if it hadn't been a line he was feeding me for some obscure reason—and both those things seemed like very low probabilities. I could lie and claim the weapon had come from the hidden base.

The trouble was, if anyone was apt to know anything about a hidden base for real, it was the people facing me. I couldn't possibly fake my way through that one.

I guess I could have said I was a Nazi agent with a new Nazi superweapon, and let them shoot me, but I didn't like that option either.

It also occurred to me that I liked these guys. I wanted their trust, and I wanted them to believe me . . . but I respected and admired them a lot. They couldn't possibly have been where they were, doing what they were doing, without a ton of guts.

So after I finished dinner, and Sandy sat down by the door, her pistol still leveled at me, I drew a very deep breath and told them the truth. I couldn't exactly tell it in order—it's hard to begin a story by saying "so anyway there I was more than thirty years in the future, not your future but a different future, when . . . "

But I got it all out, every fact and detail, and figured that if I got shot at the end of it, or more likely quietly drugged and dropped off by some quiet little asylum's gates, I would at least not add lying to all my sundry crimes.

When I finished, Al thought for a long moment, then said, "So, in your timeline . . . name me a few major American painters since World War II. Guys who would have been unknown at the end of the war but well-known by your time."

I blinked—it wasn't at all what I had expected—but then I sort of automatically started naming them. "Well, for sheer well-knownness, there's Andy Warhol. Jackson Pollock's stuff wasn't well-known and really influential till after the war, really, but he had a bunch before. De Kooning, of course. But I'm really partial to one guy's work—I had several prints of his in my place—guy named Robert LaVigne."

The way two of the guys in sheets sat up straight told me I'd said something important, but whether it was right or not was a good question.

"Jazz performers?"

"Right after the war the famous ones, I guess, are Charlie Parker and Dizzy Gillespie. Dave Brubeck a little later. I don't know jazz well, I'm just naming the guys who got a lot of publicity."

Maybe a little too casually, Al said, "How about writers?"

"Since the war?"

"Right after the war."

"Well, if you're not counting pop stuff . . . oh, I guess J.D. Salinger, Jack Kerouac—"

"Well, I'm persuaded," one of the sheets said.

There was nodding all around. "Either that or they've completely penetrated us, and we're all dead anyway," Al agreed. He looked up at me. "Happens that we were all heavy into art—to use an expression that's officially banned for being 'too jazz'—and you've at least named some likely names."

"Definite names," the sheet said.

"Likely names," Al repeated. "Who was president during World War II?"

"Most of it, Roosevelt. His vice president, Harry Truman, finished it out—"

He had me recite the list of presidents as quickly as I could. I had to come up with all kinds of other bits of trivia as well. Finally he nodded, "You tell a very consistent story. It sounds like real history. Now comes the point where we have to decide to trust you . . . Sandy, you can unfasten him, and I think we can all put the guns away. If he's not what he says he is, it's too late anyway."

They all nodded, pulled off the sheets, put the guns away, and suddenly I found I was sitting in a room full of pleasant, intelligent-looking people without a trace of threat about them.

"All right," Al said, when everyone was comfortable, and they'd passed a plate of sandwiches around, "let me explain why we didn't just shoot you. We've seen one of these gadgets before." He pointed to the SHAKK.

"About two years ago a new member of the underground turned up in the area. She went by the name of Sheila. She didn't visibly do anything for a living but she obviously always had money; that's no surprise, there are plenty of rich people in the underground. Sheila seemed to have really uncanny intelligence information—when she said 'raid here on this date,' by god the raid scored big. At first we thought she might be a police provocateur—that maybe she was getting those results because they were planting targets for us. So we asked her specifically to find us a way to hit two old high-ranking Nazis that were about due to be rotated home.

"No problem. Sheila gave us a script, and we nailed them. There were hunts and reprisals all up and down the coast.

"Now, as you might guess, besides VOA broadcasts—did you have VOA in your timeline?"

"Voice of America is a government outfit in my timeline."

"Aha. Well, here it's the outlaw radio. Plays a little jazz to lure the kids, broadcasts some salacious scandals to lure the adults, and then gives a few minutes of hard news and some real music, usually just before the radio direction finders zero in on the balloon carrying the transmitter. It's generally on the air whenever we can get a transmitter up and running."

"And your not knowing that speaks more in your favor," commented one of the guys who had been sheeted, a big burly blondish guy with a sort of potato nose.

"Anyway, as you might guess, we have other major activities here, but the biggest one is to support the forces still in the Free Zone—which it will certainly not violate security to tell you is a big swath of territory running from Dutch Indonesia up through Indochina and into Burma, China, and Tibet, where there's all kinds of rags and tags of the old Allied armies. They've held out against Hitler, and now Himmler, for a long time, though in the process they eventually lost the South Pacific, Australia, New Zealand, and the Philippines . . . "

"Uh, in my timeline, a lot of that—the South Pacific and the Philippines—were in Japanese hands," I said.

"Not here. The Japs had to use everything they had to take Midway, the Aleutians, and Pearl Harbor right after the Germans took the Azores, and they didn't get much for it. They got about the same deal out of the war as Hitler's other allies like Italy, Spain, Turkey, and Hungary did . . . little dribs and drabs of land and the privilege of not being reconstructed. Then on top of that the Japs lost too much in their first attack on the Philippines—it had to be taken by Germans years later—and they are still bogged down in China, for that matter. A lot of us think, or hope anyway, that if Germany went down, her former 'allies' would turn on her instantly."

I nodded. "About this agent—"

"Well, she made it clear early on that she really, really wanted to be taken to the Free Zone. There's usually one of two reasons for that—either someone has a missing lover or relative there and is trying to get there to find them, or the person is a German spy. And the Free Zones have enough people, by and large. They don't need bodies as much as they need skills, intelligence, and stolen weapons. So you can only go if you've got an important thing to bring them or show them.

"Sheila said she did. It was a little bound volume, in black, with all kinds of physics equations and diagrams. She copied out three pages of it by hand and sent it over there, in one of our regular courier pouches. Three months later—not unusual, it takes a while to get there through channels—we got a note back saying they had to have her come out right away."

"You've seen it?"

"I have it here. Sheila got worried that they were closing in on her, and wanted to make sure that if anything happened to her, at least the book would get through. Part of it was, she seemed desperate to demonstrate to us that her knowledge was needed in the Free Zone, and of course the more desperate she looked, the more we suspected her motivations. So one night she took four of us out to the big rocket base out in the desert east of Los Angeles—the ones the Germans won't admit is theirs, and the US government won't admit is theirs, but that lights up the sky every third week or so—and as one of the rockets was taking off, she pulled out that gadget and blew it apart with four little 'whump' noises. It must have been four miles up when she did that; she said what she had done was to put very high-velocity shots into it—apparently they home in, in a pattern, just as you describe—and they tore the fuel tanks apart, spilling fuel onto the hot engine.

"The next day Sheila shot down a plane bringing the German consul back to San Francisco after a leave, from five miles off. That did a pretty good job of convincing us, and that's when we agreed to send the pages.

"But since she had shown us this gadget, it seemed like a waste not to use it some more. We had to be careful to use it only when there would be no direct witnesses, she said, and when the whole thing could look like an accident or when we could provide covering fire so that it looked like a lucky shot. So we had a lot of . . . well, fun, wasn't it, guys?"

Everyone nodded enthusiastically. "If we'd only been able to find a way for her to travel," one of them added, "we could easily have bagged the president, or even the Führer. It was one hot death angel of a gun."

"And when we asked her where she got these things, she said only that . . . well, do you remember the war in Spain, back before World War II? She said something like that was going on, that the other side had help, and she was coming in to redress the balance. She described the help as 'what the Nazis were to Franco, these people are to the Nazis,' and she was pretty clear that she didn't mean just in technical or military help. And it sounds to me very much like she must have been—"

"A Special Agent, like Harry Skena," I finished for him. "Though I don't see why she couldn't just jump over to the Free Zone. Maybe she didn't have access to a base, or something. But—" the thought hit me hard. "You're talking about her in the past tense. Has she already gone to the Free Zone, or is she—um, dead?"

Al spread his hands; his bushy eyebrows waggled above his glasses. "To tell you the truth, when we found this gadget on you we figured either you'd stolen it from her or you were part of her team. And from the havoc you caused passing through the city—you wouldn't believe how tough it was to get the cell together tonight with Good Neighbors and cops everywhere, and apparently there will be USSS troops arriving on a plane tomorrow to help in the search—from all that beautiful, so-cool chaos you unleashed, we thought you must be a friend of hers.

"We're damn glad you're here, Mark, and one of us does some hand-loading, and we've still got some old .45s in action, so I think we can scrounge you a few magazines. We have a key to her place, and we've searched it a couple of times, but there's not the slightest clue to anything in there, and there certainly wasn't that blue-gray powder you were describing. Which I'm damned sorry about, because it would be fun to keep pulling those merry little pranks we were pulling before."

I nodded impatiently. "But where is she?"

"That's the point," Sandy said quietly. "We were really hoping *you'd* know. Because tomorrow night we make contact with a sub out of the Free Zone, and she's supposed to be there to go with the book, and she's been completely gone for ten days. It's like she just vanished into thin air."

"That could be exactly what happened," I pointed out.

"But if she was doing it of her own free will, why hasn't there been a message to us? And why couldn't she just pop back in whenever she got whatever it was done, and only be gone for five minutes in our time? And if it wasn't of her free will—"

"You think the Closers got her," I said.

"We didn't know what they were called till now," Al said, "but that's exactly what we think happened. So what I suggest is that we all get some sleep; tomorrow the library is boarded-up and closed because they'll have every Boy Scout in the city out pogging—"

"Pogging?"

"I think the word comes from 'pogrom,'" he explained. "What you saw happen with the bus today. Little bastards run out of the bus and beat hell out of 'joogers.' Which is a contraction of Jew and nigger, but officially there are no Jews anymore in America, and the black population is supposedly all on 'reservations' down South, being turned back into slaves. So the word 'jooger' is just an insult our home-grown Nazis use for anything 'abnormal.' And practically all of us in Berkeley are abnormal."

It was nice to know something was the same between the two worlds.

"Anyway," Al went on, "I vote for lying low and then trying to make the rendezvous. We take Mark along, and if Sheila doesn't show, we see if we can sub him in for her."

"I don't know any atomic physics," I protested, "and the SHAKK is useless without a reload. I might as well stay here."

Al shook his head. "Here's the part you're not gonna believe, Mark. You said that in your timeline the atomic bomb came along in 1945, and they really only started working on it in earnest after America got into the war, right?"

"Right, pretty much so. There was some research before then, but it got into high gear after Pearl Harbor."

"Pearl Harbor was—"

"Japanese sneak attack that started the war in my timeline. We lost a lot of the navy there. They bombed the harbor without warning on a Sunday morning."

They all nodded solemnly; it was news to them, I guess.

"So," Al said, "it took, what, four years to build the atomic bomb?"

"Yep. And the Germans were only about two years behind us, I remember reading once—the Soviets were in the race, too, but they were mostly running off stuff they stole from the American project, so they don't exactly count."

All of them looked at each other and shrugged. "And you're sure you remember *nothing* about atomic bombs?"

"A little bit from high-school science and from my science requirement classes, maybe," I said. "I told you, I'm not a nuclear physicist."

Al sighed. "The reason we're so amazed about this, Mark, is that obviously if the Germans had atomic bombs, they'd have cleaned out the Free Zone a long time ago. And they don't. In fact, 'atomic bombs' are on the prohibited list as 'Jewish science'—they were around in science fiction before the war, I can remember some stories I read as a kid, but they certainly never turned up in 1942 or 1943, when we really needed them, and the Germans never got them either. So this set of directions—well, Sheila said that's what it was and we thought she was kidding, giving us a code word for it."

Now it was my turn to goggle and stare. "You mean—I don't believe it. As I recall it was expensive and difficult but it turned out to be pretty simple in the long run. Hell, in my timeline by 1975 *India* had made one."

Al shook his head. "That's both the thing that makes your story convincing and the thing that makes it baffling. There is no such thing in this timeline as an atomic bomb. You say your friend said the Closers won't tolerate them? That's as good an explanation as any, I suppose."

"It's because of the radiation," I said. "Atomic bombs produce stuff called fallout, which gets everywhere—in the air, the water, eventually the food. It's radioactive."

They all looked a bit more puzzled than before, except for one guy who hadn't spoken before. "I remember radioactivity. I used to teach high-school science before the war. It was a hot new area—for that matter all the science-fiction magazines were full of it. But after the war we got told it was all a monstrous piece of—"

"Jewish science," Al finished. "Yeah, it all kind of fits. They want a world run by Nazis, and they want it without atomic bombs. So they came here, and played around . . . " Al groaned and stretched. "We have to go to bed. Tomorrow we have to get set to go meet that sub, and that will be a pretty full day of getting ready and then a long time up late. And besides, I've heard enough impossible things tonight to digest. Time agents, good and bad. Atomic bombs. A certain writer becoming a household name—"

They all laughed at that for no reason I could tell; one of them was blushing.

"—and on top of that, somebody that I think I actually hate more than I hate Nazis. Bedtime, boys and girls . . . we've got a busy day tomorrow."

It was a busy day; they'd pretty much decided that since nothing looked good, they'd fold down the cell and disperse before it got worse. One of the guys had a big old truck that he used to go camping up in the mountains—he was secretly a Buddhist and liked to commune with things, he said—and that was going to be our vehicle for the trip. He managed to slip out about midday, get back to his vegetable stand (which he found smashed to bits with "Jooger!" written in paint all over it, and all the vegetables hurled out in the street), and discovered they at least hadn't broken into his garage. As dusk was falling, he drove his truck back to the rear entrance of the Berkeley Free Library.

Meanwhile Al and Sandy and I had been getting everything incriminating into a small number of crates; the crates, in turn, would travel along with us, along with some gasoline and dynamite for destroying them if that became necessary. Our real security, however, was going to have to be not getting caught. There was just too much to destroy, otherwise.

The others had slipped away quietly during the day, except for one guy whose day cover was begging in the streets, a shaggy-haired (almost an inch long—a hippie by local standards) burly guy named Greg. He went along with one of the big tall ones to help out.

Dusk found us ready to load, and we did in about ten minutes; the truck bounced and thudded alarmingly in the potholed streets, with the three of us sitting huddled by the equipment. Al had assured me the homemade dynamite was fresh, and therefore hadn't sweat any nitroglycerin and was reasonably safe. This was very reassuring because I was sitting on a box of it.

We got the rest of the cell in without incident, and without any noise other than that of the truck. Jaffy, the driver (it seemed to be a nickname, and I never did find out his real one), kept the headlights out and stuck to back streets, just creeping along. I suppose that would look suspicious to a cop . . . if he saw it. But nobody else would phone the police, because in this timeline, America had become the kind of place where something creeping past the house, in the middle of the night, lights out, and engine barely turning, was probably official business, and you didn't want to know.

We stayed tense and quiet till we were out of the city, then, after a long while, Al said, in a quite normal voice, "We can probably talk now—no chance of a patrol out this way. We'll just have to shut up when we start to get close to Half Moon Bay."

Everyone chatted for a bit; nobody's day had been too terribly frightening, because the first day of a big dragnet search was usually given over to Boy Scouts, Jaycees, Kiwanis, and so forth pogging the bohemian areas, in the hopes that it would flush something out from cover. The cops had done the usual roundup of the usual suspects, but most of the usual suspects were "baxters," as Al called them.

"I've heard baxters mentioned before," I said. "What are they?"

"Honestly, when I saw that .45 I thought you might be one. They're people who've slipped the trolley a little bit; they start to imagine that they're living before the war, or during the war. They have a tendency to make speeches in public and to run around waving rusty weapons for which they don't have any ammunition. They're kind of sad . . . but proud, too. Magnificent madmen who won't let time kill their country."

I liked the phrase, and complimented him on it. "Thank you," he said. "I try."

"Al," one of the men sitting in the darkness said, "do you suppose—well, look, this might be our last time when we're all together, right? I mean it doesn't look good. Sheila probably *did* get caught, and you know what they say, after two days, *anyone* will talk. So . . . uh, could we all hear it one more time? I know you buried copies of it in a couple of places, but I like it when you recite it, and I'm afraid I'll never hear it again."

The truck bounced along on the rutted highway; it was clear that Reconstruction hadn't involved building anything like the interstates, or even keeping up what was already there. Under the canvas cover, it was warm from all the bodies, but cold drafts blew in from little crevices. Al was quiet for a long time.

"You really, really flatter me. Do you realize that?"

"We all want to hear it, Al," someone else said, then Sandy chimed in, and finally I said, "Whatever it is, my curiosity is overpowering now. I want to hear it to."

Al, beside me, nodded, and said, "All right then, let me get the trusty canteen beside me, so I can drink while I do this . . . and I think there will be time before we get to Half Moon Bay, for both parts if you want them."

"We want them," Sandy said, firmly, and it seemed to be settled.

He took a long swig of water. I got a funny feeling in my stomach, like something was going to happen, and then he began to speak.

It was *beautiful*.

10

I *am not a poet,* or even a poetry lover. Lit classes never taught me to like it. And I don't remember it well, so though I was to hear it a few more times, one way and another, I couldn't recite it or quote it.

So you will just have to trust me that it was beautiful, and let me tell you what was in it, and a little bit (which I mostly learned later) about how Al came to write it.

But if you want to imagine my first experience of it, you have to imagine this: Al is speaking right next to you, and his voice loses that strange, slightly whiny quality and becomes deep and resonant. Four others of the bravest people you will ever know are sitting so close to you you can feel the warmth of their bodies. The truck slams and bounces every now and then, and Al has to back up and repeat a couple of lines, but he does it so gracefully and stays so much on the beat that you feel like the bumps and jars are part of the performance.

Every so often you are reminded, by the back of

your mind, that you are sitting on about seventy pounds of dynamite.

And as the truck winds its way down the peninsula roads, taking the least-traveled whenever it can, you get glimpses, through the open canvas back, of billions of bright August stars, and of silhouettes of pine trees and mountains.

The poem was in two parts. The first was called, simply, "The Fall." It began with the assassination of President Roosevelt—a crime still unsolved—in 1936, right after the election. It narrated the following events:

Nobody was quite certain that it was the Nazis who shot Franklin Roosevelt as he rode in an open motorcade in New York City in June 1937. There was no suspicion of it at the time. Indeed, no one was even sure where the shots had come from; the street was noisy and there were so many windows open on so many high buildings that it was unknowable.

They seemed to be ready for it, all the same; within a day they had hate literature out blaming it all on the Jews, and there were anti-Jewish riots here and there around the country.

(It took me a while to figure it out, but it appeared that one critical variable in the whole thing—something that made me suspect the Closers had been working with the Nazis in this timeline for a long time—was that their subversion and propaganda was a lot more effective. They clearly were much more effective at stirring up race and religious hatred in the USA during that time than they ever were in our history.)

The new President was John Nance Garner, a Texas isolationist who was noted for devotion to the oil companies. As an isolationist, he refused to even comment on the Munich deal that surrendered Czechoslovakia to the Nazis.

But when, in October 1938, the coup by General Saturnino Cedillo overthrew President Cardenas of Mexico, and the Mexican Fascist Gold Shirts came to power, Americans found out just which of President Garner's loyalties came first. Cedillo immediately pledged to break up the Mexican government's monopoly on oil production, Pemex, which had been seized from American and European private corporations, and then to return the pieces to foreign investors, Mexico went up in rebellion—and Garner sent the army to back Cedillo. American planes bombed unarmed civilian crowds in Guadalajara; Cedillo kept power backed by one large part of the Mexican Army and by Garner.

The United States went up in a storm of political controversy—it sounded to me like the Vietnam protests but twenty times bigger. Garner had already canceled most of the New Deal, and there had been anger over that, but American troops fighting and dying to keep an avowed fascist and close friend of Goebbels in power was more than could be borne.

The Democrats had become isolationist; the Republicans outflanked them by becoming ultraisolationist. In 1940, to everyone's surprise, the Republican candidate was Charles A. Lindbergh, prominent as a heroic pilot and public conservative—and member of many, many organizations with Nazi ties.

The situation was so bad that the only nonisolationist party by then was the Socialists, and they actually carried a couple of states. It didn't matter. On a platform of "peace with honor" and "bring the boys back from Mexico," Lindbergh won.

But the news from Europe was bad—worse than anyone could have imagined.

Al's voice recounted all this in a rolling, singing

cadence, and through his eyes we saw America become imperialist, saw the army squandered in Mexico—Garner could keep the forces there but he couldn't get additional money out of Congress, so ammunition, aircraft, weapons, and lives were lost and not replaced—saw the horror of Americans presented only with a choice of an imperialist or a fascist sympathizer . . .

And gave us the horror that poured in over the radio from Europe.

(Again, it was much later that I learned from ATN sources that the Closers had been working with the Nazis since 1932. What they had done was to copy plans and devices developed by Germany at the very *end* of World War II, and transfer them back to the German Armed Forces of 1932; the easiest technology to learn is one that is an extension of your own).

The Nazis began World War II with short-range jet fighters, a Focke-Wulf fighter plane called the FW-187 that beat the Spitfire by far in every possible category, big heavy bombers, snorkel submarines with underwater communication systems so that they could coordinate while submerged—and the V-1 "buzz bomb," modified into a television-guided homing weapon.

Al rattled it off in a litany; the Germans contemptuously ignored Poland in 1939 and struck west and north. France, Denmark, Norway, and Sweden had fallen before Christmas; every one of those nations had a long-ago-prepared pro-Nazi government ready to take power, like Vichy France and Quisling's Norway in our timeline, but far better prepared; within a year, France would be rearming—on the German side.

The British Army in France couldn't be evacuated due to the stormy winter weather. There was no "miracle at Dunkirk"—most of Britain's combat-ready units ended up in German POW camps.

Again, with contemptuous ease, Hitler gobbled up Poland in the first two weeks of January 1940, after cutting his infamous deal with Stalin.

As in our world, the summer of 1940 was the Battle of Britain, but this time with a difference: the RAF was hopelessly outgunned. The V-1s could be shot down by airplanes, barely, but they were operated by remote pilots looking through TV cameras in the nose, and they hit with deadly effect; the London dockyards burned most nights.

And when the RAF rose against the V-1s, they rose to face Me-262s and FW-187s; they were hopelessly outclassed, and they fell out of the sky.

By late June, the Chamberlain government that had done so much to make sure Britain entered the war unprepared had collapsed, but instead of Churchill, the British got Lord Halifax—a man interested in negotiating a surrender.

It didn't happen, and here Al's voice rose in triumph, and I found my heart beating faster as I heard of the "miracle" that saved Britain.

It was only betrayal at the top that had made America useless to her traditional British friends, and there were people who did not like that . . . among them, Howard Hughes, the Rockefellers, and Alfred P. Sloan of General Motors. In defiance of the federal government, they organized a giant financial consortium to arm Britain against the Nazis. In a crash program, Hughes had produced the first Allied jet fighters by the summer of 1940, and Sloan had them rolling off the assembly lines at twenty per day—on money borrowed with no security from the Rockefellers. Moreover, they had copied the German use of drop tanks and gone it one better—the new airplanes, the P-100 American Eagles, could fly, just barely, all the way to Britain from Labrador.

The offer was straightforward and simple: the British government could lease as many P-100s as the Consortium could build, for a dollar a year and a promise to buy them at cost plus 10 percent within five years of the end of the war. They would cost Britain nothing while the fighting was going on.

The Halifax government, bent on surrender, tried to refuse the offer—and the Miracle of Britain happened.

The Labour Party had never wanted to surrender. Neither had the Churchill wing of the Conservatives. When it was announced that Halifax was opening negotiations and wasn't taking the Consortium's offer, British unions rose up in a general strike to put an end to that, and after an uproar in Parliament, within days Churchill was prime minister—months later than he was in our timeline.

During all this, President Garner thumped his desk, declared our business was in this hemisphere, and extended no aid to Britain. And presidential candidate Lindbergh went him one better by saying we didn't have any business in the hemisphere, either.

Garner tried to block the transfer of the planes, but the P-100s taking off from Detroit were far more than a match for the antiquated P-40s he might have used to stop them. They were touching down in Labrador within hours, refueling, and strapping on drop tanks— and what the British called "Miracle Night" happened on August 30, 1940.

Four hundred P-100s—more of them than Britain had ever had of Spitfires—arrived early in the morning, flying secretly into fields in Scotland and the northwest. Their pilots slept in pup tents on the fields while the mechanics who had flown over just two days before readied them for action.

That night, the P-100s screamed in to meet the

German attackers. They overmatched the FW-187 by far, and sent them tumbling from the sky; they were about even with the Me-262, but the P-100s hadn't had to run as far and were flying over friendly territory. It was the first great battle of jet aircraft in history, and Britain won it. The surviving Luftwaffe raced back across the North Sea with its tail between its legs.

With P-100s covering, the old Hurricanes, Spitfires, and Typhoons swarmed into the sky to destroy the deadly V-1s. London slept well that night.

The British crews were exhausted, their planes pushing their safety margins, and yet they would never get a better chance; they landed and leaped from their planes to help the ground crews refuel, strap on fresh drop tanks, and rearm the planes. The bombers had been lost, mostly, in the futile and disastrous attempts to bomb the V-1 launching sites, but every bomber that could be pulled off submarine patrol was along on the mission, too, and every old plane that could fly and carry a bomb or a torpedo.

It was still night when they left; at dawn, they swept down on the invasion fleet being readied at Cherbourg.

They had caught the Germans napping, and in short order the landing craft, the stockpiles of ammunition and spare parts, the rank on rank of Tiger tanks parked and waiting for the landings Hitler had planned for September were in flames.

Britain was saved—for now. And with the P-100s, though she would continue to take a pounding, she could fight on. Moreover, there was an excellent chance that Russia would come in on the British side the next spring, for Stalin had finally realized that his deal with Hitler couldn't last.

———

Jaffy slowed down, turned up an old gravel driveway, and stopped the engine. "Patrol ahead," he called back to us. "They've got headlights on—I think it's just routine."

We sat with our hands on our guns and watched two German-built squad cars roll by, their machine guns hanging idle. We waited a long time there in the icy dark of the mountains, and a great field of stars danced above us. There was no sound at all when Jaffy restarted the motor.

"Keep going, Al," somebody said.

Spring held more surprises. President Lindbergh, too late and too little, offered aid to Britain, and not only brought the American Army home, but warned Cedillo to stay out of the European war.

But Congress was in a different mood, and many of them seemed to feel that if the Consortium was arming the British, Congress did not need to do anything for the USA. Lindbergh couldn't even get the weapons expended in Mexico replaced.

Hitler popped three surprises, one after another, in the summer of 1941. Under persuasion of his agents, and with the offer of German help, Franco joined the Axis, swept down the Tagus Valley into Portugal, and took Lisbon in a week; a week after that, Nazi guns were pounding Gibraltar, and the guided V-1 had closed off the western entrance to the Mediterranean.

Simultaneously, the Turkish government was overthrown by a Nazi-backed coup, and suddenly Greece and Yugoslavia were under a two-front attack. It was over quickly; in less than a month Hitler's control extended from the Atlantic to Iran, and in a short time after that the attack was under way to close Suez.

Unable to supply Egypt and Palestine by any means except around the Cape, Britain was forced to evacuate forces to India and Australia, and by July, Hitler had gathered up everything in the region, including the Persian Gulf.

The drive into Russia was nothing like what happened in our timeline. The attack was announced by Stalin's assassination; it was only six weeks till Moscow fell, and in the peace treaty the USSR gave up the Ukraine and the Baltics to Hitler. The German troops were not merely home, as they had been promised, by Christmas; they were home before the leaves turned.

President Lindbergh must have been sincere, and not a German agent, for he moved more and more to actively resist the Nazi onslaught. Al's poem called him that "poor, poor, well-meaning man, not a good mind, not even a good heart, but not bad, not evil, not yet captured, driven mad hysterical naked by the drum drum drum of evil." He proclaimed the Lindbergh Doctrine: The United States would fight to prevent any of the Atlantic islands, from which our shipping and Britain's lifeline might be threatened, from falling into German hands.

On November 8, 1941, German parachute and glider troops landed in force on the Azores, in a complete and total violation of the Lindbergh Doctrine. They were under command of Air Marshal Manfred von Richthofen; I was a little startled, since in my own timeline the "Red Baron" had been shot down and killed in WWI. Clearly the Closers had been working pretty hard for a long time in this timeline.

The Battle of the Azores is about half of Al's poem; he goes ship by ship, blow by blow. The story is grim from one end to the other; Admiral King's Atlantic Fleet was far from ready, but they linked up with the troop ships and set out anyway. It was clear the force was too small—King had only three operational carriers, all carrying planes that were worse than obsolete—and so Admiral Kimmel and the Pacific Fleet were supposed to run around to link up with him, through Panama.

But as the fleets were readying, a shipload full of fertilizer blew up in the Canal, and it was out of action. German or Japanese actions were suspected, but it hardly mattered now—Lindbergh had already declared war. And in any case, the Pacific Carrier Battle Group would have had to round the Horn—the ships were too big for the locks.

The battle plan was foolish but politically necessary. Both King and Kimmel protested, but without effect—King was to sit out in the Atlantic, at the outer edge of where the P-100s could guard his fleet, and wait for Kimmel; Kimmel was going to have to race ten thousand miles as fast as his fleet could go.

But another player was about to enter the war. Argentina had secret agreements with Hitler. Just off the Falkland Islands—part of Juan Perón's reward for stabbing *los norteamericanos* in the back was to get those islands—German JU-88s, effectively outdated but more than able to carry the new air-launched guided V-1, jumped Kimmel's fleet. In less than ten minutes on that dark night, the carriers *Enterprise* and *Hornet* were ablaze, and before the remainder of the fleet escaped north they had to run a gauntlet of more than two thousand miles of air attacks, covered only by planes from the *Lexington*.

Brazil, already technically at war with the Axis because of the invasion of her mother country, Portugal, struck south into Argentina; it was a measure of how desperate the Allies were that the addition of Brazil seemed like a big gain. It was immediately counterbalanced by the entry of Vichy France on the German side.

As Kimmel desperately raced north to join King, word reached Washington of the terrible losses at the Falklands, and it became clear that Japan was about to attack Hawaii. President Lindbergh recalled the Pacific Fleet to San Diego and ordered King to press the attack without waiting for Kimmel.

There is no doubt the Germans were reading American codes. As the Atlantic Fleet pressed into striking range, now out of reach of all but the briefest support from jets out of Britain, JU-88s and heavy bombers closed in, and, in a hail of V-1 cruise missiles, the carriers went up like tinder. Some of them launched planes; some of the planes got through, and a few of the German allied ships, from the Italian and French navies, took some damage. But it was the end of American naval power in the Atlantic. Kimmel and the survivors of the fleet that had run the gauntlet of the Falklands turned back and put in at Rio, losing three destroyers and a cruiser to the new high-speed efficient U-boats on the way. Al's poem ended with Kimmel's fleet limping into Rio, and with the ominous note that worse things were brewing far to the north.

The truck pulled over to the side and all but skidded to a stop; Jaffy was out and running around in a second, and we all jumped out to join him before we quite knew what was up.

"Something moving without lights on the road up ahead," he breathed to us. "No place near here to pull the truck over out of sight, so we're going to have to tough it out."

It was very quiet, but in those mountains sometimes you can see things a long way off. We sat and waited, and finally the low thunder of engines came to us. "Heavy haulers," Al breathed, "and a lot of them. I'd say we're going to see a parade . . . "

A few minutes later they came into sight. They were moving a lot faster than I would have dared, right down the centerline, big heavy tractor-trailer rigs each carrying a tank or an APC. I counted twenty-eight of them.

We waited a long time, and then Al said, "I don't think there's going to be a lot of the city to go back to. Somebody is really after Mark, or us, or something."

"Roll on?" Jaffy asked.

"Roll on," Al said. "Nowhere behind us to go, and I'm not optimistic about in front of us. But I know there's nowhere behind us to go."

Al's second poem was called "The Gathering of Nations," and it was the story of how the Free Zone got put together. I never got much of a chance to look into the history between when "The Fall" ended and "The Gathering of Nations" began, so there were gaps in it. Briefly, it told how Patton, Bradley, and Montgomery dueled with Rommel in the Shenandoah Valley, after the "great ships of ice in the Chesapeake."

That much, I found out, referred to the secret German weapon no one had any idea of. They had had the fiords of Norway, secure against prying eyes, for long enough to build two dozen immense artificial rafts of ice, big as small islands, onto which they moved whole air and submarine bases and divisions. When the ice islands grounded in the Chesapeake early the next spring, they carried most of the Wehrmacht.

There was another reference to Patton and the American Expeditionary Force coming home to Boston on the Royal Navy—and to the RAF coming with them—but exactly what happened, I never learned.

At any rate, "The Gathering of Nations" began with Patton's Army driven west out of Gettysburg, toward Pittsburgh, and Montgomery retreating northeast toward New York. What was in the poem after that might fill many volumes—Bradley's defense of the bridges at Wheeling, which allowed Patton's forces to escape in their epic retreat, which was eventually to take them to San Diego, to their rendezvous with Nimitz, and to the escape across the Pacific to Auckland. That was exciting enough—but the Royal Navy had gone them several better, picking up Montgomery's army from Long Island and the New Jersey shore, running past the German strongholds in Delaware and Maryland. (Al's poem has a passage that brings tears to my eyes when I think about it, describing the grim decision of fifty P-100 pilots to hold the air above the Royal Navy long enough for them to get through, grabbing Marines and some of the American Navy from Guantanamo Bay, skirting down the South American coast with dozens of tankers of Texas fuel oil that had managed to sneak unescorted out of Galveston . . .)

The rendezvous with Kimmel and the attack, with the Brazilians, that led to the revenge sacking and burning of Buenos Aires—and the long voyage to Perth, Australia, straight across the Atlantic and Indian Oceans . . . all that was in there. There were moments of comedy in it as well; the meeting of Patton and Montgomery, again, in Sydney, seemed to make everyone chuckle. ("Of course you got here sooner, Monty, you rode the whole way!")

A few more verses sketched in references to other groups and outfits that had found their way there. Soviet divisions that fled over the Khyber Pass and slugged their way across Japanese-occupied India rather than be disbanded as ordered. General Chennault's Flying Tigers. MacArthur and much of the Philippines garrison. Anyone who could find a ship and get clear of the Axis navies seemed to find a way there, often against terrible odds.

I'm no judge of poetry, but from the way people responded to it, I'd say that the English-speaking nations had gained their equivalent of the *Odyssey* or the *Aeneid*.

The ending, with the litany of all the forces that were now in the Free Zone—everything from the First Marines to the French Foreign Legion to the Reconstituted Abraham Lincoln Brigade and the Irgun—left me feeling better than I had in days. I was in with good people. If courage and goodwill could bring you victory, it ought to work for these people if it worked for anyone.

There was a long silence afterward; by now we were winding down from the crest of the mountains that run like a stegosaurus spine up the peninsula. The truck thudded and shuddered regularly, and once the box of dynamite actually rose a bit under me; people were sometimes thrown together in heaps. Jaffy was being careful, but the road wasn't much more than a track anymore, and there was no light at all among the trees and in the deeper ravines; he had a couple of tiny carbide lights with red glass in front of them burning on the hood, but whenever he got to a place where he could drive by moonlight, he would stop, run around, and blow them out.

At last the winding mountain road gave way to

something a little smoother and easier to handle, and then to something that was merely a badly maintained country road. We were coming up on Half Moon Bay.

Jaffy knew a couple of ways to sneak around the town itself; Al, next to me, whispered that the town had sort of a vogue among the younger elite of the West Coast German expat community, because they had all gone crazy with surfing, and this place was sufficiently isolated so that they could slip off and do some not-quite-proper sex on the side. People who worked in the guest houses in the little, turn-of-the-century port town had become invaluable to the underground, because they could pick up so much blackmail material for the scandal files.

Half Moon Bay was also a great place to bring a sub in close to shore; they could paddle out in rubber rafts without much problem, because though the surf was reliable, it wasn't the sort of spectacular stuff that is also dangerous.

Jaffy was driving us around on back roads and sometimes through private farm roads where the underground had some arrangement; the idea was to get to the beach on the north side of town without being seen. As a result we did some backtracking and often went very slowly. It was too dangerous to talk now, so most of us just got caught up on our napping.

Finally he killed the motor. I could just smell a little bit of sea breeze. He came around and squatted in the back of the truck with us.

"We're still a long way off," Al said. "Did you see trouble?"

"Lots of it. Two groves of trees with men moving in them. Couple of guys keeping an eye on the road; one of them had a pair of binoculars. Stuff like that. I think they have the beach completely staked out."

"Shit," Al said. "Suggestions, anyone?"

What we had in the truck was more than enough to hang all of us if we were caught with it. In the aggregate it was far too heavy to move by foot. Thus we couldn't abandon the truck . . . but any hope of getting down to the beach depended on being silent.

"Well," I said, "I imagine most of you have the skills for a bare-hands night attack—"

They all nodded. "Everyone here has done a German or two, and more American quislings than you can count," Al said.

"Then why don't we each pick a direction, scout it, come back at a prearranged time, and see if we can figure out what's up? We've got hours till our friends come by."

Greg grunted. "Good as any other idea, and it won't be boring. Let's."

My target was one of the ridges where we'd seen some bored idiot lighting a cigarette; I worked my way forward carefully. This was a lot like playing Army as a kid; stay low, show no shadow, move as fast as you can without making noise. It helped that what I was going across was a huge field of pumpkins—there's a risk of tripping over a pumpkin or a vine, of course, but on the other hand it's all so damp that there's nothing to rustle, and it's so blotchy in dim light that there aren't very many shapes that show up well against it.

There were trees as I came out of the pumpkin patch. I was able to move just a little more quickly and ascend just a little faster.

There were two of them, both wearing the Good Neighbor Patrol uniform. It occurred to me that the Good Neighbors, and the local idiotic version of the Boy Scouts, probably appealed to a certain kind of personality that loved to wear uniforms and do violence but wasn't much into running any real risks to their hides.

I crawled up closer and discovered what I had was that perfect conversational pair, the Whiner and the Sympathizer. Whiner thought it was cold and damp out and he was going to get something and he had to have the cigarette to steady his nerves but if the fucking captain saw that he'd be in deep shit. Sympathizer agreed with all that and said it was really a shame that Whiner wasn't an officer himself. Whiner said, well, it was all political, what do you expect, and Sympathizer agreed.

I figured as soon as they were apart, Sympathizer was going to turn Whiner in.

Unfortunately, after I counted the thousand heartbeats I had estimated, all I knew was that they were generally watching toward the sea, when they weren't looking at each other, and that their organizational politics were like any other organizational politics; Whiner felt shafted, Sympathizer agreed, and I wondered why Whiner's shoulder blades were not itching right between them, where I figured Sympathizer's knife would go.

It was also pretty clear that these were not the last of the red-hot guards.

I came back down the hill quietly and slipped across the pumpkin patch, feeling pretty discouraged. I hadn't learned a thing, it seemed to me.

That was what everyone had found; a few younger members had been very spit-and-polish but no more effective, and mostly it looked like a bunch of disgruntled small-town back-slapping goodfellas, stuck out in the cold woods.

"They're more than enough to sound an alarm, though," Al said. "We probably ought to do something about them, so we can get the truck through. And I don't like the fact that they seem to be facing the landing point. That sort of suggests we've got big trouble."

Sandy spoke up. "I think I have an idea. Help me out with it. If you were using those guys as a guard, all you'd be doing is using them as a tripwire, right? I mean, if they run into something, they aren't going to stop it effectively, and they aren't going to do anything but run in circles and scream, right? So they're expecting to chase something that landed on the coast, and they want to make sure they don't lose it."

"Got you," Al said. "They aren't looking for anything from this side, for some reason. Well, hell, why don't we just drive the truck right into town and park by the fisherman's market? That will put us less than a mile from the rendezvous point, and at least we won't look as conspicuous as we do sneaking around in the pumpkin fields. And it will leave us a lot of time to send in a deep reconnoiter."

Driving into town was downright dull; there was a row of trucks sitting by the fisherman's market, and we just joined it. Sandy, Al, and I crept out; something made me take the SHAKK along, and Al brought the precious notebook. "We'll be back for all of you for sure," he said, "but this is because—"

"It's because luck can run out," Jaffy whispered back at him. "That's okay, man, we can understand that. Life is not always fair. Go in peace, and I hope it works out, but if it doesn't—woe to the wicked, you madman."

Al grabbed him and kissed him passionately on the lips, which startled me a little, especially since I'd figured Al and Sandy were probably an item, but like they say, some of your best friends and not always the guys you'd expect . . .

We moved up the edge of the beach—the grass came

down there in irregular tufts and clumps so that there was lots of cover in shadows and hollows. It went faster than we might have thought.

Sandy touched my arm and pointed, and a moment later Al gave a little hiss beside me. There was a man patrolling the beach with a machine gun; he didn't look any more alert or better trained than the Good Neighbors, but he sure as hell was better armed.

I felt in my pockets and found one of the pieces of rope I'd cut for the purpose, tying a little bowline loop on each end. I'd never actually garrotted anyone before, but what the heck, I was new to the timeline. Maybe I'd get to like it.

I crawled forward, the cold sand pressing moisture up through my clothes so that between the sweat and the damp I was drenched when I finally reached the shoreward end of his patrolling. I crouched in a deep shadow and waited.

He came back into the shadows for just a moment, and I sprang. The gun hit the ground as I did, but in the deep sand it wasn't noisy, and praise god it didn't go off. I had the line around his neck, braced my knee in his back, and yanked it tight enough to shut off his air before he knew what was going on. I kept the tension up as I used my shoulder to drive him into the sand on his face.

I put one loop over the other, slid it down as my opponent struggled facedown in the sand under me, and then pulled the free end tight with all the force I had. It must have finally pinched a carotid, because after a flurry of scuffling around in the sand that seemed to go on forever, he finally lay still. I yanked hard to ratchet it that little extra bit tighter, and tied it off. If he was playing possum, he'd be pretty uncomfortable and have to move soon, and if not, he'd die soon. I'd made out the American Swastika insignia on his arm and was enjoying the thought of him dying slowly.

As I rose and motioned them forward, I found Sandy was right at my ear. She whispered, "Al saw another one and went on ahead. Let's move up to him."

When we got there, he'd done a neat little bit of knife work, but then I think he probably had had more practice than I had. Slashing the carotid like that drops blood pressure in the brain so fast that the victims are dead before they hit the ground—and Al had been quick enough about it to get practically nothing on his clothes.

We crept on forward; there was a dark, vertical shadow on the sand ahead. We had to get close before we could see what it was.

"Oh, *fuck*," Al whispered under his breath, about the time I saw, too.

It was a woman, nude, smeared with dark streaks that could only be blood, tied upright to a post, facing the sea. It wouldn't have fooled anyone under any circumstances—you could see she was either dead or unconscious, and the post stuck way up above her head. It was there to freak out whoever came ashore.

"Bush league," Sandy murmured.

Al glanced sharply at her. "Explain?"

"Everyone we've hit even up close is a Good Neighbor. This isn't a professional operation. They got lucky, caught her, beat her until she told them where her pickup was. Now they're doing this kind of petty bullshit. That's all. If we can get 'em off the beach somehow, we'll be right in the clear."

"Is it—" I whispered.

"Oh, yeah, it's Sheila. Jesus, those fuckers. Can we kill some more?" Sandy asked.

"Just about for sure," Al reassured her. "One good diversion would do it . . . if we just had somebody to kill one of them at a distance, we'd be in damn fine shape. They'll all either run toward the noise or start firing in the dark."

"I could go get one," Sandy suggested, "just to get things rolling."

Al shook his head. "We have to get to Sheila, see if she's still alive. And if she is, we need time there. We'll need a better diversion than that."

All of this was in whispers soft as breathing. I was gaining a little confidence—the patrols had not been set up in any way that would let them cover each other, so I thought Sandy was probably dead right. This was some overambitious local Good Neighbor captain—probably the same one Whiner and Sympathizer had been talking about—who had launched this operation on his own. "I just had an idea," I breathed. "I'm going to try something—just take advantage of it if it works."

They nodded, once—I guess they trusted me, which was pretty flattering in the circumstances.

I crept up the sandy beach to the brush line. The question I had asked myself was, if I had no brains or judgment, what would I think was the best place for my command post? I wasn't sure what I would do when I found my hyperambitious captain, but I did know that if I wanted to make a lot of valuable chaos happen, doing something to him was probably the most efficient way to accomplish it.

There was one likely spot, and as I climbed up the grassy side of the dune, I was gratified to find tire tracks. He'd even driven up here. Too perfect.

He was there on the hood of his car—having a car at all, of course, meant he'd spent some years of assiduous sucking up to the authorities. Probably thought of it as being realistic and honestly pursuing his self-interest . . .

He was sitting there cross-legged with his radio operator on the ground beside him, and as I listened I realized he was having a great time talking military-talk with the boys out in the field. He didn't know yet that two of his pickets were dead, because he'd put them out so badly; he had a lot of men scattered all over the place grumbling and hating him, and probably a division of marines could have landed without his men picking it up. He was smoking, himself, so that as I got closer I saw the tiny dot of red going back and forth.

The problem was there were two of them. If I could get them both, for sure, silently, I could have all kinds of fun . . .

I crawled in closer, and now I could hear the two of them talking. The radioman, I realized, was young enough to be impressed with his captain.

By now I was practically up behind the car from them, and could take a better look. The car was parked on an upslope, but I didn't think releasing the emergency brake would make it roll back—it was in soft sand.

I figured any burst of noise would bring people running in here, and it could well start them shooting each other, but that would mean regular cops out on the beach and make the contact that much harder.

There was a walkie-talkie, sort of—the thing was huge, backpack-sized—just leaning up against the car. In fact there were two of them . . .

An idea hit me, and the more I thought about it, the better I liked it. Very quietly I lifted the radio and crept on back. The captain was just explaining—way too loudly, "Well, you know, Jimmy, you do get a lot of time when all you can do is wait. That's part of being in the organization; it's the mark of real discipline . . . "

Probably the captain became a Good Neighbor because the Boy Scouts thought he'd make a lousy Scoutmaster.

It took very little time to get back to Al and Sandy. They saw what I had, and I wished it was bright enough for them to see me wink. "What kind of fun can we have with this?"

Al beamed; I could see the glow of his teeth in the dark. "Allow me . . . you said the kid's name was Jimmy?"

"Yep."

"Then it's Captain Alex Laban. A stuffed shirt and a first-order moron. Let's get some radio traffic . . . "

Holding the earphone so that all three of our heads could surround it, we heard three things; Jimmy requesting people to report what was happening at their stations, people reporting nothing, and Laban chewing them out for reporting nothing in incorrect form. "That's Command Post Command Post Nothing to report sir Over," he was telling one.

Al grinned, flipped the mike to talk, and said, "Jimmy, you tell us as soon as he tries to pat your butt."

There was an amazing spell of radio silence. Then Laban said, "Who was that! Acknowledge! Who was that?" It was really loud.

Al flipped the knob around, and his grin got more deep and wicked. "Emergency, Channel 100 Emergency," he said, crisply but softly into the mike. His voice was high and squeaky.

A voice responded at once. "Situation?"

"Good Neighbor captain exceeding authority. Beach north of Half Moon Bay. I have been ordered to do things contrary to my moral beliefs. My name is Jimmy, and he's just left me alone, but he's been bothering me all night—he said it was for field maneuvers, and I had to work the radio for him, but now he's got me out here all alone and he's—he's—I can't say. It's too icky." Then he rammed the mike against his neck and made a gargling noise, and rubbed it facedown in the sand.

The voice on the other end started frantically trying to hail "Jimmy." Al flipped the channel again and asked Jimmy a question that would have been pretty blunt in a leather bar. Jimmy didn't answer. Then Al asked him if he couldn't talk because of what he was doing for Captain Laban, and whether he really liked it. Jimmy's voice now came through high and squeaky: "Captain Laban is going around to the posts right now to find out who's doing it, and if you don't stop it, I'm going to have him *kill* you."

"Has he ever—" what Al suggested seemed a bit implausible, but now Jimmy was really raving, screaming almost. I could hear him perfectly well without the radio.

The regular cops had flipped over from the Emergency Channel and seemed to be convinced Jimmy was getting raped right there and then on the beach; they started trying to talk to him. Al did a deep voice and said, "Jimmy, this is the police. We just want you to know you are not to do any of that stuff with the captain. You are reserved for us, and you will do it with us."

That got Jimmy yelling that Al wasn't the police and he wasn't doing anything and Captain Laban was going to beat his ass in.

Al sat back, smiling happily. "Except on Channel 100, these things are all very low power, so they won't interfere with each other," he whispered. "Only base stations like Jimmy's have much oomph. So all they can hear is him raving. And I would bet any minute—"

Sure enough, the captain might not have been any kind of military genius, but he'd figured out that the cops would be out to investigate real soon. Considering he had kept a possibly important witness all to himself and that there were some pretty wild accusations flying around, he behaved like you'd expect anyone of his type to do—he ordered people to go home and jumped into his car. We heard him drive away.

"He didn't even check to see whether his whole command heard it," I said.

Sandy shook her head. "The regular cops were all trained by the Nazis during Reconstruction. He knows that anyone with any sense will be taking off to hide right now. Good Neighbors are always doing this kind of thing—a lot of them are people who weren't smart enough or brutal enough to make the regular cops. We can probably sneak up to Sheila now and see if she's alive—but I'm afraid she isn't."

She wasn't. She was as cold as the night air, and her poor body was bruised, battered, and cut all over. I figured they had probably not so much systematically tortured her as they had just improvised, the way a group of sadistic children will sometimes keep coming up with things to do to a dog or a cat until it mercifully expires.

She was tied to the post too tightly to unknot, but we cut her loose and at least laid her on the ground. There was no sign of her SHAKK or of anything else except her—along with her clothes they had taken everything.

Al swore and pointed at her mouth. "Look what they did to her."

A lot of the blood on her had come out of there. I didn't see what it was, and then Sandy said, "Oh, shit, shit, don't let Greg see this, I think he had a crush on her."

"What?" I asked.

"There's this weird belief they have that some agents on our side have radios concealed in hollow teeth. They pulled out all her teeth, either looking for it or to destroy it."

I felt pretty sick, but I said, "Uh, but—you *could* have a radio in a hollow tooth—"

Al made a face. "Please. I know your people are more advanced than mine, but even I know you can't make a vacuum tube that small work."

It was my turn to be baffled and irritated. "Ever hear of transistors? I'm not defending them, but if they've gotten hold of a Special Agent before—"

"What do you know about transistors?" a voice said, very softly, behind us. "Keep your hands away from your weapons," it added.

11

"*May I turn around?*" I asked, my hands kept high above
my head.

"You may," the voice said, and I did—very slowly.

You know how sometimes a face of a public figure
stays with you forever? You see him a few times,
maybe you hear him speak, and—presto, with you forever.

I'd heard this guy twice, both times because I was
deliberately crossing a picket line to hear him. He was
the great *bête noir* of a rather large faction at Yale when
I was there, and even though he generally irritated hell
out of me, and more so out of Marie, he was always
much too interesting to ignore.

That is, as much of him as you could get to hear
before the whooping and shouting got too loud.

He was a broad-shouldered man with bushy black
eyebrows and a sharp nose and chin, bigger than he
looked at first, and he stood a little awkwardly, like
he might limp or stumble a bit when he walked. At the

moment he had a very convincing Thompson submachine gun pointed at me.

His Hungarian accent was not as thick as it had been
when I'd heard him speak at Yale, he was twenty years
younger, and even in the dim light reflecting off the
sea I could tell he was heavily tanned.

"Dr. Teller," I said. "Are transistors unknown in this
timeline?"

"You realize," he said very casually, "that your
knowledge of transistors, plus your knowledge of timelines, means that either you are what I have been pray-
ing for, without knowing exactly what it was, for
years—or else that I should shoot you and your com-
panions right now."

"He's legit," Al said, and rattled off half a dozen
passwords.

Teller nodded. "Then we had best get moving. Was
this poor woman—"

"The contact you were supposed to have," I said.
"I'm sort of the best that was available as a substitute."

"Let us pray you're good enough," he said. "Are we
ready to go, then?"

"We can be," Al said, "as soon as we pick up our
three friends from back in town. They've nowhere else
to go and, there's a fair amount of incriminating stuff
with them."

By that time a dozen soot-faced men in black turtle-
necks, watch caps, and dungarees—the very image of
the World War II commandos in the movies of my
childhood—had emerged from the shadows.

Teller spoke briefly into a handheld gadget that
looked like a cellular phone, and we hurried up the
beach, back toward Half Moon Bay. But we had gone
no more than three hundred yards when we heard the
rattle of gunfire. We picked up the pace, but long

before we got near the town there was a huge explosion. Flames shot far up into the air.

"Can we wait ten minutes?" Al asked, shuddering, as he stared at the flames. "God damn the god damn luck, Mark, Sandy, we could have taken them along with us."

Teller shook his head, and I could tell he didn't like it any better than we did. "This beach will be swarming with cops of all kinds in minutes. We've got to get off it. There's a good chance your friends died in that explosion, and if not, they will have to shift for themselves. At least they have been provided with a diversion."

Al nodded slowly and started to mutter something under his breath; we dog-trotted up the beach to where the rubber rafts lay concealed, guarded by four more tough-looking commandos.

There wasn't any surf worth talking about, but a beach that is able to have surf tends to amp up any wave that hits it, and the paddling out to sea was about as difficult, physically, as anything I'd done. They handed us all paddles, and we put everything we had into it.

There was no more gunfire behind us. Either the other three members of the cell were dead, as we hoped, or they were captured.

Al was still muttering next to me; I glanced at him, feeling sorry for him, and he must have thought I was curious. "Kaddish," he explained. "Haven't said it in years, not since I found out my mother died in a camp near Toledo."

Though there were no shots, there was plenty of noise from the shore—sirens, motors, people yelling. We could see many headlights on the road over the mountains behind us, as we topped each wave, and a little later there were headlights on the coast road as well.

Let all of ours be dead . . . please let them be lucky enough to be dead . . .

I was about to ask just how far out we were going to have to paddle—my arms were getting sore from the unaccustomed labor—when we came into the calmer water away from the beach, and I caught a glimpse of something long and thin sticking up from that water. By now there were all sorts of electric lights glowing on the shoreline.

Very swiftly, and making what seemed like a terrible lot of noise, the submarine broke the surface in front of us. I'd built some model ships as a kid, and I knew what a Salmon class sub looked like. In my time that thing would have been a museum piece, but here it was.

Lines were thrown out and tied off, and they brought us in fast. I'm no sailor, but it seemed to me that I'd seldom seen men who knew their business so well. In less time than it takes to tell, our rubber boats were up against the steel sides of the sub, and we were scrambling onto the slippery deck and down through the hatches into the close, smelly space underneath. They towed us into a cramped corner, sort of out of the way, and then the commandos were piling in as quickly as they could. The last man down the ladder was in a faded navy shirt and a pair of black pajama trousers, with bare feet, and as the hatch slammed shut he hissed, "Think I heard a plane engine, Cap'n."

"Take her down!"

"Aye aye, sir!"

The diving horn sounded, and I felt the steel deck shifting under my feet as the submarine plunged back beneath the waves.

I looked around. The commandos were sitting in a long double row, feet pressed together in the middle of the corridor, filling it completely. I heard the whine of the electric motors as the sub ran for the open sea.

When the commandos took off their knit watch caps, a second look told me something interesting about them—many were bald, or gray, or both. All had crow's-feet around their eyes, and though I could see hard muscle under the sweaters, most had at least a little bit of a paunch.

Every one of them must be in his forties.

The captain himself looked more like what you'd expect an admiral to look like where I'd come from. I suppose when a navy doesn't get any new ships or enlistees, this is what it gets to look like . . . on the other hand, they were probably the most experienced crew in history.

The silence was interminable, but I had no idea what kind of detection devices we might be hiding from, and I was not going to take any chances in my ignorance. The air got more and more stuffy, not from the failure of the recirc system—we had not been underwater for more than an hour—but from the tang of sweat and fear.

I looked across the corridor at Sandy; she was staring down at the deck, and tears were running down her face. She'd lost three of her best friends—hell, maybe one of them was her lover.

I'd been there; I knew what that felt like. My heart broke for her, and I reached out and quietly took her hand. She squeezed my hand till it felt like she'd break it, but I didn't take it back.

There was a change in the sound of the motors, and then we drifted silently. Overhead, there was a low thrum, which then became a throbbing sound.

Everyone seemed to hold their breath. Something thundered overhead like a freight train.

We sat perfectly still in the hot air, sweat running down our faces. The commandos, sitting next to me, who probably would have regarded a firefight at close quarters as all in a day's work, looked sick and drawn.

I didn't blame them. There was part of me thinking, *I don't know what a depth charge coming in sounds like, but I bet I'll know it when I hear it.*

And with that came images of the walls suddenly bursting in, icy water and high pressure, torn and bloody bodies and hands scrabbling against the pitiless steel surfaces bearing them down to the black depths—

We waited longer. The captain whispered a command, and the motors resumed for a little while, slowly pushing us forward. The commando next to me breathed in my ear, "Cap'n says we're under a cold-water layer and the tide can take us out, pass it on." I repeated it to Al, next to me. He nodded. It sounded like things were better than they had seemed to be.

The motors stopped again, and we drifted again. Twice more we heard ship's engines overhead, but never as close as the first one.

After another hour the captain started us forward again and said, "All right, let's not make too much noise, but we can talk a bit. We'll make the rest of this run submerged."

He turned to us. "I know we were a bit short on ceremony there. I was afraid the plane got a radar fix, and perhaps it did, but for whatever reason they didn't get on us fast enough. I'm Captain William Stark. Welcome to the USS *Skipjack*. I know the accommodations are not terribly comfortable, but you'll only have to bear with them for a day or so."

"A *day* or so? How fast does this thing go?" Al asked. "Or are you dropping us off someplace?"

Stark grinned at us, and we noticed how many other people were chuckling. "Well, you'll just have to see. But the short answer is, things are going to be much more comfortable than this, and the long answer is, if I told you how, you wouldn't believe it."

And that was all he said. Teller seemed very excited to get a look at the notebook Al had so carefully brought along, and as soon as he had it he was dead to the world; the commandos weren't supposed to know too much about us for security reasons. I tinkered with the SHAKK a little, but I still could not come up with any way to reload a gadget that obviously had to have a special substance that I didn't even know the chemical ingredients to.

Sandy sat in the corner, quietly weeping, and Al said he thought it wasn't so much for any one of the men who had died back on the beach at Half Moon Bay. It was more that she had lived so close to them for so long, and that some of them had been heroes to her. "Used to be a lot of those on college campuses, you know, boykids and girlkids who wanted to worship artists. God knows I was one. I kind of suspect my mother was, too."

"You—um, if you don't want to tell me, it's okay," I said, "but I'm really curious. You were saying Kaddish? I thought that after Reconstruction—"

"Oh, some of us survived one way or another. In my case I knew there were a couple of nutcase profs around Berkeley with theories about how to 'cure' people of homosexuality, and after the surrender they had been pretty fast to join the Nazi Party, even before the

Wehrmacht administrative troops got there. And I knew their 'therapy' was basically tormenting people until they said they liked women. Well, women are okay with me—I'm sort of bi, anyway—and so I knew I could fake that part of it. And I turned out to be right— once they'd locked me up for being a queer, it didn't occur to them to come back and lock me up again for being a Jew. But there were parts of the country where they gassed everybody in both categories. I just happened to have this local dodge."

He stared off into space. "I wish I'd had a little more privacy, a little more time, gotten to see more of my mother before she died," he said, "partly because I just wish I had, like anyone would, and partly because I could have written a great poem about her, I think. One of the damned miserable things about all this is that instead of ordinary deaths, you have people who become martyrs, and their martyrdom matters more than who they are.

"I think I might have been very happy if I could have just been a poet."

I nodded, and then, feeling more tired than ever, I fell asleep. As I was drifting off I noticed Sandy had shifted around to use my shoulder as a pillow, and had the stray thought that I liked her, for her courage and common sense and all the rest of it. I'd have to keep an eye on her for a while; people who are in deep grief often do a very poor job of taking care of themselves.

When I woke up, Sandy was still sleeping on my shoulder, but something was subtly different. It took me a moment to realize the floor was sloping at a funny angle, and then that the motors were making an odd noise and I could hear the hiss of compressed air going into the ballast tanks. We were on our way up to the surface.

I sat up a little more, waking Sandy. "Where are we?" she asked.

"Surfacing, I think," I said.

There were a lot of sailors swiftly, silently, running back and forth, and all of us sitting in that corridor had to pull our feet all the way in so that they could get past us. The captain appeared to be talking to someone on a sort of telephone, and it didn't seem to be anyone on board.

"Maybe we're meeting a ship?" Al suggested, next to me.

"Could be, I guess," I said, "but I can't believe they can get a surface ship this close to North America. Maybe it's a plane? That's pretty dangerous, too."

World War II subs were not terribly fast underwater, and they had limited amounts of time they could spend submerged; even if there had been an improvement or two, I didn't think we could be much more than 150 miles off the California coast.

"Well," Captain Stark said, "I see we've awakened you at last. You've all been asleep for most of the last fifteen hours; it's finally dark enough topside to do the transfer."

"The transfer to what?"

"To what's going to take you people, and the commando team, and Dr. Teller, to the Free Zone. I think you'll be pleased. Unfortunately our abilities to modify some things are limited; we've never worked out a good way to do the transfers underwater."

We all nodded, just as if he'd given us real information, and he said, "Do get your bags and things in hand, because we have to get you out on the deck and then get you over the side very quickly."

After a few more minutes, the sub was at periscope depth and cruising along slowly; they ran up a snorkel and the diesels started, which made us go faster but was no advantage—it also brought a strong smell of diesel fumes into the hull. Then, a long half hour later, the captain gave the commands; the sub rose to the surface.

"All of you, topside, now," he said.

The commandos got up as one man—you could tell they had done this before—and raced up the ladder, one after another. Dr. Teller went next, more slowly and deliberately, and then Al and Sandy, with me bringing up the rear.

The sun had set no more than two hours ago, and the night on the Pacific was warm and pleasant. There was a little fog blowing around, and, all things considered, I liked that; what I lost in starlight I was more than repaid in concealment.

There was a strange feeling, a shudder through the hull of the *Skipjack,* and it took a moment to realize that it was coming from the sea itself, that some vast force was moving beneath the water near us. The low, heavy vibration became stronger, and began to include a high-pitched component as well. Then the waves directly out in front of us took on a strange color.

Where it had had smokestacks, of course, it now had watchtowers and radars; those broke the water first, in a churning white disorder as they came out of the water, not yet connected to each other. Hundreds of gallons of warm greenish water sluiced from the sides of the rising towers and struts, and then, majestically, her bridge cleared with a booming roar.

By now the whole rising body was surrounded by a great mass of the water foaming and heaving, and there were choppy waves rolling toward us, making the *Skipjack* bounce and buck under our feet.

Then the gun turrets began to clear, the guns themselves shrouded in fabric of some kind, each turret big as a good-sized ranch house, breaking water one after another with a sound and effect like surf crashing on a great boulder. There was something about the effect that made you want to cheer, but if you did, you had nothing left to do when the main deck cleared with a thunderous roar, millions of gallons of water washing over the side as she came above the water like a ghost ship in a nightmare. It wasn't easy to keep your feet on the *Skipjack's* deck, but you only felt sorry for anyone who had to be below and miss this.

By then the Stars and Stripes had broken from her mast, and at the upper levels there were men running around, getting things in order. The lights of her bridge were visible.

We all waved; it was impossible not to, the way it is for a big ocean liner.

Though nothing could top the huge sixteen-incher turrets and the main deck breaking the surface, there was something awe-inspiring in quite a different way about the manner in which she continued to rise steadily from the waves, foot by foot, until she floated before us on the now-calm ocean.

I knew what she had to be, and a part of my brain was ready to gasp it out—a ship whose picture, heading to the bottom, was famous from Pearl Harbor in my world; the ship that in Al's poem here had carried Patton and Admiral Nimitz to New Zealand and eventually to the Free Zone . . . and then I knew how it was possible, and I turned to Dr. Teller and said very softly—"She must have been the only hull you had that would stand the pressure and could be sealed up that way . . . once you had the atomic reactors to put into her."

Teller nodded, like a proud papa, and added, "It wasn't the easiest job we've ever done. We'd have fabricated a new hull if we could, but since we couldn't . . . the worst part of the job, really, was figuring out what to reinforce and where to seal, since if we'd made a mistake and she'd sunk, we could never have raised her."

The little boat from the *Arizona* came out to us, and there was a certain amount of naval pomp and ceremony in getting us transferred to her. We all shook hands with Captain Stark,, but like any decent sub captain, I could tell he was eager to get back under the waves and away from such an obvious target.

Finally we were on the *Arizona*'s boat, whirring over to the side of the battleship.

When we arrived, there was a long, complicated process of getting netting down for us all to climb, but still, in less than half an hour we stood on her deck. From the way the commandos were grinning, I could tell they were looking forward to being dismissed belowdecks, something that happened as fast as their officers got a nose count.

Meanwhile, we three and Dr. Teller were met by a pleasant young Asian man in black pajamas who said, "Captain's compliments, Dr. Teller, and I'm to conduct you and your party to dive stations and then to the bridge once we're down and under way."

"Lead on, then," Teller said.

We crossed the steel-plated deck—I noted how heavy the gray paint was, and that now that I was looking around a little more, I could see scars here and there, places where things had been taken off or modified in a dozen ways.

We went through a double hatch, with two doors about ten feet apart. The outer one had probably not originally been in that position and might not have been on the ship; the inner one looked like it had been carefully cut from some other steel and made to fit. I realized as the man with us dogged the second hatch down that it was an airlock.

The maze of winding passages inside the battleship was utterly baffling; to judge from the number of welds and the diversity of surfaces, I doubted that anyone from my timeline who had served on the ship would have been able to find his way. They had kept the hull, the bridge, and the turrets, and I guessed they had kept the steam turbines as well, but that was about all.

Diving horns were sounding everywhere, and we felt the decks sinking below us. The young man who had guided us here grinned. "I always feel a little nervous at this point," he said. "I've been on almost every dive since the first one, but this is always the point where I realize this poor old girl was never designed to do any such thing."

We could feel thuds and bangs through the hull, and all of us must have looked a little nervous, because the kid winked, and said, "You saw her come out of the water. You know she's not streamlined. What do you suppose happens when you submerge all that steel in such irregular shapes?"

We all relaxed until Teller added, "Mind you, you're getting that groaning and thumping in the structure because it *is* a high-stress process. If she ever fails, this is when she would be likely to."

He appeared to be enjoying the thought, so I decided I wasn't going to let him scare me. That was one of those decisions easier to make than to carry out . . .

After a while, the young man said, "We have cabins for each of you, and all four of you will be sharing a head. If you'd like to freshen up before I take you to meet the captain . . . "

We followed him through more winding corridors and down a few ladders, and eventually found ourselves looking at four coffin-sized compartments with bunks—actually they might better have been described as being bunks with a door—and a phone booth–sized space with a toilet and sink, arranged so that you could use the sink if you practically stood in the toilet, or the toilet if you didn't mind a sink on the back of your neck. It looked great to me—it was certainly better than anything I'd had in a while.

We all took turns making use of the facilities, and then the young guy took us up to the bridge to meet the captain. It was another climb through a winding passageway, this time one with a lot of traffic, where many times we had to stop and press ourselves into crevices to let various sailors get by.

The crew seemed to be multiracial and multilingual, and many of them were younger than the commando unit. Probably it was easier to rotate new guys onto a big ship than to put them into a tightly knit combat unit.

At last we came to a spiral stair, and, following it up, we found ourselves on the bridge.

In some ways it was the most altered part of the ship, in some ways the least. The heavy glass of the windows looked even heavier than what I had seen on a tour, once, of the *Missouri*, and, of course, at our running depth it was all but pitch-black outside anyway, with just a faint overhead glow. The screens the men were watching were sonar and hydrophone, and there were rank on rank of instrument and gauge boards that no one had ever planned should be here when the ship's keel was laid down.

The man who turned to us was dressed in old uniform parts, often mended, but there was something—well, *stylish* about him, He looked like a guy you'd follow anywhere.

Then I got a better look at him and realized with whom I was dealing.

I suppose it was natural enough to work your way up—he couldn't have stayed in PT boats forever, and there were no offices to run for out in the Free Zone. His hair was short but still managed to be a bit disorderly; the famous, wide-set intelligent eyes were still there, and they looked right through you in a way that made you want to do whatever he asked of you.

I started to understand the reactions of some older people I knew.

Understand, I'm a little too young to really remember John F. Kennedy from my own timeline, but there was a certain kind of magic about him anyway, and of all the things I saw and people I met over in that timeline, this was the one that stuck with me. There were famous people I got to know better, and certainly there were many closer friends, but when I think back on that particular adventure across time, it's the vision of him standing there, leaning slightly on his cane because his back was bad, staring out into the black ocean depths before us.

He took a little time to show the place off—he was very proud of his strange command, and whatever didn't have to be kept secret he was happy to show us. Dr. Teller, of course, had worked on getting the nuclear power plants built and on working out pressures and top speeds—the *Arizona* wasn't fast, couldn't be fast, for though her engines could push her a lot harder than they ever did, her superstructure had enough to do just to keep the terrible pressures below the surface from rupturing her, and there was so much drag that they didn't dare to move fast. The *Arizona* could circle the globe submerged—it turned out that Captain Kennedy had taken her under the North Pole more than once and had run the length of the Atlantic in her—but her top speed was low, and her vulnerability to depth charges something that no one aboard seemed to want to talk about.

For all the slowness and vulnerability, I was to learn in the next few days that the crew had come to feel invulnerable after some of the things Kennedy had taken them through; on the run through the Atlantic, they had surfaced off Jutland, run in close, and shelled Wilhelmshaven and Bremen—"You should have heard the variety of stories the Jerries kept coming up with to explain that one," one of the intelligence staff said. "Simultaneously they had to denounce it as barbaric, cruel, and a justification for whatever reprisals they wanted to take, and declare that it had no effect, and announce that there was no such thing as an Allied warship anyway and it was just an industrial accident in Wilhelmshaven getting picked up and becoming a rumor that was also misattributed to things happening in Bremen."

This was a day or two later, and I was having dinner with him in the officers' mess, where we all had permanent invitations as a courtesy. It had taken me a long time, even after seeing it surface, even after having to travel around inside it, to realize just how large the *Arizona* was.

Besides her occasional surprise terror raids around the Axis-controlled world, and her operations in support of various rebel groups around the world, she also acted as a floating intelligence and research base, a guided missile platform, a flagship when in combined operations, and when operating by herself far from base, a sort of super-subtender. She could tow up to five submarines behind her—in fact that was where *Skipjack* was right now—while supplying them with fresh air and electric power.

All this I learned over a couple of days as I got rest, food, and a certain amount of the simple feeling of safety. We knew we were making for the Free Zone, though exactly where was secret even from us.

It was different here. I had seen Axis America only through the eyes of the rebels and as a hunted fugitive, but that was the most accurate way to see it, and its most notable feature was the cloud of fear in which you lived. Even people in the Good Neighbors and various other fascist organizations had to be afraid of each other. But on the *Arizona,* once you were aboard and it had been determined you belonged there, you were automatically part of the accepted circle. I found I could talk to anyone about anything that wasn't classified; there was an atmosphere of freedom that, in just my short days away from my own timeline, I had all but forgotten.

I spent quite a bit of time with Dr. Teller, trying to figure out the SHAKK, but all we could determine was that it wanted to be reloaded, and we had none of whatever it was that it was loaded with. "It's a pity," he said, "because what you and the two resistance people describe as its effects are things we could really use. We'll have to make sure you get a chance to work around some of our materials science people; maybe you or they will find whatever it is."

Two other things became clear from the conversation; first of all, Sheila had probably not been a

Special Agent. "Officially her rank seems to have been Time Scout, whatever that might be," Teller said. "That was part of the coded material she sent us. If I were making a guess, it's that she was more or less dropped off here and told to report back every now and then. We can only hope that this means they will come looking for her, and that they have the means to come and look."

The other was what had happened at the beach. "Understand," he said, "here I was expecting one woman on an empty beach. First I find the beach guarded, then the guard departs and an armed party comes down to look at the naked, tortured corpse of the person I came to see. I was more than suspicious—I was ready to shoot—but then you mentioned transistors."

"I don't understand," I said. "Are they a secret password or something?"

Teller laughed. "No—or yes. Your choice. We've been making them in the Free Zone since about 1950, but they're a closely guarded secret. And the important thing is that they work by principles of quantum physics—or what the current masters of the Earth refer to as 'Jewish science.' The same branch of physics is essential to understanding nuclear energy as well. So if, as you are guessing, these Closers who control the Nazis are phobic about nuclear power, they probably suppress quantum theory, which is why the Nazis have no transistors."

"And no lasers," I said.

"And no *what*?"

It had never occurred to me that I might meet a physicist, let alone a world-class one, who wouldn't know what a laser was. Unfortunately, I didn't really know myself—I knew sort of what they did, but had very little idea how they did it. At least I remembered that they were monochromatic, and the light didn't disperse at all.

Teller sat and scribbled frantically, scratching his head the whole while. "Wonderful," he said finally. "Absolutely wonderful. I shall be sure to cite your assistance."

I was a bit startled. "Do you have any way to publish?"

"Oh, eventually, eventually. The war is not going to last forever, you know, merely for a very long time." And we were off to some other subjects.

It took the *Arizona* almost three weeks to traverse the Pacific submerged, and I suppose if I had had anything that it was urgent for me to do, I'd have been screaming with impatience. But the fact was that I was very much stranded in this world, and therefore until someone found a job for me to do, nothing could be really urgent. Moreover, being here meant time enough to do a little reading in the ship's library and to do some hard thinking about what I would do when I got to the Free Zone. Other than being dead certain I would volunteer and try to make my contribution in the struggle against the Nazis and the Closers, I had no idea, nor did I really know what my options might be.

That left me with one other thing to consider—me and my place in the universe. One problem with time to rest and think is that all of a sudden things start to come into clear focus.

First thing to notice, I decided—nobody really needed me back home. The fact was that Dad looked after himself well, and even Carrie managed to do so. Robbie and Paula would miss me but would find other agencies to give them work. I was a good bodyguard, but there were other bodyguards as well. Maybe Porter would write me from camp . . . that was about it.

So there was no urgent reason for me to go home. Blade of the Most Merciful were gone—I'd had the satisfaction of bagging most of them with my SHAKK, back in the Closer base. I had liked the few ATN people I'd met, and I wouldn't mind linking back up with them, but it might happen anyway, and I didn't have to be at home to do it.

No, it was clear I not only could make a place for myself here, but I probably should, because it was also quite possible that I would be stranded here for a long time. Even if another Time Scout or Special Agent came through, it seemed to me that the chances of their finding me, or of being interested in me if they did, were pretty slim.

So I was here for good, and I was going to act like it . . . and that led to some hard self-reflection. I realized I hadn't acted like it in my own timeline. Waking up fantasizing it was somewhere else had just been a symptom— the real problem was that, miserable as my new existence as a widower was, however much I had only been able to assuage my despair by constant violent action, that existence *was* mine, and I had gone through it sleepwalking or like a tourist, not letting it touch me enough for it to fix me.

I had missed a lot of pain, but I had been avoiding life.

This would have to change; I couldn't make this new lifetime be a copy of the old, nor could I drop out into a comfortable if barren existence as I had at home. If I was going to have to live here, I would have to *live* here.

All this took me quite a while to arrive at, and if I had had anything significant to distract me, I'm sure I would have managed not to think about it.

The day that Captain Kennedy announced we were only ten days from port, I noticed there was something new and different on the bulletin board—an announcement that Al would be performing his poems that evening, in one of the larger messes. I wasn't going to miss that—having heard it once, and now having read enough to get more of the references, I probably couldn't have been kept away at gunpoint. But I did think it was kind of a shame that they had put it in such a big space, because poetry was never a popular taste as far as I could tell, and I figured maybe a dozen people plus me, Sandy, and Teller would show up.

I had badly underestimated the power of boredom; for most of the crew, one voyage was a lot like another, once you got used to the idea of cruising below the ocean in a rebuilt battleship. They had seen the films and read the books and heard the records in the ship's library; the idea of anything new, anything at all, was enough to draw them out in droves. The room was packed to the walls, and though I was not late, I couldn't find a real seat of any kind, and ended up in a corner where I couldn't quite see Al, my back wedged a bit uncomfortably—though for this, I was more than willing to put up with it.

The room fell to a dead silence; I thought Al was beginning, and then I saw people struggling to their feet and realized Captain Kennedy had come in. I heard that gentle, deep New England voice making everyone else sit, but whether he liked it or not, they were going to make room for him in the front row.

Then there was a little more excited buzz, and then a very deep silence. Al cleared his throat, took a drink of water, and said, "All right, then, the first of these is called 'The Fall.'"

It didn't have quite the same impact as the first time, for me, but it still brought tears to my eyes before he was done, and as I watched the men in the room—Asians, Polynesians, Caucasians, and blacks jammed together, all listening intently, no one making a sound, tears trickling down cheeks and eyes shut to hear better—I knew I wouldn't have missed being here for all the world.

But if "The Fall" hit them like a hammer blow, "The Gathering of Nations" was a nuclear blast; by the end of it some of them were shaking with stifled sobs, others had mouths open in wonder. I have never heard wilder applause.

They had Al read again and again, five times in all, so that everyone on board could hear it—indeed, Captain Kennedy decided to require it, I suppose in the same spirit that George Washington had made all the troops listen to Tom Paine's *The Crisis*.

After about the third reading, I bumped into Sandy; she looked much better, and without exactly saying that I asked how she was.

"Okay," she said, idly, a little distracted. "God, it's so good to see Al like this. I've been looking out for him for a couple of years and to have so much acceptance from so many people listening to his poetry—well, I think it must be something he's wanted for many years."

"Those poems are going to live forever," I said.

Sandy smiled sweetly and tucked her legs under her on her chair. "And of course the other thing . . . well, Al's a great man, but . . . you know, I've been getting a lot of attention from Captain Kennedy—which he doesn't really have time to give me, but he's such an interesting man, not like anyone I've ever met before—"

I bet, I thought, and for one moment couldn't decide whether I was more jealous of him or her. But the jealousy passed, and then I mostly felt amused; I had to admit that it was almost as interesting to see what *wasn't* changed between the timelines.

12

It wasn't until we were actually approaching that Captain Kennedy let us know that we were going into the harbor at Haiphong. That seemed to be very popular with everyone aboard; Vietnam was the heart of the Free Zone, both physically and politically, and was about as far from Axis bombers and raiders as you ever got. Then, too, there's something about being able to take leave in a city, and a city where you can feel safe . . . Hanoi was just a short trolley ride away, and I remember being a bit disoriented by the number of American sailors who kept telling me about all the places to have a good time in Hanoi.

Dr. Teller had been spending a lot of time by himself with the notebook Al had carried aboard, and as we were putting into the harbor, he said to me, "I just wanted to let you know how significant your efforts were. This notebook is exactly what we have needed for at least three years—so many things in it which are obvious once explained but couldn't possibly be learned other than by painful trial and error! You've given us a huge leap forward—"

"Sheila did," I pointed out, "and Al carried the note-book—"

Teller grinned. "I know that—in fact I've already told Al my feelings on the subject. Also that he's the great American poet as far as I'm concerned."

"It would never have occurred to me that a physicist would have much of an opinion about poetry."

His brows furrowed, and I realized he was a bit angry; his hands flew around excitedly. "You damn silly Americans! God! The only nation on earth where they think that if you're smart, you won't be interested in literature or art!"

That made me laugh, and I apologized, which seemed to help.

He calmed down, and said, "But in particular I wanted to thank you for something else. This 'laser' idea of yours—it's pointed me in a number of exciting directions."

"It's not really my idea," I pointed out, "and besides, all I told you was that it was possible."

"All!" He laughed at that. "All! That's all any decent physicist wants to know. What you've done is assured me of a place in physics of my own—"

It was my turn to be startled. "Then wasn't that notebook—"

"Hah! Oh, sure, I was a footnote. The guy who read the textbook and got it sorted out for everyone else. But I've wanted an independent area to open up ever since I got into this. I had thought it might be this nuclear bomb thing, but so much of that has been concerned with just getting things accomplished at all in a setting where doing any kind of science is so difficult—and then suddenly *this* comes along—well! I've seen a dozen ways in principle it might all be done, you see. At least a dozen. I've filled a notebook of my own thus far. You've given me something new and interesting to work on, just when this other project was about to play out . . . "

He went on like that for quite a while, and I was driven to reflect that he seemed like a pretty happy guy as he got off the boat. I just hoped he'd remember to finish up on the Bomb before he got going on lasers.

It was sort of good-bye for me at the dockside. At Captain Kennedy's strong urging, Al was going around to read his poetry, sort of a micro-USO tour, and Sandy would be going as his assistant and bodyguard. Nobody exactly knew what to do with me, so I was being sent up to Hanoi for the generals to worry about.

Kennedy gave me this big, warm, toothy smile when he shook my hand for the last time, and said he was sure it would work out, that the Free Zone needed every good man it could get. It made me feel good, and between the firm grip and the big smile I realized I might easily have voted for him myself.

I wasn't particularly alarmed when they put me in a closed compartment on the train to Hanoi, and stationed a guard outside the door. There was a war on, and I was an anomaly, and if there was anything I'd learned as a bodyguard, it was that anything anomalous, anything that just didn't fit into the pattern, was something to be watched out for.

The secure barracks in Hanoi was Spartan but livable, and the food was mostly rice with a few vegetables and some fish, but perfectly palatable. I've had better Vietnamese food in Vietnamese restaurants, but then nobody goes to French prisons to sample French cuisine either.

The next day they loaded me into a truck with a

bunch of other people, none of whom spoke English, to go over to the government building and be sorted out. I figured out from what the guards were saying that it wasn't unusual in the Free Zone to have people of highly indefinite status around—Japanese who had fled their homeland and its Thought Police to float down the China coast on rafts, Hindus and Muslims from India fleeing persecution there, pilots who deserted the air forces of the Soviet or American puppet regimes and took their planes with them, Brazilians who had forged papers to get out of occupied Brazil . . . the list went on and on. They all had to be processed for loyalty risk, with the ones who seemed least likely ending up in prison for a while and the ones who seemed most likely offered a provisional citizenship in the Free Zone and put to work on some nonstrategic project for a few months to see what happened.

On the other hand they hardly ever processed anyone who claimed to be a traveler from another timeline.

They kept me waiting most of the day in a beautiful old colonial palace in Hanoi. The walls were thick and heavy, which was how it had survived a number of Japanese and German bombing raids, and the high arches in its walls were graceful and allowed quite a bit of air and light into the room. I had a pitcher of water, and they brought me a bowl of rice and fish around lunchtime, so I wasn't at all uncomfortable, just bored.

The most astonishing thing to me was how green it all was outside. There were tall palms—Hanoi was far enough from Japanese bases not to have taken too terrible a pounding, especially because (one of those funny coincidences between timelines) it had a very strong and effective set of air defenses. So the trees

mostly still stood, and though you could see bomb
damage here and there looking out over the city, it was
still mostly what it had been in old *National
Geographics*—a city of graceful French neoclassical official buildings, bright pagodas, and thatched-roof cabins, through whose crowded, busy streets the
palm-helmeted people streamed all day long. The
ruckus outside the window—children screaming, bark-
ing dogs, crowing chickens, pigs grunting, vendors crying their wares, bicycle bells, and everywhere the
excited babble of busy human voices—was wonderful
music after the pulsing mechanical silence of the ship.
I hoped that soon I could be out there tasting and
smelling some of the sensory delights.

It even occurred to me to wish Al and Sandy hadn't
departed quite so fast—I'd have liked to have seen the
city with them, Al for his passionate enthusiasm,
Sandy for naïveté—both of which I was a bit lacking
in, but this Hanoi in the Free Zone was my first real
taste of the Orient, and it occurred to me that to see it
as a burned-out, world-weary cynic was not to see it at
all.

Finally, after a very long time, a physically slight,
neatly dressed Vietnamese man came in; he spoke perfect English with a very slight accent. "Mr. Strang. I am
General Giap. I must say, we have heard a number of
very unusual statements from a number of very
unusual people, but yours are the most unusual I have
ever seen. Moreover, we have the odd fact that you
have a certain amount of support and corroborating
testimony from many people we would dearly like to
believe. So you pose us quite a dilemma. This device
you call a SHAKK"—he pulled it from a box beside
him—"will you help me to examine it, please?"

He handed it to me, pointed to the readout, and

said, "You claim to have an implant behind your ear which allows you to read this text?"

I bent forward and showed him the implanted device.

"Hmmm. Can you remain in that position? Thank you . . . now read to me the words displayed here?"

I hesitated, then translated, using the chip on the back of my head. "Reload before firing again."

Something felt slightly funny in my head, and he asked me to translate the characters next to the fire-control switch. I looked but couldn't read them, and said so, "But I've used it enough. All the way forward for single shot semiauto, middle position for hex bursts semiauto, all the way back for full auto."

"All right, now hold still—" he said.

Again my head felt extraordinarily strange, but this time more so; I almost fell, and he steadied me. "What did you just feel?"

"Very dizzy," I said. "But not like I'm ill—"

"Look at the fire control switch again," he said.

"'One shot per pull, hex cluster shot, stream of shots,'" I read. "I don't—"

"I pulled out your translator chip, then put it back in. It proves nothing, of course, you might just be a superb actor for all I can tell, but at least it proves you are good enough to fool me. If you are acting, the slight dizziness when I put the chip in and took it back out were superb touches." He sat down and pressed his fingers together lightly at the tips, clearly thinking. "The physicists assure me that the material they have received is genuine, but of course it was not entirely received by your agency. A colleague of mine is looking at another piece of evidence; provisionally I am forced to believe you may be who you say you are."

I nodded. "I'm glad to hear that."

"So are we. We are the Free Zone only in the sense that we are not under the heel of the Axis. Some day we hope to make it mean a good deal more than that, of course, but for right now it really does not. There are no guarantees of the rights of the accused here, and if, for example, we had become convinced you were not who you said you were, we would not hesitate to use drugs, torture, or whatever coercion stood the best chance of working. We are the side of the right, I believe, Mr. Strang, but for the right to be right it must first *win*— and that is our goal just now." He got up and paced slowly over to the window. "I do hope you understand that. Should we conclude that you are working against us or dangerous to us, we would take swift and possibly violent measures to deal with the problem . . . "

"And if you become convinced I'm on your side?"

Giap smiled slightly. "One of my first postings here was in intelligence, and I retain an interest in that field. I am never entirely convinced that *anyone* is on my side." The smile he added to that was utterly without compassion.

I nodded, understanding he meant to frighten me and frankly agreeing that yes, if he wanted to, I could hardly stop him, but then I said, "Just the same, if you decided the risk of my disloyalty was low—"

"Then we have a hundred possible billets to put you in, assuming you want to join the Free Zone Forces, as you said you do."

The door opened. The next man who came in was large, strong, and looked like a comic-strip boxer, his nose a little flattened and bent, his whole way of moving as if he were looking for a fight. He wore what had to be the only perfect GI battle dress I saw the whole time I was there, and twin ivory-handled revolvers graced his hips.

He was carrying my Colt automatic. "Giap," he said, "damn all if this thing isn't perfectly consistent with the story the bastard is telling. According to his debriefing the States had two big wars after World War II, in his timeline—if you believe in all that bullshit about timeline—and shit if the serial number here isn't right up in the two millions where it ought to be. And the cops just got done checking his jacket and it's a synthetic they don't recognize. And not least, that silly watch of his is displaying consistent time but there are no moving parts except the buttons, and when we looked inside all we could find was something that looked like a complicated midget crystal radio."

Giap nodded. "After my examination of him I'm inclined to think he is telling the truth, George."

"I'm sure he is. I guess that should be I'm sure you are, Strang. How the hell are you after all this probing? We'll get your stuff back to you later today."

"I'm fine," I said, "and I'm not sure whether in your place I'd have believed me, sir. I do have the honor of speaking to General Patton?"

"You do indeed, and I'm damned glad somebody realizes it's an honor. It's an honor to speak to Giap, here, too, though he's quiet about it. Well, the question now is what we do with you. You look like you're in decent shape, and from what that crazy poet you brought with you says you might make a soldier, so I guess we can just enlist you, but it seems like something as unusual as you are would have a better use than just lugging a rifle."

I shrugged. "I don't know, sir, if you've read the interview, then no doubt you know that all I have training to be is an art historian or a bodyguard. I'm good at both, but I don't imagine you've got much need for either."

Patton nodded and handed me back my .45; he said,

"You seem to take good care of your weapon, and that's another plus for you. Since you're a bodyguard, why don't you come to lunch with us? About when I started to think you might really be what you seemed to be, I started to want to hear about your world."

"Shouldn't you take other guards—"

"Oh, I'll have them whether I take them or not. Certain other generals around here insist on having me followed. How about you, Giap?"

The Vietnamese blinked innocently. "I have never followed you, George."

"I'll say!" Patton grinned; I suddenly realized that these men were very old friends. "Will you come along to lunch with us?"

"Gladly."

"By the way," Patton added, "there are two fewer rounds in there than usual. We pulled the two you had left over from your own timeline. They looked like we should copy them."

"They're called Black Talons," I said, "and I don't know how they do it exactly, but they're supposed to have maximum stopping power."

"Well, we've got some whiz kids in our labs, and they'll figure it out. But I'd be damned surprised if a 1990 round isn't better than what we're using."

We were out on the streets now, and I had to admit I was amazed—and that I felt like I was going to earn my keep as a bodyguard. Giap and Patton walked through all the swirl of bicycles, vendors, shrieking kids, handcarts, oxen—with just me as their apparent guard—like any two tourists anywhere.

As we rounded one corner and actually went deliberately into a narrow alley, Giap turned to me and muttered, "He refuses to be afraid. And to be fair, people love him for it. As for me, I have to follow him like this because I will not let him make it look like I am afraid of my people!"

He stopped for a minute to let a little parade of waddling ducks go by, and we caught up with him. "There's a noodle house over here I like," he said. "Mac introduced me to it, and I like to visit it now and then in his memory."

To my astonishment, the place was a Japanese restaurant. Giap and I exchanged glances, and Patton explained, "Here, watch . . ." and as we went in, he said, "Hey, Jimmy, where's my baby doll?"

The Japanese man behind the counter grinned and bellowed—in a thick Bronx accent—"You keep your white devil paws off my daughter! Ruthie, get out here and wait on these gents!"

The girl who came out to lead us to our table was about eighteen and terribly cute; her Bronx accent was as thick as her father's.

"Jimmy's from New York, if you haven't guessed," Patton explained. "Used to be a steward on a Navy cruiser, then drove a landing craft, then was an artillery spotter for me in Australia, then spent a year or so sparring with Krauts on New Guinea before they gave that up for a bad business. Now that he's a little older, he's settled into being the noodle king of Hanoi."

We found ourselves conducted to a table in the back; no menu ever appeared, nor did any bill I noticed, but what did turn up, again and again, were plates full of all sorts of wonderful food. I ate sparingly, and so did Giap, but we were both a little logy by the end of the meal.

Then, as the tea was poured for us, Patton said, "All right, now all I need from you is the whole history of the USA from your timeline."

Even when you're reasonably well educated, that's

not easy to do. Unfortunately for Patton, too, military history is off in one small corner of academia, art history in another, and the twain touch rarely. He was glad to know my father had served in the Third Army and that he had commanded it, and glad to know he'd won distinction.

Patton had a certain generosity of spirit, too . . . when I told General Giap that he had defeated first the French and then the Americans in a deeply political war, he said, "All wars are political."

Patton grunted. "Not the ones that are any fun."

"Nonetheless," Giap persisted.

"Yeah," Patton grunted. "I know you're right, Giap. Ah, hell, I'm glad you got the glory, friend, but I wish to hell you hadn't had to beat my side to do it."

"Here, we are on the same side, George," he said. "Now, if you could tell us once more, a little more about this space program . . . "

The afternoon passed pleasantly enough. Two hours later, the two generals seemed ready to go. "The strangest thing of all," Patton said, "is that just now there's not much work for either of us. Though a couple of the projects we will be putting you to work on just happen to be the sort of thing that might get either of us employed again . . . "

Giap nodded. "Who did you say, again, was the first American to orbit the earth?"

I was getting puzzled by how often he'd returned to that point. "John Glenn. A Marine Corps pilot, I think from Ohio—at least that's where he went to get himself elected to the Senate."

The same flock of ducks started to cross the street in front of us, but something was different this time—

There. Under the canvas of one booth, someone had pushed those ducks out to walk in front of the generals.

I'd had a lot of practice at noticing things that weren't quite right; I had tackled both of them, the tall burly American and the frail Vietnamese, in a moment, and then was standing above them, the Colt in firing position, just as a too-late shot screeched wildly by. I'd seen the muzzle flash in the dim tent, and fired back—what came back out was a flurry of shots, and then there was a scuffle and the tent itself went over.

Police had been near the tent on the other side and had jumped on the men inside—there was a struggle and a shot or two more, but it was clear that matters were under control.

Patton was on his feet as well, his famous pistols drawn, but Giap seemed to have vanished—for just an instant. Then the booth from which all the trouble had started tipped over, and I saw him locked in a knife fight with the man who had been under there. They rolled over my way, and I stepped on the attacker's knife arm at the wrist and placed my .45 against his temple. The man let the knife fall, and we pinned him down and flagged some more of the police.

After they had taken him away, Patton said, "Well, he could be one of our bodyguards."

"True," Giap said. "But in all truth, I think I'd rather send him over to Engineering Seven. As a bodyguard. And I certainly hope he has better luck with those lunatics than we do."

"Engineering Seven is—"

"Not for discussion here in the street," Patton said firmly. "But I do believe Giap has the right idea. Come along, then, Strang, I think we've found a place where your mix of skills can be some use."

I had been bewildered at having that much attention from two senior generals; it was only later that I came to understand that because in the Free Zone officers kept the commands they brought with them and units kept their weapons, by and large, high-ranking generals like Patton, Giap, Montgomery, and the rest were usually not wanted for anything but sliding counters around on maps and talking about what could be done next.

The exception to this was an organization called the General Council, which was as much of a coordinated command as the Free Zone really had. (The local legislatures and governments that raised taxes and ran civil affairs had no military power whatsoever—they had only the choice of either raising levies to pay for the armed forces, or of starving their own forces, letting the Axis win, and then seeing what deal they could come up with. It's wonderful how a serious situation can introduce the spirit of cooperation into a legislature.)

The General Council had one hundred engineering projects going at any one time, scattered around various parts of the Free Zone. Of these one hundred, at least half were dummies, but which numbers were dummies varied from year to year as well. It turned out that Giap had mentioned Engineering Seven for me only because it *was* a dummy. "Actually," Patton said, "we'll send you to Engineering Fifteen. That's the one that's being supervised by General LeMay, who's all right if you don't mind maniacs, and has a bunch of good people working on—well, you'll see. And you have one additional duty—write down everything you remember of your home timeline. We have no way of knowing what's going to be useful, so we want all of it before any of it can fade from your memory."

"Yes, sir," I said, and took the orders that were to get

me on a plane out of Hanoi to Engineering Fifteen's offices in Singapore.

"Oh, and Strang?"

"Yes, sir?"

"Thanks for saving my life. And old Giap's, too. I'd miss the old commie if anything happened to him."

"My pleasure, sir, but you should be more careful."

The general looked at me a little incredulously. "Are you aware whom you're asking to be careful?"

I thought about it for one long instant, realized he was right, said so, and took my leave. The last I saw of him, the palm-frond ceiling fans were turning over his head and he'd pulled on a pair of pince-nez to study a map.

The flight was all space-a, meaning whenever there was room on an airplane and a more important sack of flour was not ahead of me in line, I got to move toward Singapore. The first hop was right down to Saigon, but then I was stuck there for a day, tried jumping to Bangkok, and ended up coming back on a DC-3 that was going on from Saigon to Ipoh down in the Malay Peninsula, before finally catching a flight to Singapore.

Once, on my way to a dig in India, I had passed through Singapore, and in my part of my timeline, it looked sort of like a chunk of Manhattan torn off, wrapped up in bits of Hong Kong, and stuck out into tip of the jungles, protruding into the sea. But in my world Singapore had been fought over just once in the twentieth century, and had been utterly undefended from the land side; the Japanese took it with no trouble at all.

Here, it had fallen to them at the outbreak of fighting, been retaken almost at once by Aussies and New

Zealanders (able to get there because the Japanese fleet was busy with the invasion of Hawaii), fallen again when the Japanese made their brief counterattack, fallen again to the Free Zone forces . . . and so it had been worn down by shellfire and fighting until it became one vast, grim, forbidding fortress complex, nothing like the exciting trade entrepôt it was in my timeline.

When the old Ford Trimotor I had managed to hitch a ride in touched down at Singapore, what I saw was about as attractive, esthetically speaking, as East Berlin used to be. It was from here, just three years ago, that an air sortie had sunk the aircraft carriers *Kaga*, *Graf Spee*, and *Gloire*, but only after the island had taken yet another pounding; bomb craters were still visible here and there.

I was met at the airport by an older guy named Bob, who practically talked my ear off on the way back to Engineering Fifteen; he didn't know where I'd come from and my official new title was "chief of security," so as far as I could tell what he was trying to do was make sure I knew how important Engineering Fifteen was. He kept referring to "the future of humanity itself," which after all was pretty much what the Free Zone was all about, anyway.

It wasn't until we reached the secure bunkers that I finally found out what I was guarding: the Free Zone's space program.

Just as Patton had scooped up and run with most of the American nuclear program in his long run that went past Oak Ridge and through Los Alamos, Marine General Puller, stationed on the West Coast, had had the presence of mind to grab the advanced research projects from the Consortium's Hughes Aircraft facility. One of those projects had been a group of men around

Robert Goddard and Willy Ley, and they had been working on rockets.

What they might have done had they had another year or two is an open question. What they had done here, starting from scratch with miserable equipment, was nothing less than astonishing—they had to hand-build each one, and there were innumerable false starts, but they had produced a whole series of rocket engines.

The problem was, the kind of people who could do that sort of work were exactly the kind of people who were impossible to guard. Remember what I said about hating to guard kids, except for Porter? Well, creative scientists and engineers are large kids. They want to do everything when they want to do it, and they don't see why they can't do it their way, because after all they're the smartest people in the room.

I've heard the theory, too, that being childlike enhances creativity. I couldn't say, really, except to note that I was never around adults so childlike—or so creative.

Goddard had died not long after the Free Zone was established, but Ley was here, and Wernher von Braun had escaped the Nazis to come here (partly sickened by what he saw of slave labor—he'd brought several slave workers with him—and by his own admission also because the V-1 had been such a success that long-range rocket projects had withered on the vine). There were a lot of brainy types from Hughes Aircraft, and Kelly Johnson from Lockheed was in the crowd, and some really odd characters from the Philadelphia Navy Yard who had hitchhiked to LA, missing the departure of the Pacific Fleet by no more than a few days, and then managed to sail clear to Tahiti in a stolen yacht—Bob, who picked me up, was one of that gang, and they were far and away the strangest of all.

And my job was to keep this silly gaggle of visionaries out of trouble, because they were on the brink of giving us working ICBMs and spy satellites.

To do this, besides myself, I had about twenty Thai and Malay cops. I got along with them all right.

My major job most of the time was to back them up when they tried to stop some key person from doing something stupidly dangerous. The attack on Patton and Giap had not been isolated—Japanese agents had tried to get about twenty key personnel that day, and had actually badly wounded Mao Zedong, who was pretty much in retirement these days but still valuable as a symbol for the Chinese resistance. We had given them a short, succinct answer—the *Arizona*, and the other two submersible battleships USS *Tennessee* and HMS *Resolution*, had slipped in close to Honshu on a moonless night, surfaced, and unleashed their big guns on the harbor at Yokohama, setting fire to the dockyards and leaving many ships on fire in the harbor, during a state visit from Himmler. Reportedly dinner had not been a success.

But the attack meant that once again the Axis was getting ready to move against us, and every such attack was a painful reminder of the fact that the Free Zone had once been almost a fifth of the Earth's surface, even after the loss of the Americas, and it was still dwindling. We weren't beaten yet, but we had to depend on new weapons to save us eventually.

Von Braun actually was the one who finally made it clear to me why the Germans had not closed in to destroy the Free Zone, and why they hadn't developed their weapons much beyond what they had been at war's end. "Don't forget," he said, "that Hitler may have rallied his armies around being supermen, but he came to power promising the Germans that every

German would be rich. They're still"—he shuddered, and looked down at his plate—"the German translates as 'digesting.' They've got so much of Eastern Europe where they've exterminated whole populations, and then there's the rump of the Soviet Union to be pressed into service, and they're already making noises about *Anschluss* with Canada or the United States—they're busy giving their citizens the payoff. Once they had the world in hand, that was enough for them, at least for the time being."

Six relatively pleasant months went by; Singapore was still a grubby fortress, the scientists and engineers were still loony and helpless as kids, and my assistants got more and more efficient.

I had gotten a letter or two from Sandy, and written back in a friendly way without much expecting to hear from her again (attractive young women didn't stay single long in the Free Zone, and my pursuit was at best halfhearted). On Thursday nights I played poker with the Philly Navy Yard crew, on Saturday I did some pistol practice with my guards (the newly copied Black Talon rounds were indeed superior because they spread out in a star shape inside what they hit), and usually on Tuesday I went to one of the twenty-year-old movies at the Ex Sell Lent Theetre, often with Ley and von Braun, who both had a thing for German expressionist sci-fi flicks, of which there were many. In between I stayed in shape, worried about infiltration, looked for holes in fences, and the like, and wrote out at length everything I could remember of the history of my own timeline up to the point where I stepped out of it.

At first that made me homesick, then it sent me into a period of introspection where I started to come to grips with Marie's death, and then finally it was just one more chore.

Once in a great while I'd look at the SHAKK—I had discovered that for some mysterious reason besides the drawer to feed in the powder it had another drawer next to what I was guessing was the firing chamber, but otherwise I had learned nothing more. The translator in my neck continued to work, but it didn't know the word for either of those drawers; the readout continued to say "Reload before firing again." I thought it made kind of a nice paperweight.

My new world wasn't what I would have chosen to make it, but I was fitting into it, I was useful, and, frankly, I was better adjusted there than I had been at home. And I barely thought about home, anymore.

13

What saved us finally, at Singapore, was that my whole guard force for Engineering Fifteen was there. And that only happened because it was first launch day.

FZSS Human Rights wasn't what I'd have recognized as a spaceship, but that was what she was.

Sitting there waiting for launch, anyone would have said she looked like an upside-down pile of airplanes hanging under a dirigible, and they'd have been right. But all four stages of the craft were necessary—miniaturization and cryogenic fuels weren't very far advanced in this timeline, so the ship had to be big, and it had to use every possible trick to get up there.

The day was almost windless when the Human Rights was towed out of her hangar by a motley collection of old trucks, was brought around into the wind, and started her engines. I had snagged a spot on the dirigible stage, rank having its privileges, so I was standing there next to von Braun when the ship rolled out.

Dirigible takeoffs are neat; they just rise, and as long as the props aren't on the gondola, you barely feel the engines at all. It's like floating in a dream.

Singapore looked about as good as it ever had; it was still a giant steel-and-concrete turtle sitting astride the strait, but the jungles and the dim blue mountains beyond them were beautiful.

We were going up to fifty-five thousand feet, and to make this thing work at all, we had had to decide to use hydrogen—yes, it's flammable, and it's why the *Hindenburg* burned, but on the other hand one cubic foot of hydrogen will lift four times as much as a cubic foot of helium. Moreover, hydrogen is cheap and easy to make, while helium is complicated, tricky stuff, even if you do have it coming out of natural gas wells. If there was time to get another model into the air, most of the engineers wanted to go to helium—but we'd need much better engines before we could do it.

It took almost an hour to get up to altitude and cruising speed. Singapore sits almost exactly on the equator, which means that if you take off headed east, you get almost a thousand-mile-per-hour extra boost from the Earth's rotation.

As we reached cruising altitude, the steadying cables hooked to the eight-engine prop plane below us were released, so that soon we were towing the three-plane combination; General LeMay was on the phone to the crews of the three locked-together craft, and they all seemed ready to go.

The engines of the big airplane began to turn. "Here, we may begin to get just a little nervous," von Braun said. "If all her engines do not catch, we will all look very foolish."

But they all did; as they came up to speed, the huge

airplane moved forward, until it was towing the dirigible. We cut her loose, and General LeMay stepped back and saluted. "God, I'd give anything to have that kid Glenn's job," he said, and we all laughed; it broke the tension.

All of us scrambled, packed close together, up the eighty feet of ladders and stairways through the body of the dirigible to the observation bubble on top. Rank has its privileges, and being one of the least important people present, I was one of the last up the ladder; by the time I got there everyone was already pointing and talking.

Ahead of us the eight-engine plane soared upward; it could not have left the ground on its own, but its engines were more than adequate for what was to follow. A mile or so above us, and perhaps twenty miles ahead, when it was just a dim dot to the naked eye, it plunged downward over the South China Sea, building up speed. At the bottom of its dive, near the water, it released the remaining two linked-together craft. The twin ramjets of the "third stage" caught, and we saw her soaring up on a stream of flame as the huge mothership swung away and headed back to Singapore. "Let's stay on this course just a little longer," von Braun suggested, and LeMay said, "Try to make me stop watching."

The twin-ramjet craft had gotten up to about Mach 3, still climbing, and was fifteen miles above us—the merest arrowhead on a great pillar of flame and smoke rising above the blue Pacific—when it released Major Glenn and the orbiter. The powerful rocket engines cut in with a flare we saw from where we waited, and the dirigible's observation deck echoed with cheers.

The ramjets of the "third stage" had cut out, and through binoculars we saw her loop over and head back to Singapore in a long fast glide; she would have to land with her tanks empty, for her ramjets would not operate at the low speeds she would need for landing. I didn't envy the pilot—he'd have no chance to make another pass.

I swung my binoculars back to the uppermost, space-going stage of *Human Rights*; it was as big as a modern fighter jet from my timeline, and rode a huge plume of fire and smoke; as I watched, she dropped her first strap-on tank.

"Go, baby, go!" LeMay yelled, and the bridge echoed with cheers again. "Guess we might as well head for home—we can see about as well from there."

The great dirigible swung slowly around, her engines a distant thunder through the body. It took much longer to get downstairs than it had coming up, with everyone stopping to talk and slap each other on the back.

"Got a message, General," the radioman said. "I'll put it up on loudspeaker . . . "

"Mama Bear, this is Ocean City." That was mission control on Singapore. "That crazy kid is all the way up. Says he sees the stars and the curve. And radar from Big Dog confirms. He's made it!"

Everyone cheered and clapped some more; LeMay grumbled about being stuck on a "damned hydrogen gasbag" that wouldn't let him have a cigar to celebrate.

Glenn was to make ten orbits, experimenting with the attitude controls, photographing German and Japanese strategic areas, and experimenting with radar from space. Then he was to come in for a landing on the hard-packed airfield on the north side of the island, by the Johore Strait, where the twin-ramjet stage had also landed; the eight-engine piston prop stage was a seaplane and would land right in the harbor at Singapore.

All in all Glenn would be orbiting the earth for fifteen hours; time enough for people to rest, to wait for his return, possibly to catch a plane over to the airstrip to see him come in for his landing.

It had been a thrilling day so far, and the prospect was for more excitement before it was over.

If only, somehow, it could have stayed the same sort of excitement.

We were getting relayed messages from Glenn most of the way back to Singapore, and the news was all good; the ship was handling well, he could see what he needed to see.

It takes a dirigible a long time to fight up a headwind, so Glenn had completed one orbit just as we made it back to base. LeMay got a private channel with him for the few minutes he was overhead—and then we all saw him grow pale. "You're sure that's what you saw," he said, three times. "Confirm with radar as soon as you can. We'll be in touch."

He turned around and said in a low voice, "Gentlemen, we may be a little late. I will want all those of you with top clearances in my office as soon as we're on the ground."

The big dirigible thumped and hummed as she came in for her landing, and a band was playing, not well but good and loud, loud enough for us to hear it as we approached the mooring mast. LeMay was on the radio a lot, and he didn't sound pleased, whatever the matter was.

I've said that in that timeline, from up above, Singapore looked like a giant turtle. When you got closer it looked like a giant turtle with a massive skin problem—there were bumps and blisters everywhere, low thick towers and heavy bunkers, any structure that had proved impossible to bomb out. A kind of evolution had happened to them—only the strong had survived—so that there were no tall thin spindly structures of any kind, no steeples, certainly no skyscrapers. Dead ahead of us was the "Cake Pan," the big stationary radar for this end of the island—and the place where the first V-1 hit.

There was a great flash, and flames leaped up from the Cake Pan.

They had fired them in salvos, and they had found ways to jam us; first the radar tower blew up, then the control tower, and then, suddenly, the great fortress was rocked with explosions, everywhere.

People were shouting, LeMay was trying to get anyone at all on the headset, and the pilot must have decided to try to run for it, though where you could run in a dirigible is beyond me. I don't think we took a direct hit—had we done so it would have ended in one great fireball—but when I looked outside I saw the skin of the dirigible rupturing and the blue hydrogen flame burning across the surface.

The loss of pressure sent the great airship drifting slowly toward the ground, as the wind carried it toward the roaring fires that the salvos of V-1s were starting all over the island.

I grabbed von Braun, merely because he was closer than anyone else, and shouted in his ear "got to get to the outside catwalk." He nodded, and we started our struggle that way—the floor was too smooth to climb easily and just now the door that had been only steps away moments before was a steep climb on that slick floor. We threw ourselves upward; I got hold of the door handle, he got hold of my belt and climbed up my shirt for a better grip, and we both managed to get ourselves braced above the door.

The dirigible was still sinking like a brick, and bucking up and down as her gas cells ruptured. Flames were pouring out above us.

I yanked the door open, and we both slid out onto the catwalk; for one heart-stopping instant I started to slide down the rough corrugated iron, as if to plunge under the railing and out into the sky, to drop three hundred feet onto the concrete runway. But I grabbed a post on the railing, and again von Braun grabbed me, and we fought our way up the railing, climbing hand over hand, once having to make it past a blazing gas cell that seemed to singe our backs through our shirts.

At last we reached what we were looking for—one of the securing cables that had kept the giant plane steady during takeoff. There was too much noise to talk between the thunder of the burning hydrogen, the wail of sirens and explosions of bombs from below, and the scream of the tormented propellers, for no one had been able to shut off the engines, and as the keel warped and buckled, no longer supported by inflated cells, the propellers were being brought into strange angles with the wind.

We had just taken a grip on the cable together when one of the engines, with a shriek like a coffee can thrown onto a table saw, ripped loose from its pylon and dove down to the pavement, now just a couple of hundred feet below.

Relieved of the weight, the airship shot upward for a moment, dragging us sixty or seventy feet higher as we clung to the cable and tried to keep feet braced on the catwalk.

The extra strain must have ruptured other cells, for we found ourselves sinking faster this time, the dirigible now drifting over the end of the airfield and heading down toward the harbor, some of the dragging cables already touching housetops.

We had little choice; we could stay aloft to avoid being smashed, and thus be burned alive whenever the cell next to us blew. Or we could climb down the cable to get away from the flames, and in all probability be dragged into the wall of a building at ten or twenty miles per hour, two stories up, or scraped off on an electric power line.

Something about burning does not sit well with the human mind . . . we couldn't have discussed it in that terrible din, but we were both immediately climbing down as quickly as we could go, hand over hand, the cable whipping horribly.

After a few moments I was motion sick; I leaned over my arm and threw up, but I did my damnedest not to get a drop on the cable, which could become slick.

Something nasty went by my head; I assumed it was von Braun's lunch.

I hadn't wanted to look down, but the news was slightly better—our cable was now trailing down a smashed-up street, and though there were three large rubble piles, there were clear spaces between them. Moreover, we were sinking fast now, and only about fifty feet off the ground.

Fifty feet is still an awfully long way. I climbed downward as fast as I could, taking a risk I couldn't have believed I'd be taking less than ten minutes before, for it had been no longer than that. Von Braun's shoes, swinging to and fro on the cable above me, gave me an incentive to climb all the faster, and the sinking dirigible carried us farther downward.

I was drenched in sweat, and my best suit was never going to be the same; all around me, now, the smoke of the great fires raging on the face of the old fortress was making it hard to breathe, and I couldn't see anywhere clearly enough to be sure of exactly where we were or what might happen next. But there was less than twenty feet to go, and I took a calculated risk and burned my hands a little sliding down the rope—at least right at that moment there wasn't anything too terrible to run into. My feet scraped pavement, but I hung on for an extra second so von Braun could slide down, too. We let go at the same time, but the dirigible didn't bounce up much; the cables whipped by us like mad pythons, and then we felt rather than heard or saw the great dirigible crashing to the pavement, a block of houses beyond us.

A great burst of red flame blossomed over the street and belched upward in a low, deafening roar. Every house in front of us caught fire.

"Well, we're not going *that* way!" von Braun shouted in my ear.

"Deal!" I shouted back. "I think Engineering Fifteen is *this* way from here, anyway!"

It's not a great place to be lost. We were out beyond the permanent buildings and in the free-floating shanty-town that surrounds so many Third World cities; at least the area wasn't a target for the cruise missiles now pounding the main citadel, but on the other hand much more of what was around here was flammable. Already the streets were beginning to jam up with people seeking to flee, but on that densely settled island, with no real cover except in the fortresses, there was so little place to flee to that only those who were burned out were sure they wanted to run.

Many simply came out in the street and stood around; the bombardment wasn't happening right here, by and large, and they desperately needed to know what was happening.

I caught a glimpse of one radar tower and of the

stump of one of the prewar office buildings, and now I knew where we were. Holding hands like scared kids or lovers in the rain, we rushed on toward Engineering Fifteen, taking any route we could, crashing through water-filled potholes, switching to one side or another to avoid blazing buildings.

The fire and smoke were getting thicker—later I realized that some of the cruise missiles had passed over the poor parts of the city spraying hundreds of pencil-sized incendiary submunitions, starting fires everywhere at once, overwhelming the fire crews, starting pathetic columns of refugees fleeing in all directions to block up the roads.

For a short distance we made good time following behind a militia unit that was trying to get formed up and get to its station, but after that we had to fight our way across a pile of stalled carts in a little public square. We had just made it across when we heard the Dopplered rising roar of incoming jets.

The fighters screamed in over the square, little high-speed Gatling guns on their wingtips spraying death into the unarmed crowd; as each peeled off, it let loose a bomb.

I knew before they hit what they would be, and von Braun clearly did, too, for both of us piled up against the wall. There was a hideous thud, and the jellied gasoline—napalm—sprayed into the crowd, sticking and burning wherever it went. People on fire ran in all directions, and no one fought the hundred fires that sprang up all around. From the next block we could hear the rattle of automatic rifles as the militia company tried to put up any kind of opposing fire.

"This is no raid," von Braun said. "They are going to invade. This must be what Glenn saw from orbit. Dear God, where is that man going to land?"

We fought onward through the crowded streets, struggling through panicked crowds. Twice more fighters roared in at low altitude, wreaking whatever havoc they could. There were bodies in the streets now, and the sky that had been a perfect soft blue, just an hour ago when we were off to launch a man into orbit, was now black and gray from the smoke, tinged pink underneath with the blazing fires.

But Singapore had evolved. We were in the bad part of town, and the poor were stuck, but the fortress, after having changed hands six times in twenty years, had been rebuilt and rebuilt until it was awesomely tough. As we reached the perimeter we found well-organized authorities getting people under cover, moving the frantic refugee convoys into the safety of the special tunnels, giving first aid, tagging lost children to make sure they could be matched up with their frantic parents.

There was very little panic, if any. We showed our priority badges and were given access to one of the covered tramways; in no time at all we were back at Engineering Fifteen, far inside the complex.

Bombs were falling now, and cruise missiles were still hitting, but there is something about a yard of concrete between you and a bomb that makes the bomb so much less upsetting. "You think it's really an invasion?" I asked von Braun. "Could they have made it all the way here from India—right down the coast of Sumatra—without getting spotted?"

He shrugged. "There are many ways here. But if it's not an invasion, it's a terribly big raid. German bombers out of Japan couldn't have run the radar fence, and the fleet couldn't have come from India—and those were carrier fighters—the most likely thing is that they slipped up here out of western Australia and the carriers are over on the other side of Sumatra. And these improved cruise missiles worry me. The Nazis haven't improved *anything* since they won the war. If they're getting the research habit again, and they keep it, they could bury us—they have a hundred times our facilities."

I doubted very much that they were doing research; I suspected the Closers had merely gotten impatient and slipped them some technical improvements. But since von Braun did not know of my background, this hardly seemed the time to explain it to him.

Besides, if the Closers got serious about technical aid to the Nazis, then we would probably get buried anyway.

The tram had dropped us off at the concrete blockhouse that covered the entrance to our area; a lull in bomb hits let us chance a run to the main building. As I came in, several of my Malay and Thai employees saluted smartly, and the sergeant of the guard came up to me in haste. "Sir—we've had one attack by agents trying to penetrate the compound, and we're cut off from the metallurgy building and mission control. We've heard shooting, but we can't get out that side of the building; I've got a team that's going to try to go around and get behind them—"

"Damn good," I said. "We'll go with your plan—carry on. I'll join your sortie party."

He gave me the biggest salute I'd ever seen in my life and started hollering orders. I jumped in with the ten men who were going to go around; the plan was to use one firefighting access tunnel that we had to get to a small instrument shack, then try to burst out of the shack and get to the back side of the metallurgy building. The trouble with it, other than an exposed run of about sixty yards, was that it would put us right between metallurgy and mission control—and we knew for sure the enemy was in the metallurgy building.

If they were in mission control as well, we were dead. But there had been a lot of our people in mission control, and nobody in the Free Zone ever went anywhere without at least a sidearm, and many people habitually carried a rifle or a carbine. So there was an excellent chance that mission control was out of touch but still with our side, and if we could get them to sortie—

It was worth a shot. Right now anything was worth a shot, actually.

We raced down the tunnel at a breakneck pace; I was in the middle of the party, not wanting to disturb my assistant's plans by joining the van or rear guard. Everything would depend on speed—

I hit the concrete steps under the instrument shack and leaped up them—and almost fell over the body of one of my men. I jumped to the side, went prone, cursed the fact that all I had was my .45 and the shots were coming from—

Plenty close enough. I realized I was looking into the legs of a group of Nazi paratroopers charging the shack. I fired at them, upward, through the instrument shack door, which was propped open by the corpse of the lead man, who lay in the doorway. There were just two of us alive, besides me, and only one other man fit to hold a gun.

Praise god our team leader, Prasad, was the next one through and had three vital things: a tommy gun, good luck not to get hit right off, and lots of presence of mind. The enemy were totally out of cover and virtually at point-blank range, so he got virtually all of their rush in one long burst. Prasad emptied the drum mag at them, and that gave everyone else a chance to get up there and start laying down fire. The enemy fell back to the alley between the metallurgy building and mission control.

It was then that I got a clear look at the side of mission control, and if I hadn't already thrown up from that ride on the dirigible, I would have had to now. They had dragged out everyone in mission control, put them up against the wall of the building, and shot them. Black smoke poured from the building.

Between the dead from mission control and the dirigible, our space program was gone, or would be as soon as Glenn landed.

Prasad gave quick, crisp orders; we dropped back into the tunnel, set the time charge on the other side of the door, and ran like hell. We were most of the way back when it blew behind us; we could be pretty sure it had blocked the tunnel, but it would have made us feel better to know that it had taken a few of the enemy with it.

When I got back, von Braun was crouched at the phone. "I've got a patch through from a guy in the control tower, and I'm talking to Major Glenn," he explained. He talked just a little longer, and then groaned, "Okay, fading out, we'll talk again when you come back around."

It looked like the building was being well defended, and there wasn't a lot of need for my attention; nobody was low on ammo yet, and since my whole guard had turned out for the launch, there were about three times as many armed men on our side in the compound as we'd normally have any right to expect.

"Well, then," I said, "what's the news?"

"Well, the one piece of good news—" A bomb blew somewhere near the roof, but not on it, and though the building shook, it held. We both heaved sighs, and von Braun went on. "Glenn was able to spot their fleet from orbit. They're over on the other side of Sumatra, just as you guessed, down by the Barisan Mountains in fact, where the Coast Watch wouldn't have gotten much warning of them. They must have flown in through the canyons and ravines to avoid detection. What they don't know is that we've got a wolf pack on patrol down that way—their carriers will be getting hit within an hour, and the bombers are already on their way from Borneo.

"But the bad news is a lot worse. He saw something in Florida as he passed over. There's a cape somewhere along the north coast—"

"Canaveral?" I asked.

"That's the one. Strange name—can't imagine anyone would ever work there, but it is a perfect launch site if you're going to go out across the Atlantic. And that's just what they're doing. They've got a launch facility there—looks like they have big multistage rockets. Perhaps from a career advancement standpoint I should have stayed at Peenemünde.

"Glenn saw one of their rockets take off as he was going over; the plume is unmistakable from orbit. And his radar now tells him he's got a little shadow. They're closing in on him; if he turns around and uses his engines to brake, he's going to have to drop right across their sights. If he doesn't—well, they're in a lower orbit. That means they move faster than he does. They're going to pass under him soon, and anything they shoot upward will come right into his path . . . and since orbital velocities are in thousands of miles per hour—"

I whistled. "They could bring him down with a brick."

"Exactly," von Braun said. "Could and possibly will.

He's going to keep relaying intelligence to us as long as he can, and then take his chances with them; he said something about 'every fighter pilot knows there's one way to be sure you don't miss.'" I shuddered; von Braun looked at me curiously. "This disturbs you?"

"You bet it does. I think he'll try to ram them. Which is good as far as it goes, but I suspect they've got more than one ship, and we don't."

We never heard from John Glenn again. After the war we found out the Germans had in fact lost the capsule that flew pursuit on that mission, but didn't know how or why. I like to think it's because he didn't miss.

There wasn't any chance to talk about any of that anyway; I heard a shout from Singh, my sergeant, and ran to see what he was pointing to. There were at least a hundred paratroopers coming down. "Not an invasion but a raid in force," I said to von Braun. I told him what I had seen from the instrument shack, and had to wait a minute for him to calm down after the string of oaths poured out of him. Some of those people were ones he had lied to get out of death camp, taken with him in his flight, done everything possible to save—and now they were gone.

The paratroopers were hitting the ground before I got von Braun calmed down enough. I turned to Singh, and said, "This is hopeless. They aren't after your men, and you can't save whatever survivors we have here. *Sauve qui peut*, man, that's all we can do."

Singh shrugged. "It's not a bad way to die. My family will hear of it soon. But those of my men who wish to flee, none of us will stand in their way. You, Captain, you've got to run for it, and you as well, Dr. von Braun. And I do think we can give you a few minute's start if you can grab or destroy anything that shouldn't fall into their hands."

Swift, silent, and grim as death, the paratroopers—close enough now to see the SS thunderbolts on their uniforms—were closing in on the building. Von Braun laughed. "Chances are they are ahead of me, but I'll go do what I can." He was off at a run toward the front part of the building, where his office was.

I thought I had nothing, then realized. The SHAKK. Just because I had not been able to figure out how, or rather with what, to reload it, didn't mean that the Nazis wouldn't. Moreover, I had no idea whether the SHAKK was a common technology between ATN and the Closers, or whether it might be something bad to have them capture.

I pounded down the hall to the office, grabbed the SHAKK, stuffed it into my shirt, and turned around to find myself facing a small, cruel-looking man who had a Luger leveled at my chest. "What is that?" he asked.

"Uh, cereal box prize," I explained. "My favorite toy when I was a kid. I didn't want to leave it behind. After you . . . um, you know, *do* me, could you leave it on my body so maybe it will get buried with me? It's got to be the last real Flash Gordon Ray Gun on earth, and . . . well, I just really loved it. As I guess you can see from the way I ran back here."

He seemed totally unconvinced, and extended his hand to take it—just before he fell forward. He hit the floor, quite dead, and blood spread out from under him.

General LeMay stepped into the room, putting his service .38 back into its shoulder holster. His clothes were burned and he was sooty, but he seemed all right otherwise. "Von Braun said you'd be down here; figured when I saw the gent headed this way maybe I should see what was keeping you."

"Thanks," I said, and followed him out the door. We

rushed back up the hall toward where I had left von Braun.

"Singh has a line of retreat opened up, and we've got an autogyro we can make a run in, if you're game."

"It beats staying here and getting shot," I said. By that time we were headed down the steps.

"Yeah, my way of looking at it, too," LeMay agreed.

After all the trouble leading up to it, getting out was ridiculously simple—Singh and his men covered our retreat, we ran to a hangar, and there was an eight-passenger autogyro warmed up and waiting to go. We kicked the doors open, opened a gate onto a service road, got in, started her up, and rolled down the service road to get space for a takeoff.

Autogyros are one of those things that never took off in our timeline and probably wouldn't have in theirs, except that the Free Zone couldn't do much research and the Axis didn't. Basically it's an airplane with a freely rotating wing—the wing turns like a windmill, or like helicopter blades, just from the forward motion of the aircraft. It isn't as versatile as a helicopter, but it's a lot easier to make it work, since you only need to put the rotor blade on a pivot and use a regular piston-prop engine up front. It can't hover, it won't fly backward, and it has a distressing tendency to bounce as it lands, but it will take off from a short runway, and the fuel economy's okay.

Shortly we were airborne and headed out away from the city, across the island, and on up across the South China Sea to Saigon. As we got farther away, I looked back; a great pillar of black smoke, lit by the sudden flares of storage tanks and ammo dumps blowing, towered over us, but in a few minutes, we were out over the South China Sea, the fire of blazing Singapore was not the whole of that side of the sky, and we were no longer under that black cloud. The sun came out, the sky was blue—

It was the same day on which we had launched John Glenn to orbit. I didn't know it yet, but probably he was already dead, and when I found out he had not reported in, I was hardly surprised. The whole catastrophe had taken less than a full afternoon, and the future looked miserably bad.

14

If it looked bad for me, I couldn't imagine how it looked for von Braun. To have lost the physical facility was one thing, but between the deaths on the dirigible—LeMay, like us, had thought he was the only survivor—and the massacre of technicians, Engineering Fifteen was dead for good. They had delivered rocket engines to several other projects of one sort or another, but the effort to get into space was going to be over for a long time.

LeMay's escape had required both more guts and luck than ours; he had clung to the railing until the last moment, then jumped onto a corrugated iron roof, falling about ten feet, causing the roof to bow in and deposit him in an empty house, the residents apparently just fled.

He had seen the end of the launch stages because he had been down nearer the harbor; the dirigible had scraped off its now-burning gondola onto a warehouse roof. The gondola fell into a street with a sickening smash and the fuel in the auxiliary tanks blew; he doubted anyone had survived, though you could never tell.

Freed of so much mass, the gasbag and keel structure had leaped up into the air, in flames, rolling over, and blown completely with a great roar, the burning wreckage falling back into the dockyards. "Did 'em more good than twenty bombers could have," he said.

All this time, as we talked, we were whirring up the coastline of the Malay Peninsula; there was a fuel depot at Songhkla, and if we could gas up there, we could make Saigon in the early evening. We had no way of knowing whether or not Singapore would be taken—I still thought it was a raid, von Braun still suspected it was the lead force for an invasion—but at least, for the moment, von Braun and LeMay wouldn't be captured.

I was not feeling particularly good about my performance as chief of security, though both of them pointed out that what I was supposed to do was defend against the occasional infiltrator or assassin, not against a fully armed military assault.

There was really nothing for von Braun or me to do except watch LeMay fly, and though autogyros are interesting gadgets technically, riding in them is not necessarily any more amusing than riding in any other aircraft. We sat down, and I pulled out the SHAKK to have a look at it.

That meant telling von Braun and LeMay my story—which didn't seem like a big deal since their clearance was higher than mine—and showing von Braun the chip in my neck. He nodded for a moment, then he said, "I have a thought, if you'd like."

I said sure; he took the SHAKK carefully, opened the reloading drawer, pulled out some change from his pocket, dropped it into the drawer, and closed it. The message changed instantly.

"What's it say now?" he asked me.

I looked at the display, which was now scrolling a long message horizontally, and read "'MORE RELOAD NEEDED. COPPER 35%, ZINC 12%, IRON 0%, SILVER 87%, CARBON 0%, SILICON 0%, RARE EARTHS 0%.' Well, you made it do something, but I don't know what."

"Read the numbers to me again," he said, taking out a pad and writing them down carefully. He reopened the drawer, and his change was gone. Then he rummaged in his pockets for change and started counting around in it, finally finding four copper pennies. "These are all prewar, should be all copper, right?" He set them in the SHAKK's drawer and slid the drawer home again. "Now read."

I did again. "'MORE RELOAD NEEDED. COPPER 42%, ZINC 12%, IRON 0%, SILVER 87%, CARBON 0%, SILICON 0%, RARE EARTHS 0%.' I don't see—oh, wait, it's like the Minimum Daily Requirement on a cereal box! I mean—well, never mind. It's telling us how much it has of each thing it needs!"

Some random screws from the tool kit brought iron up above zero; slivers of a broken drinking glass (we found it under a seat, apparently some VIP had had it along) got us the silicon. The carbon and some of the rare earths came from my handkerchief and the back cardboard of von Braun's notebook. LeMay cheerfully informed us we were crazy and pointed out that modern explosive powders tended to contain some rare metals; I slid in a whole clip for the .45, and it digested that, and one odd-looking pair of pliers from the tool kit, and then . . .

I looked at the message. "MORE RELOAD POSSIBLE. ROUNDS: 23."

"Gun port to your left," LeMay said. "Let's try it out."

The gun port was really made for a man with a rifle or submachine gun, but I shoved the SHAKK up against it, set it for a hex burst, and watched as LeMay brought us down to treetop level over a deserted beach. We flew low and slow as I picked out a particular palm tree, squeezed the trigger—and heard the wonderful sound of a SHAKK burst going out. The palm tree burst into splinters halfway up and fell over.

"How did you know that would work?" I asked von Braun. "Obviously when I get back on the ground all I have to do is shovel a bunch of junk into it, and it makes its own ammo."

Von Braun nodded. "Well, I didn't know that it would work at all, but I thought about the guy who must have designed it, and the people you said would carry it. They clearly could not all go back to reload every time, so they must be carrying spare ammunition—but that wasn't true. So it seemed to me that powder had to be something commonly available, but if as you say ATN operates in places where there is no technological civilization, it couldn't be anything you had to make—and yet from your description it wasn't a natural material either. So if it wasn't the finished product and it wasn't the natural source—it must be a raw material. And then it occurred to me that a gun you can reload by putting rocks and metal scrap into it would be a very useful thing indeed for one of these Special Agents or Time Scouts you were describing. At that point I had an idea to try, so I tried it."

It made sense to me when it was explained; I wondered why I hadn't thought of it. I consoled myself with the fact that I was not, after all—and here I almost laughed out loud—a rocket scientist, and, besides, art historians use a lot of scientific gadgets but we don't exactly do experiments—no matter what you feed a rat he won't start drawing in perspective.

The fuel dump at Songhkla was able to take care of us quickly; we were flying out over the water as the sun went down behind us, and before midnight the sparkling city of Saigon glowed beneath us. We had reached the command by radio, and they were expecting us.

That night was spent answering questions for the intelligence guys, over and over and over, while they took more and more notes. It was irritating, but I saw the point when I learned that the forces landing on Singapore had hit every active weapons project, bypassing all the fake "Engineering" sections that had skeleton crews and empty buildings.

"I don't honestly think they cared about anything other than getting your group," said the tall, thin, balding man with the Russian accent. "I think they didn't mind hitting some of the others, but that was a cover. By far the largest force hit Engineering Fifteen, at exactly the time when they could kill the most personnel and destroy the most material. They wanted us shut down in that area. I think there is no question."

Von Braun groaned in frustration. "Don't you see it? Don't you see it?"

The man leaned forward. "Tell me."

"They have space launch themselves already. That means they can look down on everything we do, and they can target accurately and at will. There are half a dozen sites I can name, and I'm sure a hundred that I don't know about, that are potentially their targets. They hit the facility at Singapore because they already knew it was there—and they know where everything else is. In a dozen raids or so they can destroy whatever hope we have of besting them; after that they can slowly pound apart our means of making modern war. We may linger on in the jungles for another ten years, but our real threat to them is over."

"Not quite over," the tall man said. "We will see what we can do."

We had been up all night, and we were pretty frustrated; I didn't know what we could do about anything right now, and when I went to bed, to sleep through most of the next day, I had bad dreams and thrashed around a lot.

The next couple of days were dull in another way; when the intelligence guys weren't asking me just one more time to see if maybe I remembered something this time that I never had before, I was being processed in the great paperwork swamp that had built up in Saigon. A security chief whose facility has been destroyed doesn't have a job, and since I didn't have the position, the one thing I really wanted to know— whether Singh and Prasad and the rest of them had come through, how many killed and wounded we'd taken—was now classified information that they could not tell me.

That meant floating from desk to desk a lot, and quite possibly getting myself written up as an obsessive nut who was a security risk since he seemed to want to know classified information. I wasn't doing my prospects for another posting any good, but I had to know.

Three days later, as I was walking along one of the broad boulevards, trying to enjoy the sunshine and the feeling of safety that Saigon gave me in those days, and not succeeding because I had just been trapped between two petty clerks who each thought I should have talked to the other one first, I heard a voice behind me say, "Hey, kid, you still a straight shot with a .45?"

It was Patton, big as life (which was pretty big) and striding out of the crowd to say hello. Before I knew it I was off to eat with him and his staff; he knew all about the disaster in Singapore, and, being the kind of generous and effective leader he was, suspected that I might be blaming myself.

As a result, I got to tell him about my frustrations, and in only the time it took him to bellow into a dozen phones, I had the answers I wanted—Singh and Prasad were all right, we had lost seven guards to death and two were missing, and there were about a dozen wounded, none on the critical list anymore.

It wasn't great news, but it was news.

After that he wanted to talk about my next posting; I had not been thinking that far ahead, since my present occupation seemed to consist of talking to intelligence types. He made a couple more calls, then said, "You know, Strang, you might have told me that a little force of auxiliary security guards you trained held off an SS paratroop force three times their size. It's hard to help a man who won't blow his own horn! I'm just going to have a little chat with old Giap—I have a feeling he's apt to have a use for you. And no more hiding your light under a bushel!"

I had just about enough time to thank him for straightening the mess out for me, and for lunch, before he and his three junior officers were piling into his jeep to race away. "Mims," he said—I was not to hear his voice again for a while—"I do believe we are late at the airport, and I think in all likelihood that Monty will be angry and will stamp his little footie and pout about it. Shall we thank the gentleman for helping us be late?"

Sergeant Mims, the driver who had been with Patton through all of the years, right from the start of the AEF, turned around and grinned at me. "Sir, you couldn't have known, but taking care of your problems has made the general late. This is going to make Field Marshal Montgomery very angry. So thank you for making General Patton's day!"

They roared away; the captain and lieutenant riding in the back waved a little sheepishly. I suppose they were used to this sort of thing but could never be sure who else might or might not be.

Two days later I received orders and space-a pass to take me up to Hanoi for a meeting with General Giap the next week. I wrote a thank-you note to Patton—and I *never* write thank-you notes, Mom always had a terrible time with me about that—packed my single suitcase, squared my bill at the *pension* I was staying in, and caught the next bus to the airport.

When I arrived at General Giap's office, he was just finishing up some sort of staff briefing, so I had to cool my heels outside a bit. There were a number of delicate little watercolors on the wall, quite good in the Annamese and Hmong traditions, and I studied them carefully, letting the analytic process shut off more worrisome matters for the time being.

"I sometimes wonder—does our art say anything to an outsider?" Giap asked, behind me.

"It might not say what you intend it to, but it does say something," I said. "It's a way of seeing the world, and it's interesting to see other people's ways of seeing."

He nodded, as if I had said something profound, and showed me into his office. "What I am about to tell you," he said, "is a matter of highest confidence. To be honest about it, we are giving you this post not so much because we think you can do it—we think perhaps no one can do it—but because you did rather well in a hopeless situation. General Patton was impressed with how you had trained your men; I was impressed with the fact that you actually managed a counterattack, even if an unsuccessful one.

"What we have for you to do is to guard our last possible key to victory. We will have to depend on you to be resourceful; your job, if you are willing to take it, is to think of every possible way some enemy might try to knock out the facility, and to make sure that way is blocked. Technically you will be a staff officer under General Minh, but he intends to give you a fair amount of autonomy and ability to command resources.

"What you will be guarding is the facility designed to give the Axis its death blow. The code name for the place is Engineering Forty-six. You will see one familiar face there—Dr. von Braun has accepted a position.

"As you know, we've made considerable use of nuclear energy here since the Free Zone was established. In fact we've even tested a couple of atomic bombs in underground caverns, using their neutron production to make more plutonium.

"The information you brought has allowed Dr. Teller to make a more powerful kind of bomb, the 'fusion' or 'hydrogen' bomb. How it works, I have no idea. But they say it will. And we have enough rocket motors left so that Dr. von Braun has been able to assure us he can build enough missiles to deliver two dozen of these superbombs to anywhere in the world we select.

"When those missiles fly, our forces will attempt to break out of this hellish pocket in which we have been cornered for a decade. We know we can count on uprisings around the world, and what we hope to do is to catch the Nazis with their leadership cut off, local forces paralyzed by indecision, and supply lines in complete disarray. They were never really able to occupy all the vast territory they control, especially since they decided to allocate very little of it to their French, Spanish, Italian, and Japanese allies; this is why they had to leave your country in charge of its home-grown Nazis after so brief a Reconstruction. In many, many places the underground is ready to break out and take over, so long as the local fascists cannot get support from the Luftwaffe and from the world headquarters. And once these missiles hit, they will not be able to.

"We have only a very limited amount of time. The rockets are being set up and the bombs hauled out to them as quickly as we can go. The raid on Singapore has shown us that the Nazis know we are up to something which could bring them down; and with these artificial moons of theirs, despite our best efforts, they will undoubtedly know all about what we are up to within a short while. We are getting as much air cover as possible for the area where you will be working, but we have to be alert for a possible ground attack, and, of course, we are critically short of radar capabilities—so although we can spot a high-level bombing run, airborne commandos might well get through.

"Your mission, Mr. Strang, is to make sure that nothing whatsoever happens to the missile field."

"Glad to be of service," I said.

"Understand, no one can tell you where or how the threat will come."

"That's usual in my line of work."

"I knew you would say that." He stood up; I was always startled when he did that, for he was a small, physically slight man, but his dignity and intelligence, and his fierce approach to everything, tended to make you forget that until you were standing right next to him. He smiled slightly. "And I do hope that you and I will meet again when the world is at peace. I had always hoped to be a professor of history, you know—circumstances dictated otherwise. I should like to hear what you think of my paintings sometime, over sherry in a faculty club somewhere, where the most serious violence is on the soccer field."

I shook his hand, bowed, and agreed. It had taken a very short time, and I was eager to get on with the mission. "Can you tell me, or should I wait to find out, just where this missile field is going to be?"

"I think we can safely tell you. It's in a little place you've never heard of, a provincial town north and west of here, called Dien Bien Phu."

General Minh was a big, easy guy with a big, hard job. He was happy to turn me loose on it. The next week, the only break I took was a brief dinner one night with von Braun. He wanted to know what had happened to the security forces at Singapore, just as I had, and I got from him the accounting of whom we had lost at mission control—I couldn't quite imagine that the whole Philly Navy Yard crew was gone, but they were.

I spent much of the time just walking the ground. The village of Dien Bien Phu itself had had about a thousand people before the war, but it had swollen to six times that size with crews and technicians. They were hiding as much as they could from the air (and though few of them knew it, from space), but there was no concealing the fact that Provincial Highway 41, which had been a good-weather gravel track, was now a four-lane highway. Nor, really, could the launchpads sprouting like mushrooms up in the hills be entirely concealed, though the control bunkers were at least hidden under what looked like houses from the air.

Everyone knew we would be better off putting the

missiles into silos, because freestanding as they were they could be blown over by a bomb a hundred yards away from them, and if they tipped over, the damage would put an end to their usefulness. But everyone knew we didn't have the time, the resources, even the concrete, to put them in silos. So we just kept our fingers crossed; it was all we could do.

Or almost all. The other thing I did was walk around with a French major, a guy named Bigeard, who had managed to make it to Britain and traveled all the way here with Patton. Or possibly with God. I wasn't sure Bigeard could tell the difference.

He'd been a paratrooper, made the landings behind the German lines that had slowed them down at York to allow the AEF to escape, jumped again at Cumberland, Maryland, and Petersburg, Virginia, in the spearheads of other failed counterattacks. He'd made about ten more jumps in various raids.

"No question," he told me. "There are only four decent places to jump into here. The SS might be crazy enough, you know, to jump somewhere else, but they will be no better off for it if they do. The airfield, the land across the ditch from the airfield, or along the Nam Yum below the town, up on the flatland above the river on either the west or east side. That's all. If they cannot land there, they cannot land at all."

There were a lot of kids in the village, and nobody had time to run a school, so I put the kids to stringing barbed wire around in the bushes in the drop zones, to digging pits and setting pungee sticks, and, where possible, to digging deeper holes that could be expected to flood. I did nothing to hide this from the satellites; I wanted them to think about it a lot.

That left me two holes in the defense; I couldn't very well dig pits in the airfield, but I got a bunch of proficient snipers trained to cover it. At least there was always plenty of small-arms ammunition, and we had enough people from the Himalayan fringe to ensure us all the sharpshooters we could want. I could make them very sorry they landed there, make it impossible to set up the artillery, and the airfield was away from the launching pads by some margin.

Part of the problem I was facing, too, was that if they came in overland, infiltrating from some more distant landing site (our radar fence just wasn't good enough to cover against that possibility), I needed to have patrols out, but if they landed in the middle, I needed forces concentrated. Moreover, I had to figure the enemy were likely to all be half-crazed, since there was no way they could expect to be extracted once they hit the ground, and thus this was a one-way trip to prison or the grave for them.

At dinner with von Braun, I was talking about all of this. He had kind of an abstract, distant stare, and then suddenly he said, "Did you ever continue our experiment with the SHAKK?"

"Gee, no," I said, feeling stupid because of course it was a far better weapon than the Colt automatic I was still lugging around.

"There's something I'd very much like to see about it. If it's in your quarters, do you suppose we could conduct an experiment or two more before we call it a night?"

"Happy to oblige." We got the SHAKK from my bunk, and then went back to the Materials Science Lab.

This was a much better place to work than the back of an autogyro; we were even able to figure out just what the rare earths *were*, and soon we had all the percentages moving up toward 100.

"Now let me try my experiment," he said.

Although copper was already at 100 percent, the next thing he put in the drawer was a coil of pure copper wire. There was a brief humming noise, and from the base of the grip—where the magazine slid in on my .45—a tube extended, and pellets of copper dribbled out. When the copper stopped coming, the tube slid back into place, and a cover slid across it.

"Amazing," he said. "You realize that to reshape it that way takes a lot of energy—and yet the SHAKK isn't warm anywhere, which means it somehow put out all the energy it needed without producing any waste heat at all. Now watch closely . . . next trick . . . "

This time it was copper sulfate with which he filled the drawer. Again the tube extended, and this time it spit out pellets of sulfur, followed by pellets of copper. "I suppose the oxygen in the sulfate just goes out to the air," he said quietly. "It's a large favor, but could I possibly borrow this for—oh, a week at most? I can't promise it will be unharmed, but I'm not planning to do anything to harm it."

I agreed, he borrowed it, the next week he brought it back, and that was as much thought as I gave it. At the time Bigeard and I were busy with figuring out where to dig holes.

It did occur to me that evening to try a few experiments of my own. I discovered that plain dirt, some local stone, fistfuls of hardware, and a bit of charcoal seemed to be a workable mixture; there were excesses of a few things that rolled out the tube. Then I got curious about what the drawer next to the "firing chamber"—if this thing had a firing chamber—might do, so I opened that up.

There were tiny transparent pellets in there, smaller than BB shot and looking like nothing so much as cheap caviar. They were arranged in neat rows. I touched one gingerly and it rolled onto my hand; it felt light there. I could see what appeared to be nozzles on every surface, and the inside had a strange, complicated pattern, visible by holding it up to the light, that resembled nothing so much as a microscope photo of a nerve cell.

The drawer had been empty before; I figured this must be the ammo.

I tried to return it to its place, but it wouldn't stick; a thought hit me and I pulled out a bunch more of them, closed the ammo drawer, and checked; sure enough, it said it was "93% loaded" rather than the 100 percent it had been before.

Then I took the extra shot and fed it into the raw materials hopper; in just an instant, the SHAKK display changed back to 100 percent. Now I understood what the loading powder Harry Skena had used had been—it was just the right chemical mix to produce shot without any waste. And I also knew how I could store up a lot more than the two thousand rounds the contraption held in ready. All I had to do was make pellets, in quantity, and have a few buckets of them handy. It was so simple that I did it that night; from then on I had four galvanized iron buckets of SHAKK shot always in my office.

A few experiments showed the SHAKK shots would go right through the system to become usable as ammunition again in a second or less, even while the SHAKK was also firing full auto. (Ever try to find a good backstop for hypersonic ammunition that likes to loop around inside whatever it hits? I finally found that an empty, rusted water tank filled with sand worked pretty well.) That meant, I estimated, that me and my four buckets had just over 300,000 rounds available.

I was pretty sure that if I could get to a good place

with those buckets fast enough, I could make hash out of anything coming in. The trouble was, the outer range on the SHAKK was about six miles, and that didn't allow me to cover all the drop zones, quite, let alone all the launchpads and control bunkers. So I rigged up a centrally located tower that would give me a clear view of as much as I *could* cover, and kept my kids digging holes and stringing wire. (One clever little bastard who was good at catching poisonous snakes started "farming" them in the holes of one drop zone—I figured that ought to surprise the occasional SS man.)

The day the tower was done, I decided to move my buckets of spare ammo up there, and some impulse or other made me fill up two more. I now had 450,000 rounds, give or take, for the SHAKK. I couldn't be sure it would be enough, but any more would start to take up floor space I had to have on my "flagpole," as General Minh dubbed it.

He had his own hassles—a series of long-range patrols in the back country had run into occasional Japanese infiltration, and although we had the advantage of having the peasants mostly on our side, we still had to get men out there to catch the bastards, and in operations at that distance it wasn't easy.

It turned into sort of a party, for Bigeard showed up with wine, and then of all people von Braun dropped by. Minh's patrols had reported some success, so his mood was a bit better than usual; Bigeard had been given some secret mission he was ecstatic about; I had my tower, and von Braun was all but glowing.

"I do wish I could tell you," he said. "Oh, god, how I wish I could tell you. By late tonight you'll know anyway. And in an odd way, Mr. Strang, we owe a lot of it to you. It will all be much clearer when—"

There was a roar and rattle of trucks approaching the village on Highway 41; it sounded like as many as a hundred. Von Braun raised his glass, drained it, and said, "Gentlemen, when next we speak—well, you'll find out!"

It occurred to me as he dashed away, that blue-eyed blond muscular German, that he looked like every stereotypical Aryan in every Nazi poster. His sense of humor, though, was pure twelve-year-old; what do you expect from a man who wants to go to Mars, the basic dream of so many twelve-year-old boys? I suppose it was a lesson about judging by appearances . . .

The truck convoy swung immediately into the secure compound, the area south of the village where the top secret work was done, mostly in underground bunkers. Men were running there from all over, so whatever this was, it was big.

Bigeard sighed. "Not that this is particularly fine wine, you understand, but it's the last of the Australian, and there are no good places left for grapes in the Free Zone. I suppose I shall have to kill it all myself—"

"Happy to help you," I said, and Minh smiled and extended his glass.

"I hate to see a party break up too soon," Bigeard said. We all toasted the afternoon, the minor successes of the day, and the fact that there was still some hope in the world.

There was so much commotion from the secure compound that at first I didn't realize a distant siren had sounded; by the time I was scrambling to my feet, there were sirens everywhere. Minh was on his feet, hollering for his jeep and driver, and an instant later Bigeard was forming up his battalion to get a perimeter thrown around the secure compound. The raid we were waiting for had come.

15

I *climbed my tower*, SHAKK in hand, and phoned central radar.

"What's up?"

"Planes coming in low from the north. Lot of big ones. Bombers or transports. Air Def Com says they've got fighters on the way." He hung up; I don't think he'd heard my question, I think he just knew that the answer would be the same for everyone.

I lifted my binoculars and looked; it was a minute or so, and then tiny dots swam in over the mountains.

I got the SHAKK into my hand while I watched, and the planes swept down toward the village. It was still too soon to tell bombers from transports—the Germans tended to use the same body shape for either—but it seemed odd for an attack to be led by big, slow planes unless it was paratroops.

It was. As soon as the first one was in range, I gave him four hex bursts, moved to the next one, moved to the next one, but now there were more than a hundred coming, and I couldn't sight or pull the trigger that fast. Dimly, I was aware that the ones I had shot had started to fall out of the sky, wings and engines dropping off, troops blocked by their mates trying to get out the door with their chutes. The first transport hit hard enough to blow her fuel tanks, and in the last fifty feet or so she dropped three paratroopers with no room for chutes to deploy; they hit the dirt and lay still, streams of silk billowing behind them.

I looked away in haste. The sky was beginning to fill with chutes, and I carefully swung the SHAKK from body to body under them, squeezing the trigger precisely each time. High above, the bodies pitched hard once as their brains were torn to pieces, and then hung still on the end of the line.

I could work the SHAKK fast enough to keep up with this wave, but not fast enough to hit the planes, too. I crouched, grabbed a fistful of shot, popped the drawer on the SHAKK, shoved it in, and was up shooting again; a couple of paratroopers had made it to the ground on the airfield by then, though.

I heard the rattle of rifle fire and knew my sharpshooters would keep them busy; meanwhile I concentrated on getting caught up at hitting them before they touched down.

You would think it would be like pointing your finger, but the reality was that the SHAKK round went exactly where you pointed it. I took to firing short bursts across each paratrooper, which sped the process up, and probably nine out of every ten of them arrived dead. What that must have been like for the ones who were alive on the ground is something I avoid thinking about.

Not that I'm squeamish. Whatever compassion I ever had was cut out of my heart by Blade of the Most

Merciful; I had never made a secret of the fact that my favorite thing about being a bodyguard was having a license to hurt people and a good excuse for it as well. But even I, when I think of a man finding himself landing in a firefight, in a tangle of pits and wire that he can't safely move in, trying to make his way through while the bullets are pecking in at him . . . and finding only his dead buddies, with their heads exploded, shrouded by their chutes . . . well, I have to hope that the sharpshooters at least got them pretty quickly.

The first wave had obviously been intended to secure the airfield and the area north of town; it was just as obviously a failure. What came in next, I assume, was supposed to be close air support for the invading force of corpses laid out in front of us.

That was a lot worse. The jets came in very fast, and I sprayed at them with full auto, but I didn't have much luck—only two of the ten or so augured into the empty fields behind us without releasing their weapons loads. Another let go his bombs and then blew up, which was satisfying only from the standpoint of revenge.

Bombs crashed into the village, and there I was, up on that silly "flagpole"—the shock waves made it bounce around in way that was completely terrifying. I nearly lost my balance, and one bucket of SHAKK shot did fall off.

When I stood back up everything was in chaos—buildings on fire, walls blown down, frantic rescue efforts in progress everywhere, and I could hear more transports coming in.

If they had been intending to drop on the airfield, as the first wave had, they might have taken it then, for the wind was blowing the smoke north and I couldn't see. But their target was the secure compound, and that meant they all passed directly over me as they began their drops. I pointed the SHAKK upward and sprayed two full magazines into the sky; some rounds hit the few paratroopers who were already out the door, most rose harmlessly to a height of more than ten miles and floated back to Earth to become marbles for the next generation of kids, and maybe half of one percent of them found their way into the transports.

But that was what really counted. It helped that the few paratroopers who landed arrived dead, but it helped more that rounds found their way in through the door, or through the fuselage itself, and slaughtered them inside the transports before they could ever step out. It helped that wings fell off, engines sheared away, and the planes themselves disintegrated.

Again, I'm just as glad I know nothing of the experience of anyone who wasn't killed in the air or in the plane, for what it must have been like to be surrounded by all of your suddenly dead friends, in an airplane falling to pieces and catching fire around you—well, if I really knew, I might pity them, and I feel no desire to pity Nazis.

I reloaded again and turned back to fire at the oncoming wave of close air support; this time I was luckier, because I had a slightly longer time to aim, and four ships fell apart on their approach, decorating the hillsides behind me. I tried laying a curtain of fire between the dropping bombs and the village, but there were only two early explosions—and one water buffalo, peaceably watching us humans kill each other, fell dead in the street. I had let my hand jump a bit as I fired.

There was a rattle of rifle fire from the other side of the cloud of smoke that now kept me from seeing what was happening on the airfield and in the northern drop zone. There was nothing for it—I would have to leave the tower and take my chances that there were no more coming in from any other side.

I grabbed the phone and asked for a status report. Fighters were to be there in twenty minutes, which wasn't bad, but we needed them now. There was another wave behind this one, closing in fast at higher altitude.

It didn't necessarily look like the good guys were going to win. I jumped down the ladder, one bucket of SHAKK ammo still in my fist, and ran through the village—most of the civilians and dependents had headed straight down into the shelters at the first sign of trouble, but it was still a Vietnamese country village, and so after the first bombs had hit the streets had filled up with panicked chickens, ducks, goats, dogs, and practically everything except water buffalo; they were there, too, but they weren't particularly panicked, just wandering around as if it was too much work to wonder what the noise was all about.

The smoke was thick, sharp, and bitter, for the village was mostly palm and bamboo, and in the dry season there's not much to keep it from turning into tinder. For some reason that made me angrier than ever—the thought of all these people losing everything they owned in the fires—and it seemed to put wings on my feet.

I burst from the smoke to see that there were a hundred of them on the landing field, now, taking cover behind two wrecked Gooney birds. The sharpshooters had them surrounded and were plinking away at them, but the SS men had submachine guns and could spray enough bullets to make our guys keep their heads down, and it was clear they were about to get organized to make a break for it. If they did, the line was thin enough that they might well carry forward into the village.

I leveled the SHAKK at the underside of the nearer DC-3, set it for hex bursts, and began pumping the trigger as fast as I could. In about ten seconds, the plane began to fall apart; first a landing strut fell off, then parts of the fuselage came down, and finally with a great rending crash the whole thing fell into small bits. The SS men behind it tried to run for the cover of the remaining plane, but the conventional fire pouring through the gap got some, and SHAKK rounds eliminated the others. I turned my attention on the other plane, and it, too, went to pieces, but before I had completed the job I was out of ammo. I tossed fistfuls of slugs into the drawer, as I crouched there behind a stone wall at the edge of the field, but the SHAKK did take a second to turn each fistful into ammo.

I had just thrown in the third and final handful when a German leaped over the wall, his submachine gun at ready.

My hand fell onto my Colt, the automatic flicked onto the target, and I turned out to have faster reflexes than he did. I squeezed the trigger four times in all, and the first two rounds went in right above his eyes. He was dead before he hit the ground.

There are things to be said for low-tech, too.

The interruption had given the SHAKK time to get fully ready, so I popped up and hosed down the ten SS men now running directly toward my position; they fell dead on the pavement, and I climbed the wall, hearing more fighter planes coming in.

The fighters were jets, moving very fast at the outside edge of my range, orbiting a perimeter around the village, but I fired a hex burst at each one as it passed by, and I was happy to see that by the time they had circled twice, I, or ground fire, or just the perverse nature of mechanical things, had caused two of them to have engine flameouts and to disappear over the hills trailing smoke.

There was a field telephone nearby and I used it; the man said it looked like the last wave of troop transports in this flight would be coming in on the southern side, probably trying to land below the secure compound. In a way that was good news—the secure compound was well defended and getting more so—but it sounded like I could be most effective in that direction, so I snatched up my bucket of ammo, ran back through the smoke— the village was beginning to get firefighting under way—and stopped for an instant at the tower to throw a few handfuls from the spilled bucket into my still-almost-full one.

I came out of the smoldering village just in time to see them coming over the more distant mountains.

They were not troop transports. The Nazis had taken another big leap in technology, or more likely their Closer masters had done so, and what these things looked like was a sort of distant relative of the B-52. They were coming in fairly low, and not yet in range, but I didn't think I was going to be able to get all of them. Moreover, three of our launchpads were out that way, and if they let loose with their bombs, they would get at least those pads, and probably several more. Even with the SHAKK, I could hurt them, but I could not stop them.

Bursts of heavy firing came from behind me; I ran back to the tower and bellowed questions into the field telephone, but it was nothing to be worried about— merely Bigeard and his troops sweeping the landing field clear of the remaining resistance. The enemy in the northern drop zone were already surrendering.

I dashed back, out of breath, smoke searing my

lungs and making my eyes water, so that when I got into fresh air the first things I had to do were to retch and wipe my eyes.

The bombers were closer still, hanging like metallic vultures above the distant blue-green hills. They would be able to hammer several of the launchpads before I could even get one shot off, and, in fact, if they split up and circled, they could probably get every missile in the valley—and with the missiles, the last hope for this timeline.

Behind me, the gate of the secure compound opened, and the damnedest thing I had ever seen in my life came rolling out. It was a plain old GM truck, of the kind we saw a lot of here, probably shipped to Russia, captured by the Germans, donated to Japan, captured by the Free Zone forces. The engine was hammering away trying to drag the outsized load on its back.

But the truck itself was just a frame of normality around the deep weirdness of what sat on its bed. It might have been half of a "Martian invader" from some old fifties sci-fi flick, or the metal clam-plate top of the Closer tank I had blasted, glued to a lot of old auto parts, or possibly an entire junk sculpture collection rammed together, welded at random points, and placed under an aluminum awning to keep the rain off. Behind it trailed a cable as thick as my waist, winding off a spool ten feet tall. The top had something on it that looked like a telescope poking out of an observatory in an old cartoon, except that there was a dark hole right in the center of the lens.

And just above the dome of it, three radar antennas were spinning madly. It couldn't have looked any screwier if it had had six eggbeaters, a set of Christmas tree lights, and a steam whistle attached to it; it looked like what happens when somebody scrambles all the parts of thirty modeling kits and hands a chimp a tube of glue.

Or two tubes of glue, one of which the chimp sniffs before beginning.

Driving this whole mad contraption, wearing a shabby black suit and pair of sneakers that made him look like he was trying to dress up as a punk rocker and not succeeding, was Dr. Edward Teller. As they reached the end of the cord—that was the only way I could explain that huge thing trailing off the end—Teller braked to a stop, leaped out, and ran around to an instrument panel mounted on the side.

The whirling radar antennas sped up. The dome itself crept about, moved up and down, and a bright light flashed a few times in the muzzle of the "telescope." Then he nodded, appeared to hesitate an instant, and pushed a button.

I've heard thunder up close and been on mountains during thunderstorms. Once in Oman, on a dig by the sea, I got to see a waterspout, and once in Iowa, had to take cover in a ditch when a tornado passed close by. I'd heard more big explosions than I ever wanted to hear again.

This dwarfed them. It was a brief, stuttering roar, over in less than two seconds, but in that short time it made my ears bleed; some of the older land mines around the valley were detonated by the vibrations.

I looked up to see that all seventeen of the bombers had exploded. There was no one part of them that went first—a fuel tank, bomb, or engine—spreading to the rest. Each whole bomber had become so hot on its surface that the air next to it was superheated and flashed outward, which was the first part of the explosion, and the reason why there was such a bright flash of white light first; then the heat, conducted inside in milliseconds, detonated all the explosives, the fuel, the liquids in the hydraulic lines, the lubricants, the plastic seat cushions, creating a yellow-red explosion that swelled into a great, pulsing fireball, which then evaporated into dark smoke and a rain of bits of melted metal and charred cinders.

Dr. Teller's little device fired ten shots per second at ten separate targets, under radar control, so presumably the whole thing took 1.6 seconds for the bomber squadron.

There was a very long pause while the implications sank in. Then all those of us who could see Dr. Teller began to cheer. He got up on the truck, clenched his fists over his head like a prizefighter, and jumped back down.

He walked straight toward me, for some reason or other. His hand was out, and since he extended it to me, I shook it. From the roar that his gadget had made when it fired, I was still a bit deaf, and so was he, so he leaned in close to say, "And we owe this one to you, Mr. Strang. Not to mention that I'm quite confident about the results for me as soon as the Nobel Committee convenes after the war."

"The Nobel . . . owe it to me . . . "

"Of course. You're the one who told me about the whole idea, remember? The lasers of your own world. Once you told me what they did, building one was easier than I thought it would be. The biggest problem was coming up with the device to pump it, and it took me forever to realize that you must do it with nuclear fusion—nothing else would have the power density I needed—and that it couldn't be fusion in a plasma, had to happen in a normal state of matter. Once I got the cold fusion idea doped out—took me the better part of a week, and if I hadn't gotten it last Wednesday I was going to call you and ask you for a hint—"

"Cold fusion?" I said. "This thing runs by cold fusion?"

"The amplifier does," he said. "I still need a huge current surge to start it, which is why I have that silly cord rigged up to the back there. Now, come on, there's no other way a device of this kind could be powered. That's crystal clear from the equations. You said it was coherent light—I know you didn't say coherent light, but that was clearly what you described—and commonplace in your world—"

"I don't think I've ever seen a laser one one-thousandth the power of this," I said, almost whispering. "This is like something . . ." I was going to say "something for SDI," but I suspected it was bigger, and, anyway, the term wouldn't mean anything to him. "This is like something out of science fiction. I mean, I've seen ten-watt and hundred-watt lasers—"

Now he stared at me. "But didn't you say—oh, god, no, you didn't. I've been doing weapons work so long I just assumed that if you couldn't shoot it at someone, no one would build it." He sat down; he looked as dazed as I felt. "The first day back on the *Arizona* I hit on the idea of something that would work like that, but it would be so difficult to make it big enough to use as a weapon that I gave up on that line, especially because when I thought of this other way . . . then you don't have anything like this?"

"We don't have cold fusion, either."

"Good thing I didn't call you for a hint, then," he said. He still looked a little dazed.

He was right, though. The next year when they had reorganized the Nobel Prizes, they gave him three years' worth at a clip, for 1958–60 inclusive. By that time he'd gotten over the shock a bit.

———

When Teller's laser destroyed the oncoming bombers, von Braun's group was only hours away from loading the warheads onto the missiles. I've found that when I describe my feelings to people, they just don't understand, but that night as I watched twenty-four columns of fire rise into the sky, I was only happy. I knew they had equipped them with huge warheads, gratuitously big to, in Churchill's phrase, "make the rubble bounce." In that timeline, Berlin became the site of a crater you could easily see from the moon, and Germany itself a radioactive wasteland for generations after.

Al and I had a sizable argument about that one, though we stayed friends; he just didn't have a bitter, hateful bone in his body when you came right down to it. I figured I had more than enough for two of us. Anyway, there are those who think his "Pillars of Fire" is as good as "The Fall" and "The Gathering of Nations," but I suppose I'm too partisan to see it that way. No ear for poetry, as I've said.

As the missiles tore Nazi Germany from the face of the Earth and the pages of history, the other fascist nations were not spared, either. But Germany took the brunt, and then the major Axis military facilities. Moreover, the Free Zone Forces had hundreds of tactical nukes, and they weren't shy about using them; in a few weeks' time, they had retaken the Philippines, Australia, and New Zealand, driven the Japanese out of China and the Axis puppet regime out of India, and accepted the surrender of the Empire of Japan.

Everywhere people rose against their tormentors. After Buenos Aires vanished in a mushroom cloud, Brazil rose as one nation and struck southward, avenging the wrongs of twenty years; I was privately amused to hear Brazilians blame the Argentines for the destruction of rain forests, and to see Brazil acquire a reputation as a nation of environmental nuts.

Patton's invasion of the United States ranks as a political masterpiece in its execution; his terms were so unrelentingly harsh that most of the quiet Nazis and cryptofascists, the people for whom the occupation and Reconstruction had been excuses to practice the bigotry they had believed in all along, were too frightened to allow the puppet regime in Washington to accept.

I once heard a man in a bar complaining that Patton could have taken the country back without a shot fired—but if he had, the fascists would have been voting in it. I made that point clear to the gentleman by slugging him, and used my political pull to beat the rap.

Instead of trying to mollify the fears of the eighteen million strong American Nazi Party, he provoked them into meeting him head-on. Patton announced he was going to free all the remaining black Americans in the labor camps and give them first choice of land confiscated from the Nazis. He promised that no former Nazi would ever vote, hold office, or own property again.

Then, to tempt them to try their luck, he pledged he would not use nuclear weapons on American soil—and didn't.

It still took him less than a hundred days to trap their army in the desert and tear it to pieces, and the huge losses he inflicted simply meant that any of them with the courage to fight was probably dead. It was swift, brutal, and did the job—it was like him.

Anyway, I voted for him in the first free election. It was a hard choice; I had gotten to like Captain Kennedy, too.

16

The story could have stopped right there. I learned long afterward, from von Braun, that what they had used the SHAKK to do was to chemically separate pluto-nium—they had simply put high-level reactor waste in the drawer, closed it, and let the weapon spit out all the things it didn't want, separately. In a week of this they had obtained many tons of weapons-grade pluto-nium, and that had made the difference.

The Closers who had been in that timeline probably died in Berlin, or were now so far underground we hadn't a prayer of catching them for a few generations. At any rate, they would never want this timeline or any of its descendants to colonize again—too many nukes had gone off. It was about the equivalent of an extra dental X-ray per year, spread around, and well worth it from my viewpoint.

But one day, two years later, I was at a Victory Day celebration—just as I had the year before, I told my class at Yale that I hated having to take time out to go to that thing. They never believed me, and they were right.

Patton had won the election the fall before, and there were more American flags—with stars and not swastikas—than I had ever seen before lining Pennsylvania Avenue. The postwar problems were setting in—everything was either in short supply or needed to be done now—but spirits were up.

I was walking along in the crowd and noticing that attractive women running out to kiss me was more fun than it used to be, when one very attractive woman slipped her arm into mine and said, "Hi, remember me?"

It was Ariadne Lao, the ATN Special Agent.

"I sure do. So you found this timeline again."

"Unhhunh. Where can I meet you to talk with you, say, later in the week?"

I told her my new address, and she quietly wrote it down. "Enjoy the parade—I don't think anyone's earned it more thoroughly." And she vanished into the crowd.

It was three days before she turned up; in that time, I did a lot of thinking but reached no conclusions.

She was dressed like any female colleague would be, in a simple skirt and blouse and sneakers. There was sort of a cultural uproar happening out there, as America rediscovered jazz and everything black, and as fashions stopped being either military or "normal." But it hadn't much hit the campuses yet.

She sat down, let me make and pour coffee for her—one wonderful thing the old Free Zone had had in abundance, and which they were happily exporting to the free USA—and said, "Goodness, where do we start? First of all, I really must apologize for the entire situation—you were supposed to be a local assistant for poor

Citizen Skena and instead you ended up in all of this. For what it's worth, we've given you extended hazardous duty pay that's still piling up for you back in the ATN timeline."

"Do I have to spend it there?"

"You might *want* to—there are many nice things that aren't available in a lot of other timelines—but no, it's fully convertible. You can take it in gold, silver, plutonium, germanium, platinum, or gallium and turn it into the currency of wherever you want to go; in fact we can handle that for you. In your home timeline, converting to platinum and then to dollars, you've got about ten million dollars; in this one, with postwar inflation and so forth, more like a billion."

I gave a low whistle, and I meant it; that was a pretty impressive deal.

"The question," she said, crossing her legs, which were great legs in my opinion, "is what you want to do. Let me explain it to you simply. We don't recruit a lot of people from outside the ATN timeline, and when we do it's generally someone who has been an agent for us inside their own timeline and has a lot of promise, Mr. Strang.

"Your case is truly strange. There are three categories of agents we maintain—the Time Scouts are the ones like Sheila, who go into timelines that have not yet been explored to find out whether there is any Closer presence and any possibility of getting the timeline to join the Alliance. Their skills are mostly at blending in without very many clues as to their surroundings, and then at finding the people closest to the ATN viewpoint.

"Special Agents like Harry Skena go in after Time Scouts have reconnoitered; they go in very well prepared and with specific missions—in Harry's case it was to block Blade and to find out what the Closers were up to in your timeline. They have much greater resources at their disposal, but they only stay a short while to accomplish a particular thing.

"And then there are the ones like me—Crux Ops. We have to be a bit of both, because what we are is Search and Rescue. Every so often a Time Scout or Special Agent runs into bad luck or gets careless—or sometimes is just a little incompetent. When that happens, they disappear and stop signaling. That's when we send in a Crux Op. A Crux Op always has a simple mission, three parts. One, find out what happened to our missing agent. Two, retrieve the agent or, if the agent is dead, retrieve the agent's body. And three, accomplish the agent's original mission.

"Now it occurs to us, in Crux Recovery Operations, Mr. Strang, that you have essentially done the job of a Crux Op with no training, no mandate, and no requirement that you do so. This impresses us very much. More than half of Crux Ops wipe out on their first missions, and only one out of ten people makes it through Crux Op training, and yet you—somehow—managed to be a very effective Crux Op with no training at all and no knowledge of the job."

"What was her original mission?"

"To move this world toward eliminating the Nazis and to prepare the way for friendly contacts with ATN. And, incidentally, to hand the Closers a big defeat, because they've been very arrogant lately."

I had to concede I had done at least that much.

"So here is the deal, Mr. Strang. We offer it freely. You have a job with us if you want it. We would be happy if you wanted to be a Time Scout or a Special Agent, since to do a Crux Op's job you have to be able to do either of the other as well, but what we really want you for is a Crux Op. The pay is superb, as you might have figured out from what accumulated while you were gone, and some people actually like the opportunity to see how many other ways history could have been. You have your choice of basing—here, your home timeline, or any other—and a certain amount of freedom in visiting other timelines.

"Since you are a widower, I will caution you that it generally does not work out well if you try to find a timeline that contains your spouse but in which you never met her; we won't try to stop you, but we will warn you that the results are usually emotionally disastrous. You approach her already deeply in love and knowing a great deal about her, but she is not exactly the person you loved, and you are not, perhaps, so much to her taste, and you assume too much . . . it is better to let the one you knew go than to look for another. So hunting for your lost spouse, alas, is *not* one of the benefits you can expect."

I nodded and thought about it for the first time in ages. A lot had changed for me since coming to this timeline; Marie had been part of an innocent, younger me, and I was chagrined to admit how little I had really known about her—I had known her body, her background, and her eccentricities, and I had told myself I was in love with her, but I was in love with the trappings—I never really knew the person under them.

It can happen, even in marriages that later grow deeper.

If I were to look her up now, I would want to know more before getting involved—and what I learned could easily destroy my memories.

"I wouldn't try to look up any version of Marie," I said.

She nodded, and her eyes softened a little. "It happens that my lover was killed while I was in Crux Ops training. I disobeyed orders to find another version of him. I have never regretted trying, but I have always regretted succeeding—it poisoned some memories I wish I had left pure. Once an illusion is past relevance, there is no point at all in shattering it. So I try to be very firm with possible recruits about it—because I know what kind of error it is."

I nodded; it spoke well of her, and I was noticing how much I liked Citizen Lao.

"Now, whether you join or not, we have two other proposals for you," she said. "The bare bones one is that besides the cash, we feel we owe you a free trip home, either a round-trip to say good-bye before you move here permanently, or a one-way trip if you wish to go back where you came from."

"I know I'll want to take the trip," I said, "and I assume I have some time to decide which form."

"Yes. Now, for the third . . . Crux Ops do not go directly from mission to mission. You could, in theory, you know, because the time machine would allow that easily, but we find that for mental stability, you need to have people at home—and those people should have lived about as many days as you have by the time you get back. Thus we *strongly* recommend that you return to your home timeline about three years after you left it. We can arrange to have your family and friends believe that you were on a top secret mission for the government, and we can also go back and plant documents and records so that your affairs are well taken care of in your absence, including using some of your pay to cover any debts or obligations."

"I'm much obliged," I said.

"Now, if we do that, it so happens that we have something to suggest to you. You may recall that when you left, Harry Skena had one other non-Blade person he was keeping an eye on besides yourself. Her name is—"

"Porter Brunreich," I said, "and the poor kid was having terrible luck."

"One year after you left," Ariadne continued, "her luck got worse. Her father got into a brawl in prison and was killed."

"Sounds like him."

"She has been shuffled from foster home to foster home, and institution to institution. She's thirteen, she's been out on the streets far too much, and though there's plenty of money waiting in trust funds, her relatives and their lawyers are working hard on getting their hands on it.

"Porter Brunreich is vital to the future of more than fifty timelines that are already members of the ATN. And we think there are two or three great 'trunks'— groups of related timelines—that she may be the root cause of."

I was astonished, even though I'd heard it before. "She's really smart and a terribly nice kid," I said, "but I had no idea—"

"Well, there are plenty of timelines where she doesn't do so well. In some of them she's nobody, in some of them she ends up—badly. There are a lot of ways a child who has been traumatized as Porter Brunreich has can go wrong, or disappear forever."

I thought of that and digested it for a long moment. "So there is something I could do about it?"

"Several times in her early teens she runs away from a foster home, in your timeline. Many things happen after that, some bad, some leading to good timelines. We never know everything that went into making any one timeline, you know . . . but we do know that in a few of them, you end up as her guardian."

I goggled at her. "How does—"

"It turns out that she wrote to her father while he was in prison and asked him to name you as her guardian if anything should happen to him. He did so. And thus you are."

"He, uh, had some help in this?"

"He did, she didn't." Ariadne Lao sighed, then smiled at me. "Your sister Carrie is lonely, you know, and her internal injuries won't allow her to have children, aside from all the difficulties she has in meeting men of her own caliber."

"There never was anybody good enough for her," I said.

"Spoken like a brother." She beamed at me. "I've heard my brother say the same things about me—what a charming idiot. But it is also true that not only does Carrie not meet many men who would be good for her, she simply doesn't meet many men. It's the opinion of our psychological team that if you were to take in Porter Brunreich—*and* you wished to be a Crux Op— this would be good in several regards. You would be around to take care of her, and between your fighting skills and our intelligence service we could keep her safe. She could learn to trust people again—you, Carrie, your employees, your father could become a second family. Carrie would have someone who needed her, and that's very important to your sister—who *also* is important in a number of timelines."

I got up and looked out the window across the broad green common area. "The trouble is," I said, "you make such a good case that I feel as if I'm almost being ordered to do it. And I look around here and find myself thinking, this world is so poor and so damaged by the war. They're going places, but it's going to be a long time, even with the explosive development of science.

They need all the willing hands they can get. And I have a lot of friends here, some of them people I never knew in my home world."

"Nor ever will, in your home world," Ariadne said, quietly. She put her hand through my arm and stood next to me; it made my heart thunder, but there was nothing romantic in the gesture, just friendliness and concern. "You have to remember that these people are not the same people; they were formed by different experiences out of different pathways in history. The George Patton, Edward Teller, Curtis LeMay, or Wernher von Braun you know here are not at all the same ones as existed in your world; they look like them, they may share some behavioral tics, but truly they are not the same; they just have the same name. Likewise, should you ever learn of the doings of any of your alternates, you must not be upset. Almost everyone has alters who died stupidly young, alters who were wildly more successful than themselves, alters who turned criminal. These are the possibilities in a life, not your nature—your nature is formed and expressed only in what *you* have done."

"Do I exist in this timeline?" I asked.

"Both your parents died as Resistance fighters early on. They never met."

I nodded. "That's a bad thing, but I can live with it."

"Name a crime and a person, and I can show you a world where they committed it."

"Helen Keller and voyeurism."

"Easily," she said. "There are thousands of timelines where she never lost her sight or hearing. There are thousands more where she had far more influence than she did in yours." Then she punched my arm, very lightly. "But it was a good try."

"So," I said, "are you telling me my friends here are less real than the ones at home?"

"People are real in whatever world you are in. That's all."

I thought about that for a long time. "This timeline will be kind of cold and hardscrabble for a long time to come," I said. "They have little use for an art historian. And they have all sorts of things to live down. I, uh . . . well, I have friends here. But in my own world, the heart of Europe is not glowing with radioactivity, America did not kill fourteen million of its own citizens from 1952 to 1960 . . . and I do miss Dad and Carrie, and, oh, crap, I miss Porter, too. Let me finish out the term here and then go home?"

"To quote you, deal." She withdrew her arm from mine. "And do you want to become a Crux Op?"

"Give me a little time to think. Ask me three months after I'm back."

Going home was the merest blink; I had said my good-byes, put what I wanted into a case. The Crux Ops team had fixed things for me at home, so Dad and Sis thought I'd been off with the DIA in the operation that nailed Blade, Robby and Paula had kept the agency running, and things were more or less waiting for me on return. I had even composed a telegram that they arranged to have come in the day before I landed.

I had said all my good-byes. I was going to miss Al— Sandy had found herself a straight poet and settled down a while past—but that was about the only close friend I'd made here. At least he understood where I was going; other people got the impression that it was something top secret.

I returned to my office for the last time—or at least the last time till I got my dissertation finished and got hired, things that might never happen in my own timeline. In the privacy there, three people, one of them Ariadne Lao, popped into the space. They handed me the boarding pass; I blinked into existence in an airliner bathroom, from which one of them had just emerged, after having checked a bag of my belongings for me earlier that day.

I returned to my seat, fastened the belt, heard the captain announce landing.

Something strange happened at the airport. I cried and told my family I loved them. And they broke into the most beautiful smiles; it wasn't till then that I realized how much they had been worried.

Three weeks later I had just gotten in from a simple little job of keeping Keewee the Family Klown from getting mobbed. (A man in shoes so big he can easily break an ankle falling must have someone to keep children from tackling him.) When all the potential Bad Guys have bedtimes before nine, it's not hard to get the evening over with.

I had moved back in with Carrie and Dad. Dad was already in bed, and Carrie and I were watching an old movie on TV, when the doorbell rang.

I opened it, and there she was.

She was wearing a pound of makeup badly applied, she'd obviously stuffed her bra with toilet paper, and her skirt was more like a wide belt than anything else. But her blonde hair was matted and dirty from the spring rain, and she was shivering and looked like she might burst into tears.

"Porter!" I said. "God, come in, you'll freeze."

Her face lit up, just a little, with just a hint of hope. "You remembered me," she said. "You remembered."

"Of course," I said, and whisked her in for a scrubbing

and a feeding. Sure enough, somehow it turned out that the legal papers making me her guardian had been hidden by an aunt bent on getting Porter's trust fund, and that somehow things just worked out. I recognized Ariadne Lao's gentle hand—or one very like it—and thought how I might feel about that kind of operation.

She started to improve pretty quickly, but the nightmares were something else. I never asked her what she had done to survive on the streets, except by letting her know, in the most indirect way, that I would see that she got medical or psychiatric help if there were any lingering problems or things to worry about.

It had been almost two months when I woke up—as more often than not—to Porter screaming. I knew this was going to be a bad one, because she was screaming for her mother. I threw a robe on over my pajamas and headed down the hall. Porter stopped screaming just as I arrived.

Carrie had beat me to it; she was caressing the girl's face with her single hand, leaning way out of her wheelchair to do it. Porter lay there, silent, her face streaked with tears, and I came around to her other side and held her hand. "You're dreaming about your mom's death again," I said, gently.

Porter snuffled. "She died for me."

"Yes she did, honey. She loved you very much," Carrie said, which let Porter start crying, something that we figured she probably needed to do after all that time in institutions. She held on to Carrie for a bit, and sobbed, like so many other nights, but then she turned to me and said, "We had a deal."

I thought for a moment, then remembered. "We did."

"Did you get all the bad guys? Are they all gone?"

"Blade of the Most Merciful is extinct to the last man, Porter," I said.

"But were they all of them?"

I sighed. "No. Porter, I can't keep my promise to you; there are billions of bad guys, at least, and even if they were all tied up in a row and I just walked along shooting, I could never get all of them. I'm sorry."

Carrie looked at me, baffled, and Porter said, "So you won't keep your promise."

"*Can't*, kid. It's not quite the same thing." I knew Ariadne Lao would be coming for my answer soon, and I knew that here were the two people I most cared about on Earth—the two who needed me most. I sat down and said, "I'll tell you all about it if you like," and then I took both of them downstairs, made a fire in the fireplace, and I made hot chocolate. I talked for most of the night and told them everything.

As I finished, I explained, "So, in about two weeks, Ariadne Lao will be coming to hear whether I want to join the Crux Ops. I would be away a lot, Porter—"

"It's okay, I've got Carrie to take care of me and Robbie and Paula to guard me."

I nodded. "I have to think about it. I'm not sure what I'll tell her, even yet."

Carrie said, "Porter, if I act just like a rotten bastard grown-up and go talk to Mark in the other room, will you promise not to listen in?"

Porter said, "Sure. Is it really important?"

"It's really important." Sis rolled her wheelchair out to the kitchen; I followed.

"Mark," she said, "can I ask you one question before we talk about anything important?"

"Anything you like," I said.

"Didn't you realize who your friend Al was?"

I shook my head. She told me his full name, which

was accurate, I'd seen his papers, but it was still a common name. "I don't get into poetry, Sis, I never read it or remembered it. If I ever read anything of his in this timeline it was in the Cliff Notes."

She groaned in frustration; she's loved verse ever since she was a kid. "All right, never mind, here's the important part. Porter is a child. She has a child's concept of promises—she can't imagine that an adult would be *unable* to keep one. But if you don't want to be a Crux Op, don't—and I'll handle it with Porter. If you do, do.

"All I'm asking you to do is make up your mind. You've thought for two months. You know your feelings. Just *decide*. Whichever way you do, you're aces with me, and you will be with Porter, too. But make up your mind and come and tell us."

And the chair spun around—she had gotten into doing stunts on it to annoy Dad and me—and peeled out of there before I could answer.

So I thought. I thought of places to see, and the chance, maybe, to get a feel for how the world might be different.

I thought of the Closers, and Blade, and how they had managed to make the Nazis even worse, and all the other things I knew about them. And the thought that came to me was how wrong I had been, consistently. I had thought, right up into being married and having students, that there was no real malice in the universe; nobody was out to hurt me or my loved ones just to hurt me.

That had been shattered by the bomb explosion that claimed half my family.

But I had dreamed, even then and ever since, of a safe place, where I could sit out the wars that raged across all the possible times.

And that was sheerest folly, I realized, standing there with the corner of the refrigerator pushing into my back. The Closers were everywhere, everywhen, expanding in all directions in time. That they had not intruded into most of my past did not guarantee they wouldn't strike again and again.

For that matter, those bastards were looking for Porter. I could guard her till I died, and others could guard her afterward, but it would make no difference—the Closers only had to get lucky once per timeline.

ATN was the outfit that was doing the right thing, I realized. They were carrying the war to the enemy, wherever they could. It had been the grim determination of the Athenians—and the fact that once they had repelled their own Closer invasion, they didn't decide to sit safe at home—that had saved, was still saving the many universes as places that, if not exactly beautiful or even decent, had some potential for good. With the Closers, there was none.

And I thought of what the Closers were like, finally, and of what I'd seen them do personally—and that in two million timelines they were doing similar things or worse.

You could never pay all that back, but it would be fun to try. Something had twisted permanently in me, but I wouldn't want it straightened out now, for anything. The longing to sit home by the fire was more sentiment than anything else; I wanted to carry the fight forward. Other people could be noble about it; I wanted to go bag some Closers.

I went back to the fireplace and said, "I'll only be gone for three weeks before I get first leave—"

"Told you," Porter said. "He promised."

AFTERWORD

One of Napoleon's better generals observed that God is generally on the side of the big battalions; nowhere is this truer than in World War II. The fact was that Germany, Italy, and Japan faced not just one nation with greater resources than their own, but three (if one counts the British Empire as a unit). By D Day, American factories and training camps were turning out enough men and matériel to *completely replace* every ship, gun, man, tank, plane, and round of ammunition expended in that invasion within six months. In late 1944, the U.S. government *canceled* more battleships and cruisers than the Axis ever had.

And the Americans were merely the largest force in the mixture; though the Soviet Union was badly prepared and (especially in the early months) badly led, it also had enough to beat Hitler all by itself (or rather, aided only by "General Winter"). By the time Marshal Zhukov entered Berlin, he was suffering a major problem with "artillery traffic jams"—he had so many cannon that he could not park them all within range of the enemy.

British aircraft plants and shipyards far outproduced German ones, even under bombardment, and by late 1941 the UK was shooting down bombers and sinking U-boats faster than Germany could build them.

Once the greater weight came to bear, the result was inevitable . . . unless the Axis could win very quickly.

Thus, when you set out to write a "Hitler wins" scenario, you must make him win before Allied war production can come on line, and thus you are driven to one of two possibilities:

1. Give him the atomic bomb.
2. Make up something thoroughly implausible.

I have chosen the latter, and I hope we've all had fun with it.

To make wild implausibility convincing demands mad imagination combined with a thorough grounding in fact. In this case, I had the help of the inspired madmen and madwomen of the GEnie Science Fiction Round Table, in the "Alternate Histories" area. These are people who know more strange esoterica, dispute more points more passionately, and who are more willing to help a fellow writer or alt-history freak than any others I have found. If you're on-line, drop by sometime and join the fray.

This book would have been much more difficult—and much less fun!—without the assistance of the following members of the SFRT:

Tom Holsinger, Trent Telenko, Robert M. Brown, Bill Seney, Ben Yalow, P. "Rascal" Rivard, Pete Granzeau, Leigh Kimmel, Jim Brunet, Tony Zbaraschu, J. "Oakfed" Johnson, Lois Tilton, Al Nofi, S."Meneldil" Schaper, J. "Digger" Costello, C. Irby, Bill "Sapper" Gross, Robert Mohl, Kevin O'Donnell, Jr., Steve Stirling, William

Harris, Gary Frazier, John Johnston, J. Filpus, Mic Madden, Rick Kirka, Jules Smith, Vol Haldeman, Susan Shwartz, S. "ET" Elliott, Oz Osmanski, D. "Moo" Mohney, Alan Rodgers, Ariel, Steven Desjardin, and N. Glitz.

Very special thanks, for assistance far and above the call of getting acknowledged here, are due to Bruce Bethke, Tom Holsinger, and Trent Telenko, whose extreme generosity with their time and expertise kept me out of thousands of stupidities. Any remaining stupidities can be attributed to me.

GOLD: The Final Science Fiction Collection
by Isaac Asimov

Isaac Asimov's marvelous later works are finally brought together in a single volume in this collection of science fiction short stories, novellas, and essays, including the 1992 Hugo Award-winning title novella.

FLUX by Stephen Baxter

One of Science Fiction's fastest-rising stars offers a thrilling story about a submicroscopic race of bio-engineered humans who are struggling to understand their origins and their destiny in a world disrupted by an unknown force.

THE TIME SHIPS
by Stephen Baxter

A stunning sequel to H. G. Well's Science Fiction classic, *The Time Machine.* The Time Traveler returns to the future to rescue his Elois friends from the Morlocks, the devolved race of future humans.

SOLIS by A. A. Attanasio

A stunning novel of cryonics in the far future as Charlie Outis discovers that he is a brain without a body in a world he can barely recognize.

INDIA'S STORY
by Kathleen S. Starbuck

A troubled young woman thinks she has forged a new life for herself, until she is sent between dimensions to seek out a new, more powerful teacher. Now India must travel through time and space while unknown forces vie for control of her destiny.

WRATH OF GOD by Robert Gleason

In this apocalyptic vision of a weakened America, only a small group is left to fight the rule of a murderous savage. Until their leader, a Los Alamos renegade, manages to rip a hole in Time and rescue three of the most powerful heroes from history.

SPACE: Above and Beyond by Peter Telep

This sensational novel captures the galactic adventure of the new futuristic TV series *SPACE* on Fox, following a team of young fighter pilots as they forge a fateful battle against alien enemies.